TERESA DE LA PARRA

CRITICAL EDITION

Mama Blanca's Memoirs

THE CLASSIC
NOVEL OF A
VENEZUELAN
GIRLHOOD

THE PITTSBURGH EDITIONS OF
LATIN AMERICAN LITERATURE

Signatory Organizations of the Multilateral Agreement for the Investigation and Co-Publication of Archives, Buenos Aires, September 28, 1984:

Europe
Consejo Superior de Investigaciones Científicas de España
Centre National de la Recherche Scientifique de France
Consiglio Nazionale delle Richerche d'Italia
Instituto de Cultura e Lingua Portuguesa do Portugal

Latin America
Ministerio de Relaciones Exteriores y Culto de Argentina
Conselho Nacional de Desenvolvimiento Científico
e Technológico do Brasil
Presidencia de la República de Colombia
Secretaría de Educación Pública de México

Asociacíon Archivos de la Literatura Latinoamericana del Caribe y Africana del Siglo XX, Amigos de M. A. Asturias (a nongovernmental organization of UNESCO)

Mama Blanca's Memoirs

UNIVERSITY OF PITTSBURGH PRESS
PITTSBURGH AND LONDON

UNESCO   COLECCIÓN ARCHIVOS

Mama Blanca's Memoirs

Teresa de la Parra

TRANSLATED BY HARRIET DE ONÍS AND

REVISED BY FREDERICK H. FORNOFF

CRITICAL EDITION

DORIS SOMMER, COORDINATOR

Published by the University of Pittsburgh Press, Pittsburgh, Pa., 15260

Manufactured in the United States of America

LIBRARY OF CONGRESS CATALOGING-
IN-PUBLICATION DATA

Parra, Teresa de la, 1895–1936.
   [Memorias de Mamá Blanca. English]
   Mama Blanca's memoirs / Teresa de la Parra ; translated by
Harriet de Onís and revised by Frederick H. Fornoff.
      p.   cm. — (Pittsburgh editions of Latin American literature)
   Includes bibliographical references.
   ISBN 0-8229-3835-9. — ISBN 0-8229-5910-0 (pbk.)
   I. Fornoff, Frederick H.   II. Title.   III. Series.
PQ8549.P35M413   1992
863—dc20   92-50381
                                                             CIP

A CIP catalogue record for this book is available from the British
Library.

Eurospan, London

The original-language version of this book may be purhased from the
University of Pittsburgh Press, 127 N. Bellefield Ave., Pittsburgh, Pa.,
15260, U.S.A.

,102

COLLABORATORS ON THIS VOLUME

JOSÉ BALZA *is a Venezuelan writer who teaches at Universidad Central, Caracas.*

VELIA BOSCH *is the Venezuelan editor of Teresa de la Parra's work.*

FREDERICK H. FORNOFF *is Professor of Spanish and Humanities, University of Pittsburgh, Johnstown.*

ELIZABETH GARRELS *teaches Latin American literature at the Massachusetts Institute of Technology.*

JUAN LISCANO *is a leading Venezuelan poet and writer.*

SYLVIA MOLLOY *is Albert Schweitzer Professor of the Humanities and Chair of the Spanish and Portuguese Department at New York University.*

DORIS SOMMER *is Professor of Latin American Literature at Harvard University.*

Contents

 # Foreword

SYLVIA MOLLOY

Childhood memoirs, especially when they appear to be happy, are supremely uncomfortable texts. Celebrating as they so often do "a vanished Atlantis," to use Renan's expression, they challenge the reader with their defiantly sunny countenance. How do we read these texts that seem to be telling us from the start that our critical presence is not really necessary to their good functioning, texts that posture as private edens from which, as adults, we are unconditionally banned? I believe adjectives used to describe them, like *quaint, charming, delightful*—adjectives that have been used, in fact, to describe *Mama Blanca's Memoirs*—are an expeditious means of denying our difficulty, a way of saving face before these texts instead of owning up to a reader's quandary.

This, at least, has been my experience with Teresa de la Parra's elegaic memoir. I never called it quaint or charming or dainty, but others were doing it for me thirty years ago when I first came across the book in France. Retrospectively, this geographical displacement seems apt: not only had Teresa de la Parra been born in Paris, but also, like other women writers and artists from North and South America who were misfits in their own countries—Lydia Cabrera, Gabriela Mistral, Romaine Brooks, Nathalie Barney—she spent the better part of her life there. At the time of my encounter with Teresa de la Parra, I was doing research on the dissemination of Latin American literature in France, and the *Revue de L'Amérique Latine,* published in the twenties, had caught my eye. A hybrid publication if there ever was one, half literary review, half society column, destined for both academic Hispanists and rich Latin Americans living in Paris, it often published Teresa de la Parra. Indeed, the French version of this book, *Mémoirs de Madam Blanche,* was first published there in installments before coming out as a volume in 1929. Before that, the *Revue* had published fragments of *Ifigenia* on a fairly regular basis.

In addition, since the *Revue* was a rather lavish publication and indulged in glossy photographs, one of its issues carried unforgettable photographs of a stunning Teresa de la Parra. She was, as became clear to me, a member of the Venezuelan aristocracy, one of those Latin American women writers (Victoria Ocampo is another good example) so often and so unjustly dismissed as "rich ladies who write." But she was also, as was not so clear to me then and only became so with a little paraliterary sleuthing, a much less conventional figure than these photographs would indicate and the officials accounts of her life would lead one to believe. As in the case of Gabriela Mistral, Teresa de la Parra's sexual difference, I was to find out, was something critics did not speak about or else busily masked by manipulating the author's life into a socially acceptable script. Thus the biographical fictions—to whose fabrication the authors themselves not infrequently contributed—stressing the most salient aspects of conventional femininity: Gabriel Mistral, the mother and teacher, Teresa de la Parra, the charming social butterfly.

One wonders about the part played by childhood, as theme, in these strategic repositionings of self and gender, and of self and sexuality. Doris Sommer has suggested a provocative reading of *Mama Blanca's Memoirs* in conjunction with Gallegos's *Doña Bárbara*. Might one not also pair the novel with Gabriela Mistral's *Ternura* (*Tenderness*) or, in another vein, with Norah Lange's *Cuadernos de Infancia* (*Childhood Notebooks*)—all three, in a way, self-protective texts that, while complying with the "feminine" imperative imposed by custom, manage to keep the last word to themselves? Critics hailed all three books as conforming to their views of women's literature; and, in the case of Lange and Parra, they especially welcomed these childhood memoirs as timely amendments to previous literary "mistakes," to deviations from prescribed gender norms. Parra's ironic *Ifigenia,* questioning conventional heterosexual married bliss, and Lange's cheerfully hedonistic and wildly exaggerated *45 días y 30 marineros* (*Forty-five Days and Thirty Sailors*) had been corrected, as it were, by these books on childhood, more superficially traditional and, in the eyes of critics, doubtless more "womanly."

And yet, as anyone willing to crack the surface of these wilfully coded texts knows, these two childhood accounts—especially that of Teresa de la Parra—are definitely sending out mixed messages, definitely calling out for an intrusion on the part of the reader. The reader as voyeur: not an original stance, to be sure, but one that takes an additional meaning if contextualized along gender lines. Indeed, scenes of voyeurism or—better still—of oblique vision, abound in *Mama Blanca's Memoirs,* the best known, of course, being the striking scene of "María Moñitos" in which child and mother, united in (through) the looking-glass as the mother curls the child's hair, at once comply with patriarchal norm and subvert it. But perhaps it is another scene of voyeurism, a relation involving two women, that is my favorite in *Mama Blanca's Memoirs* for its rich implications. I refer to the scene in the introduction in which a little girl, slipping into Mama Blanca's house uninvited, calmly spies on the old woman—a premonition, perhaps, of the literary voyeurism that will take place years later, when the little girl, turned Mama Blanca's editor, decides, not without misgivings, to publish her very private manuscript.

Two things strike me in this introduction, so eloquent in its celebration of this odd yet well-matched pair, the eccentric old woman and the inquisitive child. One is the notion of female bonding and female legacy, a legacy by-passing genealogy in favor of affinity. Mama Blanca has written her memoirs with the children in mind; yet she bequeaths the manuscript not to her biological offspring but to the girl who was her friend: "It was written for them, but I am leaving it to you." The other thing that strikes me is the sense of confidentiality, of necessary concealment, that surrounds this exchange. Mama Blanca writes "clandestinely," she entrusts her manuscript to her friend in the utmost secrecy: "You read it if you want to, but don't show it to anybody."

What is so private, one wonders, about these memoirs? What is it that cannot be revealed? What has this indiscreet editor, who confesses to having cut, trimmed, and conditioned the memoirs for publication, suppressed from the book? These is no answer, of course, to this question, beyond the literary illusion it creates. I have often wondered why Teresa de la Parra felt the need to resort to that tired device, that of the found manuscript, larger than the text we actually read, to launch her story. And I find no other explanation but that she needed it to establish a prefatory space (in my view as important as, if not more than, the novel itself) in which to highlight the *relation* between women that seems to animate all her writing; the conspiratorial female pact, the collaborative effort, in which "the touch of [her] fingers and those of the departed had blurred."

"I feel like an unbound book whose pages are in complete disorder," wrote Teresa de la Parra, the year she died, to the Cuban anthropologist Lydia Cabrera, the beloved "Cabrita" with whom she shared many years of her life. Nowadays, when I think of Teresa de la Parra, that is, I think, the image of her I prefer—the image that has come to replace the glossy society portrait of the *Revue de L'Amérique Latine:* the scattered pages, the unfinished manuscript asking to be deciphered, offered up for my conspiratorial reading, for my collaboration.

"It's Wrong to Be Right"
Mama Blanca on Writing Like a Woman

DORIS SOMMER

Fortunately, the mistress of a plantation paradise remembered in *The Memoirs of Mama Blanca* (1929)[1] was hardly ever right, especially when it came to naming her six little girls. Her apparent frivolity, secured by a backdrop of cozy colonial relations throughout this series of vignettes that don't add up to a coherent story, cooled the enthusiasm of critics who had applauded Teresa de la Parra's first novel, *Iphigenia, Diary of a Bored Young Lady* (1924). It was much longer and seemed more ambitious in its story about the daughter of a decaying elite family who returns from Paris to Caracas. Like her, Parra herself had returned to the New World. Born in Paris in 1889, she lived on the family plantation in the outskirts of Caracas from the age of two to ten years. That was when her father died and her mother took six children to live with relatives in Spain. As a young woman, Parra came back to Caracas before moving to Paris again, and then to the sanatorium that never cured her of tuberculosis. She died in 1936.

Unlike the author, *Iphigenia*'s protagonist learns to stifle an adventurous spirit enough to make a proper, financially secure marriage. That is, she chooses to be right in the language of her class expectations, reducing the classic heroine's sacrifice to a parodic register of daily domestic capitulations. Venezuelan critics lauded the book, perhaps more for its censure of anachronistic mores than for its lasting literary charm. The country's intellectuals had despaired of the almost feudal order perpetuated by Juan Vicente Gómez, dictator from 1908 until his death in 1935. Opposition peaked in 1928 when National Student Week ended in riots, followed by repression and exile for the leaders who would come back in 1936 to found the first democratic parties in Venezuelan history. Small wonder that one year after the riots the plantocratic idyll of the *Memoirs* left the country's most passionate readers cold, even offended or betrayed.

But Parra herself always preferred the second, little, book. And readers would gradually concur, although sometimes with a condescending tribute to an assumed female simplicity. If women's writing is, or should be, supremely simple and transparent, *Mama Blanca's Memoirs* was hailed as exemplary. Parra's lover in Paris, the Ecuadorian diplomat and writer Gonzalo Zaldumbide, observed, "Woman that she is, she'll never manage to create anything different from herself. Instead of telling stories, women write confessions; there is no disguise that doesn't reveal them."[2] Perhaps their plans for marriage failed because as, Juan Liscano remembers, Zaldumbide never appreciated her subtlety. "Oh, if you only knew how to love me with a woman's soul," she complained in her goodbye letter.[3] Or perhaps, as Velia Bosch speculates, and Sylvia Molloy affirms, on the basis of the intimate relationships with Gabriela Mistral and Lydia Cabrera, Parra finally preferred women, body and soul. Surely more elusive than transparent, this disturbingly beautiful woman moved easily through colonial manors in silk pajamas and cigarettes, and took advantage of modernity to publicly reminisce about tradition. *Mama Blanca* is a monument to Parra's enchanting contradictions.

Mama Blanca refuses the self-delusion of being right, and so refuses the unheroic sacrifices of *Iphigenia*. Instead, the much-loved mistress of the plantation (whom José Balza intelligently credits with deciding everything) prefers to be patently wrong about the names she gave her own creations. In effect, she ridicules the pretense of any possible transparency between a system of arbitrary signs and her flesh-and-blood, delightfully unpredictable, referents. "Poetic" and impractical, this mother enjoyed the whimsical opportunities for finishing touches: she "scorned reality and systematically subjected it to a code of pleasant and arbitrary laws." In the very first paragraph of the memoirs, the eccentric old lady recalls how absurd—almost perverse—her mother's choice of names seemed to the girl of five:

Blanca Nieves, Snow White, the third of the girls in order of age and size, was five years old at the time, dark of skin, dark-eyed, black-haired, legs tanned to the color of saddle leather by the sun, arms darker still. I must blushingly confess that, wholly undeserving of such a name, Blanca Nieves was I.

By referring to herself in the third person, which inexplicably coincides with the first, Blanca begins by dramatizing the liberating distance between the child referred to and the linguistic referent that cannot, or should not, catch up to her. The mother dictated absurd connections, not because that would change reality ("reality never submitted") but because reality didn't matter. So, far from imagining language as an unexamined extension of nature, this linguistically irresponsible mother knew that "her generous hand broadcast a profusion of errors that had the double quality of being irreparable and utterly charming." Throughout this surprising little book, the distance between the child and her name, a distance repeated already in the disjunction between the narrator's third-person voice and her autobiographical subject, and in the unstable difference between error and charm, will provide a space and a mandate for the conciliatory work of time-honored tolerance and of love.

Closing up that space of verbal surprises is quite literally a discursive dead end, death itself. As if to underline the paradoxical reasonableness of irrational and antiallegorical naming—and of the generally liberating gap through which referents can escape finally unnamed and unmanageable in any allegorical system—Blanca Nieves tells what happened once "by mistake." It was the only time that her mother forgot her disdainful precaution against reality while naming her little girls. Tragically, she named one Aurora, the one who would die just as her life was beginning.

The charming, whimsical genie that carelessly whispered our names into Mama's ear happened to be right in one instance. His accuracy proved fatal. It's wrong to be right. To reap happiness it is not necessary to sow truth. Poor Mama, you knew it, you bore it tattooed on the tenderest fibers of your heart. This having been accidentally right once was to cost you floods of tears.

Aurora at seven was like the golden daybreak.

The self-identical sign, like a simple-minded equation too redundant to repeat, cancels the enabling gap between the girl and the controlling symbolic order.

Luckily for the narrator and her name, that inseparable companion, they were a mismatched couple, "a walking absurdity." And if that was a joke at her expense, she puts it into a mitigating context on the same first page of the memoirs, comparing it to an even better (or worse) joke: an older tomboy of a sister named (what else?) Violeta. Violeta was so rough and ready, she was more like a brother in disguise than a sister. And of the six little girls who saw themselves at the center of the universe, this was the only one who almost satisfied their father's insistent desire for a son. "I believe that in Violeta's body lodged the spirit of Juan Manuel the Desired, and this was the main reason he had never been born: for six years he had walked the earth disguised as a violet. The disguise was so transparent that everyone recognized him, Papa first of all." One hint of Parra's care to keep categories like sex and gender open to surprise combinations, in these semiautobiographical memories, is her making all six children girls. Although Parra was in fact one of six, the two eldest were boys. Parra's idealized recollections surround one little girl with five others, so that gender attributions are not simply a matter of biology—so unlike Domingo F. Sarmiento, who erased his brother Honorio from *Recuerdos de provincia* (1850) in order to be singularly male in a house full of women.[4]

The jumble of sexual identities and gender roles, where the terms are not so much mismatched as available for mix-and-match permutations, is not only an effect of the now aged narrator's dynamically "disorderly, pantheistic soul"; it was also the entire plantation's acknowledgment of normally missed encounters between one system of signification and another. Everyone in Piedra Azul could see that the father's second daughter was also his son. And this liberating mistake, as we will see in the critical essays that follow Parra's text, is part of a general phenomenon here in which the sign doesn't quite manage to describe its referent, but rather leaves a space for interpretation—a space, that is, for indulgence and for play.

Teresa de la Parra's reluctance to assign definitive meanings to words, and her framing of what might be called a feminine lineage by an introduction that stages a transfer of text between the aged Blanca and the young girl who will edit the memoirs, suggest a tradition of women's writing. Besides her detours around Latin America's founding fathers, whose positive programs demanded the arbitrary precision of binary oppositions,[5] Parra's book and her three lectures on the "The Influence of Women in Forging the American Soul" follow a trail of continuity. The lectures, which she was invited to deliver in Cuba and Caracas about her life and work, show Parra in good company rather than a token spectacle of her female self. She mentions Delmira Agustini and Gabriela Mistral as admirable contemporaries and then arches back to America's beginnings, with Queen Isabel's humanizing influence and Doña Marina's multilingual agility, to linger on the accomplishments of Sor Juana Inés de la Cruz, to quote whole poems by the pseudonymous "Amaryllis" ("How many Amaryllises have lived since then behind our latticed cities watching life go by!"),[6] and to remember her own illustrious grandmothers and aunts for their services to the nation.

This catalogue of foremothers arouses speculation on the possibility that finding and pausing at imperfect meanings may be a common feature among the most interesting women writers of Spanish America. I cannot help thinking that it is because of their keen sense of irony from being over- (or under)whelmed by a verbal system that cannot correspond to their lived experience. By dramatizing the incommensurability between experience and expression, women writers keep pointing to a gap between available words and the world, a valuable pointer for rereading male Latin American writers as well. Perhaps women's obsessive discourse of disjunctions derives, in part, from a certain feminine distancing—either reticence about public scrutiny or playfulness before a language of stable authority.[7] In that case, being a woman and therefore marginalized may be—how ironic!—a real aesthetic advantage, somewhat like Eve's fall and expulsion from paradise (followed by Adam), a transgression that makes women creatively compensatory. This is the way Blanca Nieves, at least, understands her humble superiority over her "brother" Violeta.

If women, more consistently than men, are exiled from the athletic paradise where signifiers reach what they signify, it is possible that their conscious frustration may become an impetus to play with possible miscombinations. In other words, thanks to women's disobedience and deterritorialization, they are already aware of the arbitrariness of authority.[8] It may easily, and correctly, be objected that this kind of distancing or defamiliarization is a characteristic of all writing, and that language, by its allegorical nature, necessarily dramatizes the absence that it hopelessly strives to fill in. Nevertheless, differences matter among the many possible ways to manage that tension between desired but unattainable presence (of truth, of authority, nature, etcetera) and the absence left by the shortfall of words that don't reach their referents. Indifference to the variations would be strangely to lose sight of the same deconstructive terms that bring the absences into focus. Rómulo Gallegos, Parra's contemporary and Venezuela's national novelist, may be as keenly aware as she was that language can be treacherous; but his punitive policy for traitors is quite unlike her bemused benevolence. Faced with the restlessness that makes writing run away with lived experience, she manages, not by consigning them both to closer quarters, but by acknowledging the futility of authorial discipline.

This is not the first time to notice a woman's bemusement or complaint about an uncooperative language. Gertrudis Gómez de Avellaneda's *Sab* (1841) dismissed an entire glossary of racially identified color categories as inadequate to describe Cuba's most typical resident. Signification was an indirect process in which, for example, black, white, and yellow couldn't quite describe Sab; and yet they suggested him by a double play of composite and default. Indirect too is the entire circuit of writing and reception for this story, ultimately written by Sab himself and meant for his beloved but delivered, for safekeeping, to her cloistered cousin.[9] It is as indirect as Mama Blanca's writing for her children, not to them. "Now you know, this is for you," she confides to her young friend, the future writer. "It is dedicated to my children and grandchildren, but I know that if it came into their hands they would smile tenderly and say: 'One of Mama Blanca's whims,' and they wouldn't even bother to open it. It was written for them, but I am leaving it to you." If aged Blanca is as anxious about the legitimacy of authorship as is Avellaneda's enslaved persona, one strategy is to stay private while going public. It is to appeal to a legitimate reader who mediates toward the ideal one.

On the same tangent of women's circuitous communications, I am tempted to add that soon after Avellaneda's novel, three Argentine women took advantage of the political vacuum following Rosas's defeat to clear some discursive space for themselves in the journal called *La Camelia* they published anonymously and dedicated to "liberty, not license: equality between both sexes [*secsos*]" (April 11, 1852).[10] One strategy was to introduce themselves, indirectly of course in their anonymity, with analogously (in)appropriate signs like those Avellaneda used for Sab: "Without being pretty little girls, we are neither old nor ugly."

In that same generation, writers like Rosa Guerra, Juana Manuela Gorriti, Mercedes Rosas de Rivera, and Juana Manso were taking issue with their Unitarian fathers and husbands over the unitary and limiting language that was sure to reproduce some of the same abuses they opposed in Rosas. In its stead, the women cultivated a heterogeneous national discourse, in which Indian languages, Italian, Galician, English, and Gaucho dialects made a heteroglossic mix with standard Spanish.[11] At the same time, they staged complaints about specious associations forced by particular words, associations like *family* and *fatherland*, or *feminine* and *frivolous*. If home was the site for establishing civilized social relations, as the male "Generation of '37" never tired of saying, then the women demanded consistent and balanced foundations for the new national family. Wives had to assume equal responsibility and equal rights; otherwise the celebration of an unexamined domesticity would backfire and mire the country in barbarous feudal habits.

From this tangent, it is easy to note the unmistakable difference between these women's struggle for consistency and Parra's straying. Her almost aggressive defense of incoherence is the other side of their demand for greater harmony and coherence between family and state. Whereas they and perhaps Avellaneda may feel their marginality with regard to authoritative language as exclusion, she feels it as a liberation. This constitutive distancing from absolutes may be common to all literature, but it is not always as self-reflexive or as promising as in Parra's work, and to other degrees in the work of Avellaneda and her Argentine contemporaries. It doesn't always provide, as it does for them, a negotiating point from which to wrest a release from the prison-house of language, or at least an expense account for redecoration.

From her particular cell, disobedient Sister Juana Inés de la Cruz (1648–1695), the model for generations of naughty novice writers including Teresa de la Parra, had time to reflect on her own relationship to language. The prospect of strategically manipulating the impossibility of language obviously appealed to her, and never so much as when she was preparing her famous response to Sor Filotea. The superior had just instructed her ward to desist from debating with church authorities and also from pursuing the secular study of literature and science. These were unauthorized activities for a woman who had joined a religious order. But the feminized signature on the strident reprimand reveals some reserve, because Juana's superior and confessor was a man, the bishop of Puebla. Signing as "Sister Friend of God," he was probably attempting to cover over his requirements by casting them as appeals to the nun's sense of common decency. Earlier, the bishop had encouraged his spiritual charge to be more daring, when he urged her to dust off a forty-year-old provocation by the Portuguese Jesuit Vieyra about the nature of Christ's virtues and then had her criticism published and circulated. Sor Juana's brilliant casuistry was more proof of women's ability than he would later want to have. As candidate for archbishop of Mexico, competing with a Spanish Jesuit who was Vieyra's personal friend, and also as a man whose ecclesiastical career boasted special attention to the education of women, the confessor was eager to demonstrate his special contribution to Mexican society through women's accomplishments. But once he lost the competition to the incorrigibly misogynist Spaniard, the Mexican bishop chose to make amends by making Sor Juana repent of her presumptuousness in daring to argue with men.[12] She was, however, hardly the pious pawn to be moved as he pleased. Sor Juana's response to his reprimand was to use "Filotea" as the legitimating vehicle for a public hearing. Heaping one self-legitimating argument on another, she overdetermined her right to write.

Many readers remember the scant autobiographical details about her irrepressible, God-given intelligence (anthologized time and again): how she would steal off behind an older sister to learn to read and write; how she would punish herself with unwanted haircuts and deprivation of dessert for not learning fast enough; how she dazzled the doctors at court with her wit and erudition; and how she entered the convent as a sanctuary for learning, free from the responsibilities of marriage and children. Other readers are beginning to value the impressive tradition of foremothers that Sor Juana constructs (mixing and matching Catholic saints with pagan and heretical victims of the church) in order to license herself in their company.[13] This kind of self-celebration through other notable women evidently appealed to Parra, who repeated the scheme in her talks. But Parra may have learned too from the nun's literary critical arguments (hardly ever acknowledged as far as I know) about the instability and the infinite interpretability of any text, including those called sacred. When her confessor suggested that she dedicate herself to the exegesis of sacred Scripture, he seemed to have forgotten that the terrain would be as slippery as that of the profane letters in which she dabbled. Holy Scripture is no less fraught with grammatical difficulties, she complained, such as using plurals for singulars, switching from second to third person, giving adjectives a genitive rather than an accusative case, and substituting feminine for masculine genders.[14]

This last category calls special attention to itself by its boldness and baldness; it is the only one that appears without examples. Certainly not because examples of gender slippage don't exist in the Bible; Sor Juana must have known some to conceive of the category at all.[15] Instead, it is likely that she omitted the target examples because her target here was the confessor himself, the male authority, disguised in the epistolary cross-dressing of Sor Filotea, who was hoping to simulate an identification with the (in)subordinate nun and to gain her confidence. Sor Juana, of course, has no choice but to let him have it his way. At the same time, though, she takes advantage of the transparent fiction to dramatize how unstable and flexible attributions of gender can be. And so, excusing herself, with a wagging tongue barely contained in her cheek, she ends her response by reminding her confessor that if she has transgressed against gender proprieties, it is because he taught her how it is done. She begs "forgiveness for the homely familiarity, and the less than seemly respect in which by treating you as a nun, one of my sisters, I have lost sight of the remoteness of your most illustrious person; which, had I seen you without your veil, would never have occurred."[16] To be sure, it would have been less strategic for the bishop to have attempted a more naked intervention, because it would have ensured his absence from the convent. In order to feign his presence there, he absents himself as a man by covering over the difference. It's not that his game fails to convince his ideal reader, but that the bishop himself is reluctant to play it to the logical end. Sor Juana, by comparison, has no hesitations and forces him into the next move. The confessor may have been criticizing her for presuming the kind of ecclesiastical authority reserved for men, but what he acts out is his equal flexibility as a gendered sign. To enter into debate with her, he had to "(a)veil" himself of a female identity, neither superior nor inferior to his opponent.

I will not insist on many more examples, primarily because it would take too long and also because it may not be necessary. Nevertheless, Sor Juana's inspiration, the catalogue of matriarchs that she and then Parra prepared in their self-presentations, lead me by an irresistible mimetic desire for remembering good company to mention some works that dramatize what might be called a feminist distancing in language. One favorite is *Balún Canán* (1957) by Rosario Castellanos, a novel narrated by a seven-year-old girl who can't seem to make the racial and sexual codes in conflict around and through her coincide with the scenes she puts together. Her initial ingenuous confusion never clears up; it becomes fixed, replicating the fragmentation of a Mexico that never manages to congeal into a society, and replicating also the national language that excludes, more than it includes, Indian territory. By way of the discursive clashes in the book—between Indians and whites, women and men, workers and landowners—Castellanos writes an anti-bildungsroman, a personal history without development or goal. Another favorite writer is Clarice Lispector (1926–1977), that ingenious narrator of the domestic uncanny, who makes perfectly quotidian situations gnawingly grotesque by the same kind of static focusing and disturbing repetitions that can make women's lives unbearably familiar. With her, I also remember Luisa Valenzuela, whose best stories in *Cambio de armas* (1982) defamiliarize a politico-linguistic system that doesn't correspond to her logic of loving.

But perhaps the most dramatic example of what I would like to call an aesthetic tradition of feminine estrangement is the testimony given by Rigoberta Menchú, the young Quiché woman who learned Spanish in order to organize a multiethnic resistance to government expropriations and violence in Guatemala. She, even more than the childish narrators or the social pariahs, is a newcomer to the system of language in which she must defend herself. Her special treatment of Spanish is often a reminder of her social marginality, not a marginality to one particular ideological code from a sense of belonging to another, but a repeated posture of the linguistic bricolage that combines native traditions of the Popol Vuh with Catholicism, ethnic exclusivity with national struggles and with Marxism, because she has learned that no one code fits or contains her. The lack of fit is also the mark of her advantage as a new speaker, one who maintains her distance from and in language, who translates unheard-of expressions to express unheard-of experiences. Not all those experiences are meant for a Spanish-speaking readership, though. And Rigoberta's most telling reminder of her difference is a cautious reluctance to get everything right, as cautious as Mama's deceptively irresponsible habit of naming little girls.

Paradoxically, perhaps, the writer who most cleverly keeps us (and herself) at a safe distance from a hegemonic Hispanic culture was the one who seems to have fit in most effortlessly. I am referring again to Teresa de la Parra, writing through a childish narrator who knows, without bragging, that she and her sisters were at "the center of this cosmos." That's why, she explains, defamiliarizing the familiar form of address, everyone referred to them in the royal second-person singular: "*tú*." Defamiliarization here doesn't suppose a lack of familiarity with the modern world, as in Menchú's case, or a grotesque decomposition as in Lispector's. It assumes a virtually divine sense of security that turns everything into raw material available for manipulation, an absolute security that recognizes with more humor than horror the space between, say, regal and familial appeals for attention. It is also a security that authorizes simultaneous linguistic differences, holding them together with the loose bonds of indulgent love, since, as Avellaneda, Castellanos, Menchú, and many others would also discover, no one code is entirely adequate to the narrative.

Those horizontal bonds, dramatized by the episodic organization of the memoirs, by the scene of writing and rewriting in the proliferating mirror where Blanca and Mama strew stories and straight hair, and finally by the narrator's caution against confusing change with progress, all these may remind us of the genre's capacity, according to Benedict Anderson, to create an inclusive cultural space for the modern nation. Novels included everyone, horizontally, in one flexible and secular concept of calendrical time.[17] If Latin America's founding fictions of the nineteenth century and the populist romances that revised them for anti-imperialist projects tended to take the inclusions for granted and to strain forward rather than moving laterally, pulling time into straight, rational lines that go from barbarism to civilization, and if the recurrent pattern of Boom novels can be visualized as a vicious circle that reaches the end of patriotic history to find out that *end* no longer means *goal*, this feminist novel stops the dynamic or the dizzying movement. Instead of a straight line or a circle, the shape of *Las Memorias de Mamá Blanca* is fanlike. It unfolds a bit wider with every page to make room for the next speaker, only hinting that the central fulcrum is being manipulated by one who was born in the center. But the design she produces is hardly the hegemonic or pyramidal structure of founding fictions. It is an acknowledgment of the mutual dependence of every fold on the others.[18] Anything less would fail to capture the polyphonic airs of a society so admirable for its complexity.

Notes

1. See Teresa de la Parra, *Las memorias de Mamá Blanca* (Caracas: Monte Avila Editores, 1985).

2. Reported in Velia Bosch, Introduction to *Las memorias de Mamá Blanca* (Nanterre: Edición Archivos, 1988), p. xxvii. See also Nelson Osorio, "Contextualización y lectura crítica de *Las memorias de Mamá Blanca*," in ibid., pp. 237–49, esp. 246. Juxtaposing Parra's novel to *Doña Bárbara* by Rómulo Gallegos, Osorio concludes that Parra's language praises nature, colonial life, women, and *simple language*, as if those terms reinforced one another.

3. Quoted by Paulette Patout in "Teresa de la Parra, París, y *Las memorias de Mamá Blanca*," in ibid., p. 165.

4. See Sylvia Molloy, *At Face Value* (Cambridge: Cambridge University Press, 1991), p. 154.

5. See Doris Sommer, *Foundational Fictions: The National Romances of Latin America* (Berkeley and Los Angeles: University of California Press, 1991).

6. Teresa de la Parra, *Obras completas* (Caracas: Editorial Arte, 1965), p. 503.

7. Although Julia Kristeva assumes woman's challenge to symbolization differently from Parra's performance (as a presymbolic "semiosis," an "archaic, instinctual, and maternal territory" of language that challenges meaning by cultivating meaningless phonic and rhythmic, poetic, excesses), Mamá is subversive, not because she's indifferent to meaning, but because she competes by exaggerating its opacity. Nevertheless, Parra's evocation of Cochocho's style does respond to Kristeva's celebration of semiosis. See Julie Kristeva, "From One Identity to Another," in *Desire in Language: A Semiotic Approach to Literature and Art* (New York: Columbia University Press, 1980), pp. 124–47. For a useful review, see Deborah Cameron, *Feminism and Linguistic Theory* (New York: St. Martin's Press, 1985).

8. Regarding "author-ity," the editor of the memoirs comes "to the melancholy conclusion that this compelling need to sign a book may not be the manifestation of talent, but perhaps, perhaps, a weakness of the autocritical faculty."

9. See "Sab c'est moi," in Sommer, *Foundational Fictions*.

10. This and other references to Argentine women's claims for sexual equality come from Francine Masiello's very informative essay, "Between Civilization and Barbarism: Women, Family, and Literary Culture in Mid-Nineteenth-Century Argentina" in *Cultural and Historical Grounding for Hispanic and Luso-Brazilian Feminist Literary Criticism*, ed. Hernán Vidal (Minneapolis: University of Minnisota Institute for the Study of Ideologies and Literature, 1989), p. 530.

11. Ibid., p. 535.

12. The best narrative I know of this fascinating triangulated power play between two men over an apparently defenseless woman is in Octavio Paz, *Sor Juana Inés de la Cruz: Las trampas de la fe* (Barcelona: Seix Barral, 1982); or *Sor Juana, or The Traps of Faith*, trans. Margaret Sayers Peden (Cambridge, Mass.: Belknap Press, 1988).

13. There is Saint Paula, for example, whom Jerome, the patron of Juana's Carmelite order, repeatedly honors for her sanctity and her learning. On the next page is Hypatia, the Alexandrine mathematician and astrologer whom the church fathers ran out of town for improprieties of doctrine, and perhaps of gender too.

14. Sor Juana Inés de la Cruz, *Respuesta a Sor Filotea*, trans. in a bilingual edition: *A Woman of Genius: The Intellectual Autobiography of Sor Juana Inés de la Cruz*, trans. Margaret Sayers Peden (Lime Rock, Conn.: Lime Rock Press, 1982), pp. 80–81.

15. See P. Paul Jouon, *Grammaire de l'ebreu Biblique* (Rome: Institut Biblique Pontifical, 1923). On pp. 148–49 there are several examples: e.g. Gen. 31: 5, 6 is feminine, and Gen. 31: 9 masculine. Ruth 1: 9a and 1: 9b. See also *Journal of Biblical Literature* 105 (1986): 614.

16. Sor Juana, *Respuesta*, pp. 98–99.

17. Benedict Anderson, *Imagined Communities: The Rise and Spread of Nationalism* (London: Verso, 1983).

18. See Luce Irigaray, "The Mechanics of Fluids," *This Sex Which Is Not One*, trans. Catherine Porter (Ithaca, N.Y.: Cornell University Press, 1985). Here she turns around Lacan's privileging of metaphor over (continuous) metonymy.

Mama Blanca's Memoirs

DEDICATION

To you who, like Mama Blanca, reigned sweetly over a
sugar plantation, where the chapel bell rung by your hand
called the workers to Sunday morning mass, where at ves-
pers, above the chirping of the crickets and the winking of
the fireflies, the benign smoke from the mill floated upward in spirals of prayer and where, distant and devout,
standing out against the mists of my earliest memories,
you herded your sheep in green pastures, like the patroness
in some primitive altarpiece.

FOREWORD

Mama Blanca, who on her death bequeathed me fond memories and some five hundred sheets of linen paper written in her fine, wavering English handwriting, was no relation of mine. Those pages, written toward the close of her life, and which I cherish tenderly, have the humble, monotonous simplicity that characterized her domestic existence, and, unbound, bulky, were fastened together at the back with a narrow silk cord whose color time and the touch of my fingers and those of the departed had blurred.

It was not kinship that bound me to Mama Blanca, but mysterious spiritual affinities that in the commerce of souls weave the brief or enduring web of sympathy, friendship, or love, which are separate stages in that supreme joy of mutual understanding. Her name, Mama Blanca, ringing on my shy, fervent lips, admirably suited her generous, smiling person. It had been conferred by her oldest grandchild when he first began to talk. Because children and the common folk, either out of ignorance or because of their dislike for abstractions, know how to harmonize things with life—to bring words to life—and have the unique gift of transforming language, that name which described at one and the same time the whiteness of her hair and the indulgence of her soul, took such hold that everyone, regardless of age, sex, or station, ended up using it. It was not at all unusual for a beggar with her basket of crumbs, or a peddler with his pack, after knocking and peering into the patio with the indispensable greeting, "People of peace," to ask the old servant who came to the door if they could talk with "Mama Blanca" for a minute.

That door, which was almost always ajar and seemed to smile on the street out of the gloom of the hall, was a constant reflection of her hospitality, a natural sign of her love for the poor, a pleasant survival of a more fraternal time before bells and locks existed, and it was also the cause or circumstance that gave rise to our great mutual affection.

I became acquainted with Mama Blanca long before her death, when she was not yet seventy nor I twelve. Our friendship began, as in fairy tales, by our asking each other's name from a distance, our voices muted by the sound of the water singing and laughing as it fell on the leaves. I had been playing about the neighborhood when suddenly it occurred to me to peep into that silent old house. I walked into the hall, pushed open the heavy door with its great knocker and wooden bars, stuck my head in, and stood gazing at the pictures, the rocking chairs, the ornaments, and the circle of flower-pots in the middle of the courtyard, where ferns and geraniums rose to the well-curb and swayed contentedly in the spray of a modest iron fountain. There, farther back, framed in the open window of the dining room, sat the mistress of the house, her robe and hair snow-white, daintily dipping ladyfingers and cookies in a cup of chocolate. For some time I had stood watching her, this fairy god-mother of fountain and flowerpots, when with a sidewise glance she spotted my head sticking through the door. Startled but smiling, she called out affectionately from her table:

"Now, isn't that nice! Prying into other people's business like some pilferer or bird who comes right on in without so much as by your leave! Don't run away now, come tell me your name, my pretty, curious little maid."

I shouted my name several times before she heard it, and as she was gay of heart and loved surprises and trivial adventures, she called back in the same tone and with the same smile:

"My name is Mama Blanca! Don't run away, don't run away, come here, come in and visit with me and have a piece of cake."

In my first swift inspection I had noticed that, for all its fragrant cleanliness, the house had a kind of tumbledown air, which won my confidence. The joviality of its mistress dissipated my last doubts. Consequently, on being found out and cross-examined, instead of running away like a dog caught in some mischief, I yielded first by calling out my name, and then, without the least hesitation, I walked in.

Seated facing one another at the big table, eating cookies and nibbling ladyfingers, we talked for a long time. She told me that when she was little she had played with my grandfather and his brothers and sisters, for they had been neighbors for many years. But that was in another part of town and long, long ago. She told me I looked like people she knew who had been dead for a long time, and when I, just to be saying something, told her we had many roses in my house and a parrot named Sebastian who could call out everybody's name, she took me to make the acquaintance of her patio and backyard where there were roses, too, but instead of Sebastian, armies of ants—ay-ay-ay!—who were inexorably finishing off her roses.

Born on a sugar plantation with a cane mill and coffee sheds, Mama Blanca knew so intimately the secrets and hidden delights of country life that, like her fellow soul Jean de la Fontaine, she could quiz the flowers, toads, and butterflies and engage them in witty and charming conversation. Showing me around the patio and the yard, she commented as she went:

"See, these daisies are vain, coquettish young ladies who like people to see them in their low-necked dance frocks. Those violets over there are always sad because they are poor and have no sweetheart or pretty dresses to show off at the window. They only come out during Holy Week, barefoot, dressed in their violet robes like penitents keeping their vows. Those gardenias are great ladies who ride about in their fine carriage and know nothing of what goes on in the world except what the bees tell them, who flatter them because they get their living from them."

And in this way, my curiosity and hunger slaked with violets, daisies, cake, and ladyfingers, Mama Blanca and I walked hand in hand down the highway of our great friendship. From that afternoon on, at the slightest excuse, I left my house, whipping around the corner, making straight for that friendly hall, shouting as I crossed the doorstep as though I were proclaiming the most exciting news:

"Here I am, Mama Blanca, Mama Blanquita, here I am."

Nobody could understand how at my age I could spend hour after hour in the company of a person who might have been my great-grandmother. As always, people based their judgment on outward appearances. Seventy years had passed so lightly over that soul that it preserved intact all the freshness of adolescence, without its

disquieting preoccupations, and along with this the generosity of
the tree laden with fruit ripened by the grace of heaven. Her friendship, like prayer on the lips of the mystics, opened up to me limitless
horizons and satisfied mysterious anxieties of my spirit. I do not
believe I exaggerate when I say that I not only liked her but I loved
her, and as happens with every love worth the name, in the last
analysis, what I was seeking was myself. For my tender years that
long sociable existence, filled with adventure, travel, wars, sorrows,
joys, wealth, penury, was like a museum imbued with melancholy
grace, where I could view to my heart's content all the thrilling
emotions which life, with kindly forethought, had as yet withheld
from me—even though at times, perhaps to amuse itself with my
impatience, it dangled them before me in the distance, smiling and
winking a malicious eye. I had not yet learned that, contrary to what
the rich and mighty of this world think, life's splendor comes not
from what it gives but from what it promises. Its many unfulfilled
promises flooded my soul in those days with a vague joy. Without
realizing it, I was seeking this joy hour by hour in the peace of the
countryside during those rich moments when dreams flower in the
unbounded world of music or poetry, and in the charm that sweetly
flows from things and tales of other days. As Mama Blanca possessed the priceless gift of narrative evocation and the disorderly,
pantheistic soul of the nonprofessional artist, her friendship led me
on sentimental journeys. In a word, I had fun with Mama Blanca.
That's the compelling reason for my selfish attachment and my
continuous visits.

With her poor trembling fingers and almost no training, she
played the piano with marvelous intuition. A few days after the
beginning of our friendship, she took upon herself the long, daily
chore of giving me lessons, the two of us seated every afternoon at
the old piano. After the class, we had tea, and she would bestow on
me yet another exquisite gift:

"I always prayed that God would send me at least one little
daughter. As He has a mind of his own, and likes to work miracles
when folks don't bother Him, He has sent me one now, when I am
seventy."

I should point out that Mama Blanca, whose maternal affection overflowed the limits of her home and her family, reaching out to include everything lovable, people, animals, things, lived as solitary as a hermit and was as poor as a poet or a mouse. After the death of her husband she had set about squandering her fortune in the most persistent and disastrous ventures on the stock market. Her love for a kind of vast (never realized) munificence—in which, amid damask and velvet, she would bestow gifts right and left, like fruits plucked effortlessly in some promised land—had embarked her upon these ventures. Therefore, if her unhappy speculations never brought her the taste of wealth, which is savorless and fertile in disillusion, they did supply, in full measure, thanks to the magic charm of her imagination, the truly splendid part, that of the dreamer, which was Mary's choice in the Scriptures. Faithful to her vice, in her poverty she played the lottery.

Her sons lamented her living alone in such straitened circumstances and urged her to come and live with one or the other of them in their comfortable and more or less finely furnished houses. But Mama Blanca's stubborn answer was always the same:

"Old folks are in the way. Whenever you want to see me, just come. My door, like the door of the poor, is always open."

That "old folks are in the way" was a subterfuge. Her maternal devotion, always ready to share any grief or adversity, had never succeeded in wiping out her sacred horror of all that verged upon vulgarity. I am thinking especially of vulgarity of soul. Mama Blanca's daughters-in-law, who formed a solid front by reason of their need to outdo one another, most of them having been educated in Europe, spoke a number of languages fluently, traveled, went in for sports, did not dress badly, lived only to shine in society, and were secretly ashamed of a mother-in-law who lived in a brick-floored house with a sloppily dressed old servant and who was, alas, neither intelligent nor educated. Mama Blanca, whose all too evident shortcomings in everything that stood for material success were responsible for her reputed lack of good judgment, managed to conceal behind her halting French (picked up in one of the Ollendorff manuals) the temperament of a magnificent artist and a subtle, exquisite intelligence nourished not so much on books as on nature and on life's daily banquet. This was why, with pleasant irony in the face of the menace of her daughters-in-law, she had chosen to hole up in her brick-floored house and her ivory tower: "Old folks are in the way."

Her fine black eyes set in her delicately wrinkled face never lost the sparkle of youth and often gleamed with flashes of mischief. Her words, whose harmony came both from the musicality of tone and the infinite grace of their thought, combined a balance of tenderness and irony.

She poked gentle fun at everything because her wise heart knew that kindness and gaiety are the sugar and salt with which life must be seasoned. And all things received a grain of each.

I doubt that ever a queen wore her robes of velvet and ermine as gracefully or as regally as Mama Blanca wore her poverty. She told me that she had learned the art in her earliest years from an old relative she called Cousin Juancho. Immaculate always, her love for whatever gave pleasure to the eye led her to contrive innumerable devices to conceal the ravages of time or accident to furniture and household articles, only at some opportune moment to lay bare the deception with a witty phrase.

One day a jardinière of old porcelain which held one of her favorite plants got broken beyond repair. She covered the upper part where the mishap had occurred, tying it around as best she could with a plaid silk handkerchief. Stepping back a few paces she looked at it and, facing the dismal result of her best efforts, inquired sweetly of the jardinière:

"Poor old fellow, got a bad headache?"

And for the rest of its days the pot wore a human air of humble, comic resignation.

Overflowing with Christian faith, she approached God with a familiarity worthy of those image-makers of the first centuries of the church who, in their zeal to convey to the faithful the holy ire and the sacred justice of the Lord, unhesitatingly sculpted their stone images tearing their whiskers or casting Adam out of paradise with a well-aimed kick. But Mama Blanca's God was never wrathful nor capable of the slightest act of violence. Deaf at times, absent-minded, he reigned without majesty in a gay heaven, filled with flowers, which everyone could enter after a little arguing, a little good-natured coaxing at the gate.

Music was always her great passion. Sometimes, seated at the piano, her fingers managed to establish that current of divine communication between composer and player, and then like a saint in ecstasy she would rise from the earth, transfigured. At such moments reality, however imperious, did not impinge upon her. On one occasion as she wandered happy and lost through the subtle maze of Beethoven's *Moonlight Sonata* she was brought word that a man who owed her money, after relentless hounding by her sons, had finally come to pay his debt, cash in hand. Barely turning her head to the doorway, and with a severity reserved for such cases, Mama Blanca answered the old servant who had brought the message:

"I have told you a thousand times that I am not to be disturbed for any reason when I am at the piano."

"He says . . ." the servant began.

"I don't care what he says," Mama Blanca cut her short. "Tell him to come back some other day."

And she returned to her ethereal wanderings in the moonlight. It hardly seems necessary to add that the recalcitrant debtor never came back and that Mama Blanca, when she came back to earth, deplored for many a day, almost in tears, the unfortunate timing.

The infirmities of her piano, whose worn strings from time to time refused to respond as they should, brought an indulgent smile to her lips at the thought of its long fidelity which had finally succumbed to time. Her own shortcomings produced in her a gentle distress that flowered into homilies if I happened to be at her side. In this event she would break off her playing, remove her glasses, lean her elbows on the keyboard, cross her hands on which time had left its blotches, and say in an admonishing tone, moving her eyes toward the name of the composer on the book open on the piano:

"You see? I could have interpreted him, for I understand him, but I don't have the ability. These old fingers are no help to me, nor were they ever, for in my time, my child, we didn't get a methodical training. Now you study hard, so you can master the notes, and not they you. Listen to what I say, and never forget it: this is the only mastery which brings rewards and leaves no regrets nor enemies."

How true, Mama Blanca. You could have ruled the notes and many other kingdoms not of this world, for you had genius that nobody ever suspected, and it was undoubtedly this indifference to the opinion of others that purged your soul of any tinge of vulgarity, as in a new baptism of beauty and grace.

Early one April morning, as though leaving for a picnic, to the hushed music of the fountain and the chirping of the birds in the eaves, without suffering or complaints, Mama Blanca set out for that heaven which during her lifetime she had prudently arranged to her own taste, a reflection of her inner joy. Sleeping, her lips parted in a quiet smile, she had gone to join the choir of the blessed. When her coffin, light and flower-strewn like her spirit, passed easily though the hall door, as it moved from sight one seemed to hear her voice overhead saying to those who remained:

"Goodbye for now, and I'm sorry for the trouble."

Obeying her repeated admonitions not to forget, once she had gone I hurried to her wardrobe to claim the mysterious manuscript on which, all her life at odd moments, she had secretly worked, like a child playing with objects meant for serious use. As she knew in advance that I would always seek the shade of her spirit, she had told me again and again:

"Now you know, this is for you. It is dedicated to my children and grandchildren, but I know that if it came into their hands they would smile tenderly and say: 'One of Mama Blanca's whims,' and they wouldn't even bother to open it. It was written for them, but I am leaving it to you. You read it if you want to, but don't show it to anybody. I couldn't bear to have my dead die again with me, so I came up with the idea of keeping them in here. This is the portrait of my memory. I leave it in your hands. Keep it a few years more in my memory." And thus it was kept for some years.

Since the publication of memoirs and biographies has become one of the more fashionable indiscretions, cutting here, padding there, according to the taste of biographers and publishers, I have been unable to resist the trend of the times, and so I have undertaken the easy and destructive task of arranging the first hundred pages of these *Memoirs*, which Mama Blanca called "the portrait of my memory," to bring them to the public. As can be seen, their author was a celebrity only to my admiring soul. This is their only advantage over other writings of this kind. While I have been arranging them I have felt the eye of the reader fixed upon me like that of the Lord on Cain. It may very well be that they have lost their pristine freshness and taken on a frozen, stiff pretentiousness, as so often happens with writings designed for publication. In attempting to condense and correct, I may very well have chaffed the grain. Like a flight of harried butterflies, the original phrases left the imprint of their bright wings dusted onto the old pages: the wings of life. In this new version, only a few are still flying. Not following the profession of letters as I do, Mama Blanca wrote with the fine abandon of those writers whose pages flit lightly down the years and never lose their freshness. I have often observed this same quality in the letters of persons who never aspired to set foot in the solemn shrine of literature, and I have come to the melancholy conclusion that this compelling need to sign a book may not be the manifestation of talent, but perhaps, perhaps, a weakness of the autocritical faculty. I know in advance that most of my colleagues and readers today will not reproach me for the pruning I have carried out in the interests of smoothness and clearness: on the contrary, they may think I could have done more. As I like approval, this pleases me. In our days, the gifted spirits tend to produce in the shadows, employing disturbing forms and, with their backs turned to nature, brilliant but incomprehensible works. To penetrate their meaning one must struggle hard, trying the doors with seven golden keys. And when one finally reaches the inner sanctum, what one wearily finds is a veiled question mark suspended above an abyss. As for me, and I say it with the satisfaction of a duty observed, I have always carried to cubist expositions and dadaist anthologies a soul garbed in humility and thirsting after faith. And just as at spiritualist séances, I have never seen or heard anything around me but darkness and silence.

The hermetic school, in combination with the lack of time which governs all the hours of our day, has ended by placing the pleasure of the spirit and the satisfaction of ideas completely out of our reach. It may be that this alliance, together with the multiplication of the machine, marks the final stage of our redemption which, as I see it, consists in killing thought by the herculean effort of thinking. Adam's and Eve's sin was pride in their intelligence. In punishment God made it the source of most of our suffering and misery. Free of intelligence and its malevolent pleasures, humankind will be liberated from a Pandora's box of serpents. Since death, obliterator of all suffering and our chief punishment, is hateful only because of the image which thought reflects in its distorted mirror, once the mirror is broken, most accursed of serpents, death will perish, and we will come to live with the serene trust of vegetables and gods. Mama Blanca loved healthy gaiety, and her passion was the happiness of others. I am sure that she will look on and approve with a glad heart the publication of these somewhat deformed memoirs, knowing that this is my infinitesimal contribution to the achievement of our redemption.

But as I wrote this last phrase I saw the shade of the voyager to eternity hovering beside my table. Laying a finger for silence on a melancholy smile, she whispered in a tone of gentle approval:

"Sh-h-h. That's enough excuses. You talk too much. Why didn't you learn at my old piano to make mistakes without apologizing? My memory depicted life, which is motley, delightful, and contradictory. You are showing it in a manner which I am sorry to say does not favor it at all. After sinning, like Lot's wife, out of stubbornness and disobedience, you have denied me several times out of respect for people, like Saint Peter. I could say to you sternly: 'Go thou and sin no more,' except that I don't hold with upbraiding sin too severely. If it were forbidden, its absence might leave the world an arid desert, for what would life be worth without the grace of forgiveness and tolerance?"

MAMA BLANCA'S MEMOIRS

Blanca Nieves and Company

Blanca Nieves, Snow White, the third of the girls in order of age and size, was five years old at the time. She was dark of skin, dark-eyed, black-haired, legs tanned to the color of saddle leather by the sun, arms darker still, and I must humbly confess that, wholly undeserving of such a name, Blanca Nieves was I.

My name and I being inseparable, we constituted a walking absurdity that only habit, with its kindly indulgence, made acceptable, without obvious sarcasm or perplexity. As will be seen, the person who was responsible for this flagrant misnomer was Mama, whose poetic temperament scorned reality and systematically subjected it to a code of pleasant and arbitrary laws dictated by her imagination. But reality refused to submit. As a result, Mama's generous hand broadcast a profusion of errors that had the double quality of being irreparable and utterly charming. Blanca Nieves was one of these mistakes which for a long time made everybody laugh heartily at my expense. Violeta, my sister, who was thirteen months older than I, was another but far greater mistake of this same nature. But you shall hear about this later. Suffice it to say for the moment that in those remote times my five sisters and I formed a rising staircase stretching from seven months to seven years, and from our enthroned stairway we ruled over all creation without ostentation. The boundaries of this domain were those of our plantation, Piedra Azul, which, to the best of our belief, existed for the sole purpose of enfolding us in its bosom and displaying day after day new surprises to our admiring eyes.

Since time began, we and Mama, under the aegis of Papa, a kind of equestrian deity with leggings, spurs, chestnut beard, and broad-brimmed Panama hat, had lived in Piedra Azul, beyond whose fabulous confines none of the six of us had ever set foot.

Besides Papa and Mama, there was Evelyn, an English-speaking

mulatta from Trinidad, who bathed us, made our clothes, repri-
manded us in Spanish devoid of articles, and who from the crack of
dawn went about encased in corset, starched blouse, apron, and
leather belt. Everything about Evelyn, from her whalebone armor,
her stubborn, kinky hair, brushed and pulled back as smooth as she
could stretch it, gave off an aura of order, symmetry, authority, and
a faint smell of coconut oil. Her footsteps were always preceded or
followed by a faint swish-swish that testified to her love of starch
and her positivistic spirit as firmly embedded in reality as an oyster
in its shell. By the law of contrasts, Mama admired Evelyn. When
the latter walked off with her accompanying rustle, holding one or
two of us by the hand, Mama would often raise her eyes to heaven
and exclaim softly and intensely in a tone of thanksgiving, with the
lilt she gave to everything she said:

"Evelyn is my rock of Gibraltar. What would I do without her?"

As I learned years later, Evelyn, "my rock of Gibraltar," had come
to Piedra Azul from Trinidad for the sole and exclusive purpose of
teaching us English. But we girls were blissfully unaware of such an
arrangement, for the simple reason that at that time, Evelyn notwith-
standing, we hadn't the slightest idea that there was such a thing as
English, which anyone could see was an unnecessary complication.
On the other hand, in a spirit of justice and compensation, when
Evelyn scolded: "You've gone and dirtied clean dress, you stubborn
thing, sitting on ground," we were not at all disturbed by her
omission of the articles, which were equally unnecessary.

In addition to Evelyn, like a kind of general staff under her
command, there were three nursemaids. They helped her to bathe,
dress, and put us to bed, and they succeeded one another with such
rapidity that I have only vague and confused memories of those
black faces and those names that were as familiar as they were
unusual: Hermenegilda . . . Eufemia . . . Pastora . . . Armanda. . . .
Independent of the general staff, there were two housemaids,
Altagracia, who waited on table, and Jesusita, who made the beds
and "cared for Mama's head" hour after hour while she, with her
lovely wavy hair unpinned, swung gently in the hammock.

In the kitchen, with half an old sack tied around her waist as an
apron and a rusty piece of tin in her hand to fan the fire, always in a

bad humor, Candelaria queened it. With a tamal or a cup of fresh-brewed coffee in his hand, Papa often remarked: "I don't care who leaves as long as it isn't Candelaria." The years went by, things happened, but Candelaria stayed on with her old sack and her tin fan, ambulating that perennially furious spirit of hers between mortar and coffeepot amid the rattle and bang of kettles.

Beyond the confines of house and kitchen came the overseer, the tenant farmers, the hired hands, the sugar mill, the cows, the calves, the mangoes, the river, the butterflies, the horrible toads, the fearsome, semilegendary snakes, and many other things that it would take too long to enumerate here.

As I have said, we six undisputedly occupied the center of this cosmos. We knew very well that, starting with Papa and Mama and including the snakes, Evelyn, and Candelaria, each and every thing, animate or inanimate, was secondary to us and existed only to serve us. All six of us knew this with complete certainty and with magnanimity, without the slightest vanity. This perhaps was due to the fact that our beliefs, clear and deep-rooted as they were, came to us through our senses and never overstepped the established boundaries out of pride or ambition. How true it is that idle knowledge gives rise to vain desires and creates vain souls. We, like the animals, were devoid of one or the other.

Our social position in those early days was, therefore, similar to that of Adam and Eve when, absolute lords of the world, they emerged innocent and naked from the hand of God. However, we six had several advantages over those two. One of these was Mama, who—and I say it quite impartially—at the age of twenty-four, with her six little girls, and her flounced dresses, was a sheer delight. Another no less estimable advantage was that, while Evelyn was having her lunch, we could sneak off and with complete impunity gorge ourselves on all the guavas we wanted without God casting us out of paradise under a torrent of curses and punishments. Poor Papa, without suspecting it or deserving it, took on in our eyes the thankless role of God. He never scolded us; and yet, out of religious instinct, we paid his supreme authority the tribute of a mysterious fear tinged with mysticism.

For example, if Papa was shut up in his office, the six of us, who paid no attention to such details, would seat ourselves in a row on the porch beside that sanctum sanctorum, and raising our legs in time to the music, we would shout in chorus: *"Riqui-riqui-rán, los maderos de San Juan . . ."* A clear, powerful voice—Papa's—would unexpectedly thunder from the secret recesses of the study:

"Keep those girls quiet! Let them play somewhere else!"

As though silenced by a spell, for a second or two we sat rooted to the spot, eyes wide and hand over mouth, until finally, all together, we ran as fast as our legs would carry us to the other end of the porch, like mice who had heard a cat meow.

At other times, on the contrary, we would clamber into the swing that hung by its four ropes from a rose apple facing that pleasant corner of the porch where, between palms and pillars, Mama had her hammock, her rocking chair, and her sewing stand. All of us standing on the swing, holding on to the ropes or to one another, we swung out as hard as we could, celebrating our prowess with shrieks and squeals of fright. Instantly, from the folds of the hammock in her billowing white dress with lace ruffles, her hair falling in cascades down her back, the latest novel of Dumas *père* in her hand, Mama would pull herself up with Jesusita's help:

"Girls, for heaven's sake don't be so naughty! Two or three of you get off that trapeze this very minute. It can't hold so many, and the littlest ones are going to fall. Get down, please, get down! Don't upset me! Don't worry me!"

Enchanted by the gentle cadence and the prolonged holds of her words, as though they were the music of a lullaby, we swung back and forth to their rhythm: Up . . . down . . . up . . . down. Delighted with the rise and fall of the swing, and our own disobedience, we blew Mama kisses and loving smiles until finally, attracted by the noise, Evelyn appeared and—swish, swish—stopping the swing with a firm hand plucked us off the ropes like ripe grapes from the vine and set us on the ground.

When Mama set out for Caracas in a two-horse chaise—a heartbreaking occurrence that took place every fifteen or sixteen months, to return after a three weeks' absence as slender as ever and with a new baby in the chaise, as though she had really bought it in the store—when Mama left, as I say, during that mournful interregnum of three weeks and sometimes more, life under Evelyn's military dictatorship was an unpleasant thing indeed, an interval as dark and gloomy as the tomb.

But when around nine each morning the stable boy appeared, leading Papa's horse, Caramelo, while Papa, seated across the yard with one leg crossed over the over, strapped on his spurs, we whispered the joyful news in each other's ear:

"He's leaving! He's leaving! Now we can play *riqui-riqui* on the railings."

There was decidedly a latent misunderstanding between Papa and us that was to endure for a long time. The truth of the matter is that we never disobeyed him but once in our life. But that single time sufficed to disunite us without scenes of violence for many years. This great act of disobedience took place at the hour of our birth. Even before he married, Papa had solemnly stated:

"I want a son who will be named for me, Juan Manuel."

But instead of a son, there had come, trailing clouds of poetry, a succession of nature's gentlest manifestations: "Aurora . . . Violeta . . . Blanca Nieves . . . Estrella . . . Rosalinda . . . Aura Flor." Father was not a poet, but he was a kindly soul, and he suffered that flowery deluge with such magnanimous resignation and such self-effacing generosity that from the first moment it wounded our pride and was irreparable. The misunderstanding was an established fact.

Yes, Don Juan Manuel, your silent forgiveness was a great offense, and it would have made for far better relations between you and your six little girls if from time to time you had shown your disappointment in word and act. That resignation of yours was like a huge tree that you had felled across the pathway to our hearts. So you shouldn't complain if, as you rode off in the morning until you disappeared from sight in the green cane fields, your remote silhouette seen from the railing—rising and falling with Caramelo's gallop and crowned by your broad Panama hat—meant no more to us than that Bolívar in battle dress with drawn sword, who, galloping on horseback like you, hung above the closed door of your study and from his mahogany frame all day long majestically directed the glorious battle of Carabobo.

 **Visitors**

I trust that none of you laughed as you read the list of our names—an incomplete list, for at the moment in time to which I am referring it was not yet ended. To laugh at our names, however mirth-provoking they might be, would indicate a lack of understanding. To be sure, none of them sat well upon us, but they suited Mama, who was born around 1831, to perfection. As she baptized us with them, they became a further adornment, as though they were lace or ribbons, and afterward she gazed upon herself with satisfaction. Because Mama was pretty, Mama was vain, and you must know—gentlemen of the classic symbolist and futurist schools—that Mama was an incorrigible romantic. Artificial flowers enchanted her, velvet even in hot weather, the rustle of silk, and any book, whether prose or verse, in which metaphor followed pompous metaphor like drifting clouds across the summer sky. She nearly wept with nostalgia and melancholy as she declaimed:

> *The troth, my Adela,*
> *Which here one day*
> *You pledged, and I*
> *Pledged you . . .*

Mama's soul was the abode of the most delightful bad taste. It was her chief charm. The manifestations of it were as transparent as water, like ripe fruits ingenuously waiting for the first passer-by. They differed completely from those in vogue today, hidden under lock and key, haughtily and cravenly, in the buttressed fortress of a sterile esoterism, where, removed from all human contact, they wither away in their pride.

Mama was a romantic without apologies and without knowing it. As I evoke her image through the haze of my memories, her white dress, her straw fan, her blue and pink bows, I am convinced that she never made an effort to imitate the romantics. On the contrary, I would say that the romantics were always imitating her. It is my opinion that like tobacco, pineapple, and sugarcane, romanticism was an American product that grew, sweet, natural, and unknown, amid colonial languor and tropical indolence until the end of the eighteenth century. Around that time Josephine Tascher, without being aware of it, as though it were an idea germ, carried it in the lace of her shawls and gave it to Napoleon in that intense form we all know, and little by little the troops of the First Empire, aided and abetted by Chateaubriand, spread the epidemic right and left. They can laugh at me as much as they like, but I firmly believe that Mama and Napoleon were very much alike. What could be more like that boundless determination of Napoleon's to seat his brothers one by one on the proudest thrones of Europe than that determination of Mama's, boundless too, to seat her little daughters on the thrones of Creation? To be Estrella, Aurora, Blanca Nieves—isn't that exactly the same thing, from a certain point of view, as being king of Spain, of Naples, or of Holland? Only Mama, bless her heart, set out on her conquest of thrones without military fanfare or human sacrifice. She drove off, as I have said, in a slow-paced chaise, in her taffeta hoopskirt, her muslin shawl, on her head a little toque covered with cherries and tied under her chin with a great bow. As the chaise started up, she waved a silk-mittened hand and launched her unvarying farewell address:

"Goodbye, my darlings! Goodbye, my beauties! Mind what you are told! You all be very good, and when I come back in the afternoon I'll bring you candy!"

Ah, her peaceful achievement was much more lasting, and our kingdoms, which were not the fruit of usurpation, were to endure, happy and unenvied, for the length of our several existences.

From time to time we had visitors in Piedra Azul. Visitors who came for dinner, or visitors who came for several days. These latter were, as a rule, uncles, cousins, or close friends of Papa's and Mama's, old acquaintances whose familiar faces did not frighten us. But, oh! those visitors who came to dinner. That was terrible. It began with Evelyn's bathing and dressing us all at an early hour and repeatedly and severely enjoining upon us that we were not to play in the dirt, nor get our feet in the chickens' watering trough, and to make assurance doubly sure, she ended up by locking us up in a big carpeted room where our cleanliness would run no risks. There, happily unaware of what was in store for us, sheathed in pantalettes that reached to our shoe tops, and with wide, stiff skirts much shorter than the pantalettes, looking like a flock of sugar bowls or compote dishes upside down, we walked proudly back and forth. Finally the visitors arrived. The minute we laid eyes on them, we all ran to a corner, where we stood with our backs turned, forehead stubbornly pressed to the wall, or hid our faces in our arms in an attitude of supreme modesty that evoked no praise. With even more than her usual lilt and grace notes, Mama would say:

"They're just little backwoods girls! They're real savages! They run from their own shadow! They've never been off the plantation!"

I don't know which affected us more, whether the frightening sight of those unfamiliar faces, who talked to us, smiled at us, and were determined to kiss us and see our faces, or the unwonted attitude Mama assumed from the moment the visitors were announced. Mama was cordiality personified. Her social charm, normally limited to the four walls of Piedra Azul, overflowed its banks at the first opportunity and became a veritable torrent, a flood of politeness, smiles, attentions, and compliments. Like us, she too got dressed early in the morning and nervously inspected the whole house, finding dust and spots everywhere, changing the table covers, putting bouquets everywhere.

Papa was the only one who was not affected, and wore the same clothes and the same appearance as every other day. From a rocking chair he watched Mama's nervousness and fussing, and commented, half serious, half smiling, half exasperated, half indulgent, on the comedy that was being staged:

"Now the usual monkeyshines have begun! You know, Carmen María, it wouldn't surprise me one bit if some day the visitors were to find a bouquet, an antimacassar, and a dish of preserves in ——."

Here Papa made reference to a room in the house that is not mentioned in polite society, where we now are.

But Mama paid no attention to Papa's ironies. Her amiability was too firm, too deep-rooted for jokes or jeers to touch it. Mama was amiable out of sheer generosity, out of a wish to adorn herself, and because, being fifteen years younger than Papa, she had not yet learned that in contests of amiability, as in all contests, it is better to give than to receive, and that the more amiable takes a horrible advantage of her adversary by keeping for herself the better part.

After having obstinately and modestly refused to let the visitors see our faces, when we were sure that nobody was paying any attention to us we ran to hide behind the parlor door, and there, unobserved, between laughter and muted sighs, we could watch the performance to our hearts' content.

I can assure you that it was no mean sight to see Mama, aquiver with bows, polite phrases tripping from her lips, her eyes rolled heavenward, pouring from a crystal pitcher, in which pineapple peel floated, golden cups of cane liquor, and then passing them out with languors and smiles. The visitors took them from her hand, tasted the liquor with the tips of their tongues, and instead of saying, coldly and pretentiously, as they do now: "This champagne cocktail is delicious," they commented nobly and simply: "This cane liquor is magnificent."

Mama, beside herself with happiness, insisted that they have some more, and her attentions, her smiles, were such that I confess it made me want to cry. It grieved me to see through the crack of the door the love that Mama was lavishing on the visitors, and I felt the need to give vent to my jealousy with moans and tears. Most of my sisters felt the same way. So while the merriment in the parlor rose and swelled with the cane liquor, behind the door a private drama was taking place: the forgotten flock of compote dishes was suffering in silence a deep grief full of disappointment and surprise.

🦰 Maria Frizzletop

I

Far more than in her own person, Mama's vanity had its abode in our six heads. When I say "heads" I am not including in this word the front, or face, but solely the upper and rear section which, in most persons, is covered with hair. As far as the faces were concerned, they were not always quite up to the mark; there were snub noses, eyes that might have been bigger, eyelashes whose length left something to be desired, a mouth or two that would just get by. But from the brow up, the marvels were wondrous to behold. Mama's vanity could glut itself there. Down the back of one spilled a cascade of bronzed silk; the head of another literally ran over with shining ringlets as black as jet; another resembled a golden lamb, and the neck, the ears, the forehead of another were hidden under a mass of chestnut curls.

When visitors arrived and we, as I have described, hid our faces, presenting to the spectators an uninterrupted view of our hair, we may not have been very polite, but I am sure that instinctively, in some secret and mysterious pact with Mama, we were performing an act of smuggest vanity.

Everyone grasped with sincere admiration:

"What beautiful heads, and every one different. They look like a choir of angels!"

By way of answer, we buried our faces deeper in our arms. The motion set in play shimmering curls, ringlets, waves, earnests of facial beauties which in reality did not exist. What we were doing, thus exploiting the curiosity and credulity of the public, was not too unlike the publicity campaigns of artists and merchants today whose products fall short of the claims for them. The visitors always remarked:

"What enchanting children!"

And they went off convinced of our beauty without having verified it. Mama, glowing with satisfaction, answered with effusively deprecating phrases, until in conclusion, and as though the matter was unimportant, she added:

"Yes, they all do have pretty hair. And it is naturally curly. The one whose hair is a little straighter than the others is Blanca Nieves, that one, the darkest of them . . . but her curls . . . are natural too."

The first part of the statement was true. The last was a brazen, touching lie. Dear Mama! It is true that the poor thing began by timidly enveloping her lie in a euphemism, which was in the nature of a tribute to truth, and it is also true, as someone has said, "that a woman's first duty is to look her best." In her efforts to perform my first duty for me, she was certainly not committing a reprehensible act, quite the contrary. I am not saying this to excuse her: her act was deserving of praise, and all the more so if one bears in mind that onerous and daily task glossed over by her lie, which nobody knew better than I.

Mother Nature, who had been so prodigal in the matter of hair with my sisters, had behaved toward me—and only me—like a cruel, heartless stepmother. But as Mama was a mother, she defied her in a struggle without quarter that was renewed each morning. In the afternoon, from two to three, the stepmother was defeated and thwarted. If company was expected, she was defeated and thwarted starting at eleven in the morning, and thanks to the maternal miracle, my poor black string-straight hair waved gracefully and hypocritically before the strangers' eyes in ringlets as close curled as those of all the others. Nobody who was not in on the secret could have distinguished between the false and the true.

Mama felt keenly the injustice of which I was the innocent victim. She suffered, too, because of the unrelenting deception this injustice laid upon her, for she was not a person given to lying. Indeed not. But she did it with the greatest naturalness in cases of this sort where a lie was indispensable.

In her struggle with my uncooperative hair, Mama displayed admirable zeal and determination. But like all great warriors, she had her moments of dejection. There were times when, as she settled herself with me in front of the mirror, about to embark on the complicated series of operations I shall enumerate, she had a momentary sinking of the heart and in a plaintive voice, hand and comb lying listless in her lap, out of sheer discouragement she would reproach me in this manner:

"But where in the world did you get such straight hair, Blanca Nieves, my darling daughter?"

I hadn't the vaguest idea where I had got it, but feeling guilty, I timidly apologized, answering in the same words and the same gentle tone:

"Where *did* I get it, Mummy?"

But Mama's suffering because of my straight hair was nothing compared to mine as a result of her determination that it should curl, come hell or high water. That morbid concern of hers for my hair meant that my head was in her hands a large part of the day, and her hovering over my innocent, unwaved hair at certain hours of the day curtailed my freedom and poisoned my fun. Every five minutes I seemed to hear that matinal phrase, as solemn and inexorable as a judgment:

"Blanca Nieves, come let me put up your hair!"

This was followed at noon by its corollary, equally solemn and inexorable:

"Blanca Nieves, come let me fix your curls."

The two phrases succeeded one another, daily and regularly, like the rising and setting of the sun.

In addition to that pride, vanity, or love of beauty—powerful motives, indeed—Mama was animated by an even more formidable force: faith. Yes, gentle readers, faith. Mama believed in slippery elm. That is to say, in the face of the evidence, she was convinced that by assiduous use its reputed properties would in a brief space of time make my hair curl naturally and permanently. This was my perdition. Every week a load of her cherished bark was brought down from the mountain, with its smell of the woods and damp earth, as pleasant as it was menacing. Braving Candelaria's foul temper, Mama would take it to the kitchen, put it into a saucepan, boil it, and then strain off the pale infusion in which my head was to be soaked for the next week. It was kept in a bowl until the new supply arrived and a fresh brew was prepared.

Each morning the procedure was to pronounce her importunate sentence upon me, armed with bowl, comb, and a supply of curl papers. In vain did my hair and I give her viable and daily proof of the utter uselessness of the slippery elm tea. Undaunted, she continued to find evidence of the progress of numerous, imaginary curls. She so cherished my poor hair that her tender, mystical soul waited confidently for the slippery elm to perform its miracle. In the last analysis, it was a kind of religion, and I was the propitiatory victim whom she, like Abraham, bravely sacrificed on the altar of my beauty.

Perhaps I am exaggerating a little when I speak of the cruel sacrifices imposed on me at the age of five by my false curls or, to put it another way, by my arduous obligation to look beautiful. Certain scruples assail me. Perhaps I have let myself be carried away by that universal urge to occupy the limelight. I have wanted to hold your attention by my sufferings and win your sympathy. The truth of the matter is that I don't deserve it. To be sure, my straight hair occasioned certain sacrifices; but in return it afforded me opportunities for delightful conversations with interesting persons of exquisite physical charms and moral attainments. Traveling the rough road of my straight hair, I had an early encounter with Our Lady of Poetry. Even though neither then nor later was I able to find refuge beneath her cloak, nevertheless she smiled pleasantly on me from a distance, and in reply I smiled at her, also from a distance. The discreet, mutual smile still endures.

You shall hear how things happened and how the bitterness of privation was followed by the delights of secret abundance.

Around one o'clock in the afternoon, while Evelyn was having her lunch, we took advantage of that brief moment of freedom to have as much fun as we could. Under the trees in front of the house, under Mama's absent-minded vigilance, we furtively gobbled guavas and rose apples while we played "candles." From the rocking chair where she sat, a novel in one hand and her palm leaf fan in the other, Mama from time to time raised her eyes to see what we were doing. But in reality it was I who, without seeming to, was worriedly watching her to see what she was going to do. Suddenly it happened. Closing the book, she called out:

"Blanca Nieves, come let me fix your curls."

But Blanca Nieves never heard. Her head which from early morning, bristling with curlpapers, had looked like an artichoke in cream sauce, bobbed from tree to tree, asking this one and that one for "a little candle." Mama waited patiently for the artichoke to come nearer to repeat more loudly:

"Blanca Nieves, are you deaf? Come and let me fix your curls."

As a deaf person does not answer nor turn his head when called, the bristly artichoke, with back turned, ran as fast as she could, munching a guava and begging for a candle. Mama waited a few seconds more before pulling out the plaintive stops of her voice:

"How much longer are you going to try my patience, Blanca Nieves? How much longer are you going to torment me?"

And melodiously singing out her despair, she fanned and rocked, leaning her head against the back of her chair. It was just like in one of those old Italian operas. But unfortunately for me, and to uphold the honor of outraged obedience, the opera never lasted more than five minutes. With martial bearing Evelyn advanced, the whirlwind of her starched skirts extinguishing all the little candles, took me firmly by the arm and led me into Mama's presence. Whether by temperament I was not inclined to noisy displays of rebelliousness, or whether they seemed to me beneath my dignity, or whether, under the circumstances, I felt them useless under the firm clasp of Evelyn's hand on my arm, my body moved forward without resisting. But my independent soul, my inviolable soul, which Evelyn could not take by the arm, did indeed resist! For a little longer it stayed on under the trees, eating its guava and clamoring for its candle, while my cross, mute head with its dozens of curlpapers there in Mama's room, surrendered itself stoically into her hands.

II

"There's no rose without its thorns," as the saying goes. And they're right. True to this well-known aphorism, every day, forgetting about the rose, I started out pricking my fingers on the thorns and only afterward, surprised and overjoyed, bent down to take the rose in my bare hands and breathe in its perfume ecstatically. This poetic image was renewed each day without past experience depriving it of its delight.

To comb my hair, Mama settled herself in a high chair with me in front of her on a stool. Her knees were my back-rest, and as we talked we looked at ourselves in a long mirror which hung nearby and reflected the scene. No sooner would her white hands begin to move about my head unwrapping the curlpapers, than her lips, reflected overhead, would break into a story. This was a sacred rite. The comb sang as it moved through my hair, already disentangled earlier that morning, while the voice calling up images sang between Mama's lips, and soon, to the double lure, the stubborn, reluctant soul stole quietly back, alighted alongside us on the surface of the mirror and, like a boat on the river, gently drifted downstream on the tide of the story between enchanted banks. The contemptible little candle and the vulgar guavas were left far behind.

As the curlpapers piled up in Mama's lap, my head began to flower into ringlets, and my generous heart would have wished to lodge not one but a dozen souls to carry them along on such a delightful journey.

I fully believe, though I cannot prove it, that Mama was a real poet. Only instead of setting down her verses on the printed page to be read by profane eyes, something almost all poets do, she worked them with grace and originality into ringlet strophes. Her public was not large, just me and my image reflected in the mirror, but it was so attentive, so attuned to the rhythmic phrasing, that Mama's poetic and narrative art could take pride in its accomplishment, its objective fully and triumphantly achieved. Really, what does it matter how many share an emotion? One million or one are just the same. The important thing is to feel that the emotion has been intensely shared, and the most beautiful of poems would have been worth writing even for a single good reader. With regard to Mama's stories, I was that single, perfect reader or collaborator.

The personages and events of these stories were never original, I must admit. One after another there came from Mama's lips fairy stories, tales of mythology, fables by Samaniego and La Fontaine, ballads by Zorrilla, scraps of Bible history, novels by Dumas *père*, and that sweet poem by Bernardin de Saint-Pierre, *Paul and Virginia*. Poor Mama, who for all her isolated, rustic life was well read, as they say, laid hold of everything her memory could turn up. Then it became my task to give unity to the whole. In my hours of dreaming, as I recalled the more thrilling incidents, I invited those personages I thought most noble or interesting to take part in my spiritual jousts. As nobody ever refused, Moses for example might be defeated by d'Artagnan, or sweet Virginia sadly shipwrecked in Noah's ark, then rescued just in the nick of time by the heroic efforts of Beauty and the Beast.

The sudden interruption of my games—that is, the transition from the pleasures of play to those of poetry—caused a momentary shock to my sensibilities and, as I have said, gave rise to a sharp but brief annoyance. It was an imperious annoyance that needed to show its authority, and if it consented to hand over to Mama the material possession of my head, it was at the price of the absolute and moral possession of hers. Its commands were as peremptory as they were unpredictable.

"Mama, today I want you to tell me a new story about a white horse, but one which you have never told me before."

Mama had to set off at a gallop up the slopes of memory in search of a completely new story to which a white horse could be hitched.

At other times my desire was to wander slowly through familiar lanes awash with nostalgia where I could greet and smile at friendly faces. Then I demanded an "old story," but stipulating tyrannical changes that reflected the varying states or desires of my spirit. Certain days were reserved for my two favorites, to whose main characters I have already alluded. One of them was "Beauty and the Beast"; the other—my real favorite—was *Paul and Virginia*, which I had renamed "The Story of the Two Children." Through Mama's art, fiction and reality were harmoniously mingled in these two stories, cross-fertilizing each other with a wealth of fact and fancy in nice balance. In this way my imagination could travel paths of fancy dotted with familiar landmarks to give them verisimilitude. The stage for Paul's and Virginia's star-crossed love, for example, was our plantation of Piedra Azul. Virginia's cabin stood on a hill known as the "the cliff," which I could see through the window in Mama's room from the stool where I sat by turning my head the least bit. Paul's cabin stood a little farther off, overlooking a cornfield that was visible only from the front porch. Many a time I jumped up, my hair half combed-out and half still in curlpapers, to snatch a glimpse of Paul's place, then hurried back to my stool to pick up the story where it had been interrupted. Instead of taking a ship for France—pretentious word whose meaning was vague— Virginia, as natural as could be, set out for Caracas in a chaise just like Mama's. On her return, she was caught in a river flood. It would be hard for me to describe today how that fatal accident upset me. The exact location of the scene heightened the intensity of the disaster. The familiar setting lent the events the august prestige of real history. Thus hallowed, the hill, the cornfield, and the river became objects of veneration to me, and I never looked at them without a feeling of devotion and love.

"Beauty and the Beast," too, entranced me and set a flood of delight running through my breast for analogous reasons. The Beast, with its long tail, black hair, big ears, and the sharp teeth it used for gnawing bones and eating raw flesh, was the exact image of Marquesa, our Newfoundland dog, who was a kind of benevolent big sister whom we all adored. When the moment came to describe the Beast, I never failed to ask with a lump in my throat:

"It was like Marquesa, wasn't it, Mama?"

Mama understood my heart's need and satisfied it to the full:

"Yes, it was exactly like Marquesa."

The boundless, humble, and hopeless love of the Beast for Beauty moved me beyond words. That passion, in which my own affections were involved, became harrowing in proportion as the Beast's sad fate grew more tragic. For this reason the real ending of the story displeased me, and for a long time I had insisted on radical changes in this detail. To change the Beast into a prince before his marriage to the Beauty seemed to me unworthy and, furthermore, a complete lack of consideration for poor Marquesa. Beauty's noble impulse was thus reduced to the commonplace. In a word, those brilliant, princely nuptials offended me by their banality. Perhaps in this I was obeying the natural instincts of the public which is moved by love only when love is garbed in poverty, insignificance, or mediocrity. Marriages sponsored by poverty are always joyfully and warmly attended by the common folk, whose hearts overflow with good wishes, and the gifts on such occasions combine, as a rule, the noble impulses of the heart and the pleasant virtues of thrift. And even though there was no question of sending gifts or attending the wedding personally, on this matter I was inflexible. Before the story began I would stipulate:

"You remember, Mama, the Beast is to remain Beast, with his tail, his black hair, his ears and everything, and he is to marry the Beauty like that. He is never to become a prince. You won't forget?"

Mama took due notice.

Naturally, *Paul and Virginia* at times had a happy ending. Virginia, miraculously saved from the flood waters, married Paul and they lived happily ever after. But if it so happened that my soul felt a vague, voluptuous desire to immerse itself in grief, then I let things take their course.

"Mama, let it rain terribly hard, and the river rise, and the little girl drown, and then everybody die."

Mama unleashed the elements, and the scene was covered with crepe and corpses.

III

When I emerged from Mama's room, it was with head as woolly as a lamb and soul aquiver with emotion. Not for me the shouting and the running; I went off in a corner by myself to savor to the full my emotional jag. Apparently at such moments my lips gaped open slightly and my eyes rose heavenward in an attitude of ecstasy that called forth the scoffing of my sister Violeta and the meddlesome solicitude of Evelyn who, full of concern, came toward me exclaiming—without the use of articles, naturally:

"Shut mouth, Blanca Nieves. Come play with others."

With one fell swoop she sent tumbling to earth a multitude of gardens, castles, and princesses. But Evelyn had not the faintest idea of her work of destruction. The golden gates of my inner life were barred to her watchful eyes. Her vandalic, victorious arms, always on the side of reality, never embraced the delightful phantoms that bring us dreams, doubts, and neurasthenia. Violeta, whose positivistic soul completely coincided with Evelyn's, was at one and the same time her disciple and her enemy. Evelyn respected her. Rather than run the risk of arousing her defiance by grabbing her authoritatively by the arm, as she did the rest of us, she prudently preferred to turn a blind eye or a deaf ear. There were frequent verbal skirmishes between them, which on occasion passed from word to act, but they understood, feared, and respected each other. Evelyn, who saw in Violeta's independence and rebelliousness signs of great intelligence, considered my contemplative attitudes a sure sign of feeble-mindedness, and did her best to correct or conceal them. Violeta, with her pitiless six years, emphasized my failing by calling me "Flycatcher" on every occasion.

If ever anyone had a name that did not suit her, that was Violeta. She and the modest, sweet-smelling little winter flower were two opposite poles. Ever on the alert, always ready to stand up for her rights and occupy center stage, she did not know what modesty was. Sarcasm gleamed in her brilliant eyes, shaded by a shower of black curls, and her tiptilted nose denoted aggressiveness, or at the very least insolence. Her answers were quick and to the point. Her fondness for controversy led her to mix into arguments and quarrels that had nothing to do with her. She could throw stones great distances, turn somersaults, and climb trees. One day they found her trading slaps with one of the overseer's sons, and they were separated just as victory was in her grasp. When the story came out, Mama was quite upset, while Papa, highly amused, laughed uproariously at the incident. I believe that in Violeta's body lodged the spirit of Juan Manuel the Desired, and this was the main reason he had never been born: for six years he had walked the earth disguised as a violet. The disguise was so transparent that everyone recognized him, Papa first of all. For this reason, from time to time he greeted him with hearty laughter.

My admiration for Violeta was in inverse ratio to her contempt for me. It was only natural. I could appreciate the accuracy of her stone throwing and the elegance of her acrobatics, whereas she could not see those brilliant cortèges of princes and fairies which, behind my gaping lips and ecstatic eyes, attended the marriage of Paul and Virginia. Compared to her I was what any poet is in our days compared to any soccer or swimming or boxing champion: nothing. But my poor, trampled, concealed superiority had its charms. My unapplauded fantasies, transfixed by Violeta's arrows, rudely shattered by Evelyn, like a pruned tree only flowered in the darkness with greater lushness and intensity.

One day a disastrous plan occurred to me that was destined to lay my pride, wounded and crushed, in the dust.

Whether the cause was the reckless generosity of a soul longing to share its wealth and invite to its feasts even the least deserving; whether it was vanity or a desire to be admired by one whom I admired so much; the fact is that one day I called Violeta aside and told her that I was going to tell her a story. If she would only listen to me, she would see what pleasure my words would afford her. With a patronizing, skeptical air, Violeta condescended to hear me. To be sure, her positivistic soul was not equipped to savor the delicacy or discover the deeper values that lie behind symbols and fictions, but there is no denying that I overdid it. Like those hosts who ply their guests with food and wines, and wines and food, I laid too heavy a burden on Violeta's indifferent attention. I wanted to dazzle her with my gifts, and I gave too much. My generosity was my undoing. Nothing was omitted from the story I made up in her honor: fairies, magic wands, talking animals, Adam and Eve, the Flood, and a Beast that was not only an enchanted prince, but also our beloved black dog, Marquesa. And to cap it off, all this jumble of events had taken place right there at Piedra Azul the night before! After listening a little while out of indulgence or politeness, Violeta, whose utilitarian soul moved with complete ease in a practical, matter-of-fact world, could stand no more; she cut me short and told me without mincing words that one had to be very silly and a complete "flycatcher" not to realize that all those things were nothing but lies Mama made up so I would sit still like a dummy and let her put up my hair. If it had been her, she would have settled matters long ago, giving Evelyn a good bite on the hand when she came to take her away from play and giving the sacred bowl of slippery elm tea a swift kick. That was the way to do things, and the next day nobody would have bothered her with curls and fairy stories. As she stated her views, Violeta was drawing her self-portrait, accurate to the last detail.

In the face of her words, which had gone winging toward the truth as unerringly as her stones toward the fruit, I was left speechless. How could I convey to the rough, uninitiated soul of Violeta the unbounded pleasure of the world of symbols when I myself forgot it every day? Humiliated and unable to answer, I gathered up my treasures in silence, while Violeta, poised on one foot like a heron, hopped away parodying, as she went, to complete my discomfiture, the opening words of my story:

"Once upon a time there was a Blanca Nieves . . . Once upon a time there was a Negra Nieves . . . Once upon a time there was a Flycatcher Nieves . . ."

From then on, whenever my generous heart needed someone with whom to share its delights, it sought the easily held attention of Estrella and Rosalinda, my younger sisters. Though less brilliant, they were a gentle, attentive audience. If their applause did not wholly measure up to aspirations, my pride came off satisfied, or at least unwounded.

IV

As a consequence of the aforementioned subterfuges, efforts, and sacrifices by which Mama disguised my straight hair, I had worked out my moral code on the basis of my hair. Like that of every decent or well-born woman, it was firm and strict. My hair in its natural form—that is to say, uncurled—came to represent in my eyes a kind of nakedness, and if I felt respect for my curls it was only out of modesty, believe it or not.

For the sake of clarity I will say that, thanks to the principles that Mama without realizing it had inculcated in me at the tender age of five, my honor, contrary to prevailing concepts, had its seat in my hair and in no other part of my person. There it had its firm foundations, there it had its shy, modest abode. For the sake of my virtue I would have defended it to the death. Moved by the same high motives, Mama seemed to respect it and to make it respected even more than I, as I shall explain.

One day Violeta and I were playing together. As usual, her despotism was lording it over my submissiveness, and she had already called me "Flycatcher," "Snow Black," and several other less malicious names which, as they did not reflect on my honor, were of slight importance. But a moment came when, in view of the fact that, for some reason, I did not submit to her domination as quickly or absolutely as she wished, she gave a scornful look at the flock of curlpapers with which Mama had just adorned my head, and enveloping her words in a sarcastic smile, she let fly with an expression she had never employed before:

"Maria Frizzletop."

Indirectly, this was an offense to my honor. In the face of such an affront, quivering with outraged dignity and bravery, I took a few steps forward, and with every intention of returning the insult, said to her, red in the face and haughty:

"So I'm Maria Frizzletop, am I? Maria Frizzletop? Then you are Maria Curlylocks!"

Naturally, instead of taking offense, Violeta shrieked with laughter. And quite right. As an insult, what could have been more pointless than "Maria Curlylocks"? What a mountain of curlpapers, fairy stories and slippery elm tea it took for me to approximate those same curly locks! It was as though a person who earns his bread by the sweat of his brow tried to insult a rich person calling her "Maria Millionaire" or "Maria Plantation Owner." My feeble insult as such was worthless. And the heroic attitude I had assumed to utter it made it, by contrast, all the more pitiful and inept. This did not escape Violeta, but her aggressiveness was insatiable. My defeat was not enough. Instead of relenting, she resumed the attack, singing:

> *Maria Frizzletop asked me to her house.*
> *All she had was bananas and rice.*

and added with cruel aim: "Old Straight Hair."

With this she reached out her hand and seized, pure sacrilege, one of my paper butterflies between her fingers. But God help the bully the day the worm turns! When I saw my ravished curlpaper, I was filled with righteous wrath, and, to Violeta's complete surprise, I hurled myself like a bolt of lightning at her head and grabbed two handfuls of curls. Her insolent, surprised head, shaken this way and that, tried in vain to free itself. In a counterattack Violeta's nails dug themselves into my ears but, without letting go of her curls to avenge my ears, I bit her in the neck. It was a melée of bites, pinches, shakes, when suddenly one of our four feet slipped, and down went the two of us. The fight continued on the ground and went on unabated until we rolled into a mud puddle the rain had made in front of the chicken yard where the fray was taking place.

When they finally separated us, we were covered with mud and bloody marks from her nails and my teeth. Evelyn picked us off the ground, took each of us by the hand, and distributing her scolding and her attentions equally between the two of us, washed us, told us we ought to be ashamed of ourselves, and changed our clothes. By the time Mama arrived, having been informed of the matter, we were wearing clean dresses, and as far as I was concerned, satisfied that the offense to my honor had been washed away by the fight, just as my arms and legs had been cleansed in the wash pan, I was willing to make up. Mama, echoing Evelyn, said our behavior had shocked and pained her. That would have been the end of it, but, as I have said, Violeta's aggressiveness or fighting instincts knew no limits. I, the victim, was willing to let matters rest, but not she, the aggressor. This time her belligerence was to cost her dear.

Turning to Mama, and speaking in the tone of a victim, which was bound to set off a new argument, she said:

"Look, Mummy, just look. See the teeth marks where she bit me, just like a mad dog."

And, to be sure, there was a purplish half moon on the side of her neck. Naturally, I had to answer:

"Mama, that was because, look, how she scratched both my ears."

"Ah, that was because she grabbed me by the hair first, and shook me like a devil . . . like this . . . like this . . . like this!"

"But that was because she had pulled out one of the curlpapers which you, Mummy, had done up my hair in with all that work, and she called me 'Maria Frizzletop,' and then she called me 'Old Straight Hair.' "

That did it. Now the drama began in earnest. On hearing my last words, pale and trembling, Mama turned to Violeta, hardly able to speak:

"You . . . you . . . you . . . said she had straight hair?"

And in the sublime tone of a tragedienne, she went on:

"Violeta, you have no heart! How you have wounded me! How you make me suffer."

Then something unheard of followed. Mama, who had never in her life punished us, dropping her voice to a lower register and, with the solemnity of a judge pronouncing sentence, said:

"Now, so you will stop being bad and not be cruel again to your little sister, I am going to punish you. You hear me? You're going to sit for one whole hour, by the clock: up there!"

And, extending her arm like a living statue of Justice, she pointed to the top of a secretary whose height, in comparison to ours, was awesome.

It would be hard to say which of the three things was most terrifying, the "one whole hour," the height of the secretary, or Mama's outstretched arm.

Like most despots and bullies, Violeta was a coward at heart who hid her weakness behind a false reputation. Mama's tone and extended arm were theatrical enough to frighten anybody, I will admit, but in any case Violeta did not live up to her reputation or succeed in coping with the situation. While Evelyn, under Mama's orders, carried out the sentence, Violeta, terrified as she was hoisted in the air, forgot all her dignity, all her famed rebelliousness. A whimper began to come from her mouth which opened wider and wider, until, from the top of the desk, the cynosure of her audience, pathetic in her defeat and misery, she let out an ear-piercing wail:

"Aa-ay! Ay-ay-ay-ay-ay!"

The room began to rock with the cries of grief. It was as though she had been dropped on live coals, or some invisible hand there on the heights were applying some torment to her.

At the sound of her heartbreaking lamentations, the room began to fill up with spectators. All the members of the household appeared, frightened or curious, to find out what was happening. First came Aurora; and behind her, hand in hand, Estrella and Rosalinda, my favorite audience who were never seen one without the other. One by one, the three nursemaids, or general staff; then Altagracia, then Jesusita; then, carried along by the crowd, majestic in her indifference, came Marquesa; and last, Aura Flor in her nurse's arms—in a word, everybody who could come, came. The only ones who were absent were Papa, who was at the sugar mill, and Candelaria, whose bad temper kept her tied to the stove like a dog on a short chain. That never-before-seen tragedy, I don't know if you can understand it, was terrible. Violeta, aloft on her throne of ignominy, rubbed her eyes with her two fists, tears streaming, and a mouth, big enough to house all the woe of the world, opened wide without pride or modesty to the back of her throat, emitting piercing shrieks. As the audience grew, the dramatic intensity of the scene grew most cruelly. By becoming common knowledge, the punishment took on the quality of degradation. I can truthfully say that on that fateful day I came to know all the horror of an auto-da-fé. Mama, seated beside the secretary, or scaffold, had begun knitting just to have something to do. From time to time, she raised her head to remark with asperity:

"Scream all you like, you're staying there one whole hour."

The screams were redoubled.

The auto-da-fé took its cruel course. In her severity Mama was the Grand Inquisitor; Evelyn, the executioner; I, the infamous informer; and Violeta, disarmed Violeta, the poor heretic seared by the humiliating glances of the audience, accomplices of the executioner. I was aware of my share in the tragedy, and my remorseful heart suffered horrors. Everything about Violeta filled me with immense tenderness. Her poor little polished shoes, so recently changed by Evelyn, dangling helplessly in space, like two hanged men, oozed grief to my eyes; her knees, like two abandoned orphans; her clean dress, the starched ruffles of her pantalettes, a button in front of her dress that had not been fastened, were mute objects that aroused my pity, added to my remorse, until finally my eyes, traveling upward, discovered a terrible thing, and I could stand no more. In time to Violeta's sobs, the purple half moon where I had bit her rose and fell on her martyred neck, redeemed by tears, and, as I say, I could stand no more. Overcome by remorse, I too opened my mouth wide, and my breast began to rise and fall with sobs struggling to escape. I too dug my fists into my eyes, I too burst forth with all the strength of my lungs and my remorse.

"A-a-a-ay! Ay-ay-ay-ay-ay!"

This was the unexpected dramatic climax. All eyes turned with surprise toward me. Even Violeta from her pinnacle in the midst of her shrieks turned on me an astonished look veiled in tears. Mama, surprised and, I think, a little touched, raised her head from her enforced labor and asked with feigned impatience:

"You, too? May I ask what you are crying about, you silly Blanca Nieves?"

"A-a-a-ay! Ay-ay-ay-ay-ay!"

Violeta and I were now engaged in a duet. Mama in silence returned to her knitting, but she began to realize that she had bitten off more than she could chew. Her stern justice was rising like a tide and threatened to engulf her, knitting and all. For when she saw me begin to cry, Aurora, the gentle Aurora, who at the age of seven was all maternal compassion, began to weep in silent sympathy. Seeing Aurora cry, Estrella and Rosalinda, out of a spirit of imitation and love for Aurora, both began to cry at the top of their lungs. At the sight of that epidemic of tears, so tragic in reality and so funny to watch, the servants all began to laugh, holding their sides and writhing. Confronted with such humiliation, the chorus of our howling rose. Meanwhile Aura Flor, allied with the servants, bound to the laughter of her nursemaid, beat the air with her tiny fists, leaping, crowing, drooling with delight, while Marquesa, wagging her tail, sniffed the air in search of the cause of so much woe. The bedlam was terrific. The only one who seemed unmoved was Mama, but I am sure she, too, was keeping a tight rein on herself not to burst into tears. Beyond doubt, she had bitten off more than she could chew. She now had no choice but to drown in her justice, and so she did, but with an air of elegance. Dominating the deafening hurly-burly of tears and laughter, she turned to Evelyn and asked:

"Go look, Evelyn, and see if the hour is up. I think it must be."

And she winked an eye, which we all saw clearly through the

bitter prism of our tears. Evelyn went out and was back in a second to say:

"It's up."

"The hour is up," Mama had to shout to make herself heard above the din. "Violeta can come down now."

But it was as though she had not spoken. Given over to the voluptuousness of unstemmed tears, nobody thought of stopping. Like all vertigo, it had its charms. Ah, but Mama knew how to attract the multitudes. Artfully, while Evelyn compassionately assisted Violeta in the descent from the Cross, she fell back several steps to the door of the room, and raising her two arms above the tempest and with the ringing voice of great orators, she employed her supreme recourse:

"Now, girls, you all listen: The first one who gets here without crying can come and bathe with me in the millstream which they're going to open now because it's eleven o'clock."

Oh, blessed words! The collective weeping turned to collective joy. The faces, still drenched with tears, still tremulous with sobs, outshouted one another:

"I'm first, Mummy, I'm first."

And each of us struggled to clasp Mama's skirt. Violeta was among the first, because her pragmatic spirit had no room for rancor, which is a waste of time, and because *millstream* was a magic word. That mass of water which, when no longer needed in the mill, rushed forth and like a monster hurled itself into a pool, roaring and swooping up everything in its path, ferns, branches, green fruit, little girls, Mama, and Evelyn.

Here Comes Cousin Juancho

I

Cousin Juancho, "your humble servant," was one of the visitors who used to come for long stays. Sometimes he spent weeks with us. He always arrived toward evening, mounted like a country gentleman on Caramelo. His presence did not frighten us, nor did Mama pour out the cornucopia of her charms at his feet.

In addition to arriving like a squire, Cousin Juancho arrived complaining. He led off by complaining about everything with greater or less indignation, and wound up gently bestowing the most generous advice on everybody.

It was always the same. His feet were no more than out of the stirrups and on the ground than, after greeting us all affectionately, he began to rant about the state of the roads, the dust, the lack of bridges, the shrunken rivers, the deplorable custom of playing ninepins alongside the taverns, and wound up by gently urging Papa to sell Caramelo and order a thoroughbred from Europe, to try to ride bouncing up and down in the English fashion while wearing a white pith helmet, and to plow up all the cane in Piedra Azul and plant cotton, grapes, and tobacco in its place.

As you see, Cousin Juancho tempered the fury of his complaints with the gentle rain of his advice. His conversation, shuttling from pole to pole and shot through with lofty, profound thoughts, formed a kind of well-woven carpet into which, winking an eye at us behind Cousin Juancho's back, an occasional witty anecdote was knotted.

He was a cousin of our paternal grandfather, and we represented the third generation that, faithful to the rhythm of his name, still called him "Cousin Juancho." This relationship, which had nothing to do with age, fell naturally on the ears of all relatives, friends, or

acquaintances, out of some mysterious concordance, and came naturally to all lips, the way you might shout "welcome" to cordiality.
His company, which brought in its wake the most unexpected incidents, provided everybody with hours of delightful recreation.

Years after he was dead, Mama still used to say, "Cousin Juancho
was a man with many fine qualities and extremely learned."

And she smiled inappropriately, instinctively summing up without realizing it the whole history of that life and the secret of that
soul, in which continually and jovially, like two good friends, the
sublime and the ridiculous met.

When through the tender green of the plantation cane fields his
venerable head appeared against the horizon, on the road from
Caracas, Papa, Mama, everyone at Piedra Azul shouted joyfully to
one another:

"Here comes Cousin Juancho, here comes Cousin Juancho!"

And they all flocked happily to the railing to watch his leisurely
approach through a pair of field glasses.

How did it happen that, being as "learned" as Mama said he was
and knowing so many things, Cousin Juancho was not in the Senate
or Congress, dazzling the nation with his intelligence, stirring it
with his eloquence, and safeguarding it with his virtue? Nobody in
the family could account for this. They felt it was one of those
mysterious tricks that life so wantonly plays, "just because."

The truth of the matter was, there was neither injustice nor mystery about it. Cousin Juancho could not govern or direct anything,
not for lack of ability, but because of too much thinking. His learning was his ruin. In his delightful conversation, his thoughts leaped
and frisked like a squirrel from branch to branch of human knowledge. It was impossible to follow him or get the better of him. He
knew everything with perfect aplomb. The time, the place, or the
category in which the idea belonged made no difference; nothing
fazed him. He brought the same assurance to a discussion of Roman law as to the reasons for the fall of the Girondists or the
independence of America, the laws that govern the movements of
the planets, the best way to get rid of moths, or the proper amount
of garlic and parsley a cook may permit herself.

In these discussions he led his breathless adversary up hill and

down dale till he pinned him down on some definite point, and
there he defeated him nobly—that is to say, without rubbing his
nose in the dust. If, for example, the topic under dispute was the
future of coffee in Central America, in five minutes, without knowing how, Cousin Juancho and his adversary were in Jerusalem a
thousand years before the birth of Christ. Excited, his arms raised
heavenward, his cuff links jingling and his coattails flapping over
the walls of the holy city, Cousin Juancho would ask his opponent
in a tone that allowed of no evasion:

"What influence would you say predominated in the first temple
of Solomon? Were the workmen who built it Phoenicians or Chalde-
ans?"

His opponent hadn't the vaguest idea. Cousin Juancho, who
knew the answer, then inquired with kindly generosity:

"If you don't know, my son, then why do you argue?"

And he departed the field victorious and magnanimous.

His definitions were always admirable, and his topics of conversation, sprinkled with anecdotes, dates, and sententious remarks, trod
upon each other's heels, infinite in their variety, without anyone's
ever noticing the lightninglike transitions. He was like a moving
train; or, better still, like a dictionary: the same sort of partial unity
within a similar general disorder. Who of you, on a lonesome,
boring afternoon, has not opened at random the pages of a dictionary? I recommend it. There is nothing pleasanter or more restful to
the spirit. The words, joined elbow to elbow, seem to mock one
another. Each is proudly self-satisfied, and laughs at his neighbor,
without suspecting that some other neighbor is laughing at him.
Exactly as people do. To go from *cat* to *catonian*, illustrated with an
austere Roman head, stopping off in between at *catabaptist* and
cataplasm, is a pleasant diversion. The dictionary is the only book
whose delightful incoherence—so like that of Mother Nature—is a
relaxing change from logic, oratory, and literature.

That was Cousin Juancho—an unbound Larousse, with all the
pages loose and half of them upside down. Which is tantamount to
saying that he was highly entertaining and incapable of organizing
or creating anything but chaos.

With the same speed that he changed themes of conversation, his moods fluctuated. He would become utterly indignant at the drop of a hat, without such indignation having the slightest consequence. He went from rage to smile with the same ease as the dictionary from *cat* to *catabaptist*. One of the most characteristic traits of Cousin Juancho's moral physiognomy was his perpetual outrage against himself—or, rather, against his bad luck. He insisted, his eyes flashing, that from Job to our time there had never been an instance of so unrelenting an evil eye as that which pursued him. And he was not altogether wrong. Without ever approaching the stark tragedy of which Job the sublime was the victim, Cousin Juancho's days transpired beneath a modest drizzle of misfortune. His heavens never cleared up.

Years after the period I am describing, after we had moved to Caracas, he came to see us every day. Rare was the occasion when he entered without tossing his hat dramatically on a table, hands pressed against his temples, wild-eyed and declaiming in a trembling voice:

"You'll never guess what happened to me today."

Something unique, incredible, that couldn't happen to anybody in the whole world except this most wretched Juan of all, the god of ill fortune, the Jupiter of bad luck.

And he would tell what had happened.

Although the details of his calamities were infinitely variable, basically, fundamentally, they were always the same. It was the usual story: Cousin Juancho, animated by the best of intentions, had endeavored, with his innate and unalterable nobility, to lend some service or assistance out of the goodness of his heart, but unforeseen circumstances had conspired to make him appear in the eyes of the whole world as a selfish, thoughtless creature, devoid of any trace of moral elegance.

Incapable of explaining himself calmly, he would grow furious. He would start by heaping insults, more or less justified, on the person or persons whom, with intentions as generous as they were disastrous, he had tried to help. He would call them ingrates, low-born trash, scoundrels. As a result of such outbursts, his supposed shortcomings were made more manifest, and the animosity of his victims grew.

For example, let's say Cousin Juancho was walking down the street, at his usual nervous gait, when he saw some elderly, infirm lady coming in the opposite direction. He, who was gallantry personified, would immediately try to move aside, with the idea of making a deep bow and leaving the lady the full width of the sidewalk.

But what would happen? Just as he was on the point of carrying out his maneuver, one of his feet would slip on a fruit peel or some other snare of the devil. Instead of moving to the left, or into the street, as was his intention, he would skid to the right or against the wall. Whereupon he would stumble against the lady, landing on her chest, pulling her mantilla askew, while the bit of fruit peel that had occasioned the disaster lurked between the sole and the heel of his shoe, where neither he nor anyone else could see it. The fragile victim, tossing her head in the air, would expostulate:

"What a way to walk! Have you no manners? Don't you know you always yield the sidewalk to a lady, whichever side she is coming from?"

In the face of such manifest injustice, Cousin Juancho would lose his self-control. Outraged not only by the undeserved reproach, but most of all at the lesson of politeness addressed to him, the master of etiquette, he would return an angry answer, his indignation carrying him to the outer limits of his inborn chivalry. The lady would retort in kind. Hat in hand, Cousin Juancho would go on arguing excitedly and without yielding an inch, pale, stammering, the target of insults. Not until he got home would he discover the fruit peel that had been the cause of the incident.

If after a long trip on horseback, he reached a hotel—or lodging as it was then called—weary and longing to rest, it was his fate to sink into a chair that some other guest had just broken and artfully put together. As was inevitable, Cousin Juancho would fall over backward. The sound of the fall brought the owner of the establishment, an angry argument ensued, after which Cousin Juancho, furious and bruised, would have to pay for the chair and massage his aching body with camphorated brandy.

Let us assume that an upright, discerning man came into power who, cognizant of the merits and ability of our excellent Cousin

Juancho, was on the point of naming him to an important post. When the appointment was ready for his signature, the faithful friend and minister would die suddenly of a heart attack or ruptured blood vessel. Cousin Juancho would sit up for two nights with the body of his ex-future protector, send a wreath of flowers that upset his budget for a month, deliver a moving eulogy at the grave of the departed, do everything he could for the widow, and mourn for weeks the irreparable loss of his sponsor and his appointment.

II

Famous not only for his misadventures, his ire, and his learning, Cousin Juancho was famed above all for his sterling eloquence. Scorning declamation and false rhetoric, he possessed the divine gift of the word—that is to say, everything that came from his lips glowed with life and stirred his hearers. I believe that this gift of the word was the origin of both his happiness and his misfortune. Every day, like Don Quixote, he would set out at full gallop to root out the evildoers, without thought of self, mounted on his most brilliant phrases, heading for utopia. He would return glowing with satisfaction, having out-argued every adversary he encountered, and having wasted his friends' entire afternoon. He never set the least store by time or money. He scorned them equally; they did not exist for him. He was always late, and rarely if ever did he have a bank note in his lean billfold. Of all the miseries the world holds, the only one he was spared was the misery lurking behind wealth, honors, and success.

A born conservative even to the slightest detail, out of a spirit of contradiction and his utopian inclinations he had enthusiastically enlisted in the ranks of the liberal party, which heaped ingratitude and disappointments upon him. This ingratitude had prevented him from taking an active part in any enterprises of a positive nature. Thus detached from reality, his soul, corroded by disillusion, crushed beneath the weight of human iniquity, had preserved in all its fragrance and candor complete faith in itself. He had the virgin innocence of those who have never worked. Never having tested his abilities except in the field of discussion, he truly believed them to be unlimited, and as his heart, overflowing with altruism, had never been soured by the failure of any undertaking, he continually humiliated the self-seeking and avaricious by distributing right and left with lavish hand every kind of imaginary largesse. His rages, even the most terrible, even those that turned his face purple and made his eyes start from his head, were impregnated with unbounded generosity, and his diatribes against everything abstract and collective took on, as they came from his lips, a tone of cordial brotherhood.

When he spoke of the conservatives, he would shout, shaking his right arm, making his cuff links click like castanets:

"They are nincompoops, enemies of progress, completely unfit to govern; it's their fault we're in the state we're in."

And when he spoke of his coreligionists, the liberals:

"They are barefaced thieves who are leading us to complete ruin."

His mellow baritone voice, that might have filled academies and congresses with the fairest flowers of eloquence, echoed through the corridors of Piedra Azul, fervid and kindly, as though he were calling out from afar to liberals and conservatives alike:

"Hello, how is everything going? Remember me to the family!"

Cousin Juancho was an archive or walking encyclopedia of everything that had taken place in the social or political world of Venezuela during the first seventy years of the nineteenth century. Unfortunately, or perhaps fortunately, he never wrote if he could help it. Even though in his conversation he was continually harping on politics, the tumult of his thoughts prevented him from bringing any story or thesis safe to port.

Except for two or three favorite stories, which he related with a wealth of details to the very end—wholly unnecessary, for his hearers already knew them by heart—the others, that is to say, the new ones, rarely got to the point, although they rambled up a thousand bypaths.

For example: after affirming that the conservatives were all incompetent, he began to give certain highly interesting details about the resignation of President Vargas, which he alone knew, and everybody listened with eager attention, knowing beforehand that the frail story hung by a thread. And so it was; if he happened to notice that Mama or some other person was absentmindedly trying to rub a spot off her dress, that was the end of President Vargas.

Still talking, he would go over to Mama, or whoever it happened to be, look at the spot, and then break off his narration:

"You've got a spot on your dress. I noticed it a while ago. Don't worry, it's not fruit juice, it's grease, even if it doesn't look like it. Don't touch it. You listen to me: spread out the dress, put magnesia on the spot, and then a piece of tissue paper with a weight on top . . ."

President Vargas's resignation was indefinitely postponed.

Years before, in a halcyon moment, Cousin Juancho's golden dream had come true. He had been sent to Europe on a special mission, although of brief duration and with very little salary. He boarded ship in a radiant mood. After duly cursing the heat and the seasickness of the first few days, during the rest of the long crossing he talked from morning till night so agreeably, argued so shrewdly, held forth so wittily in scintillating paradoxes, that he was the life of the voyage and the delightful common denominator of the most varied groups.

If he had been able to carry out his diplomatic mission, he would have continued to charm his hearers as he did his shipmates. Meeting in a huge bare hall with his colleagues, all of them solemn and garbed in black, in a chill silence such as prevails in the Protestant churches, Cousin Juancho would have taken the floor and quickly broken the ice. Cuff links jingling, coattails flapping, after eloquently holding forth on the balance of power in Europe and the future United States of Spanish America, he would have gone off on a tangent and wound up praising the excellence of the soap of Marseilles. In the bare hall, now glowing with human warmth, his delighted colleagues would have listened to him with interest and hearty applause.

Between ourselves, and meaning no offense to these gentlemen, everyone knows that the one objective of delegates to all congresses and assemblies, from the times of Assyria and Babylon down to the League of Nations of our own days, is to skillfully conceal from the public the utter uselessness of such meetings, while at the same time assuming to themselves maximum importance. Cousin Juancho, always more upright, more honest than anyone, would have broken the conspiracy of silence. He, however, would have done something useful, for he would have amused his colleagues with his agile, unexpected, and unique leaps from the future unity of Spanish America to the excellence of the soap of Marseilles or the properties of sesame seeds.

But it was not the will of God that Cousin Juancho should honorably and conscientiously carry out the diplomatic mission assigned him. The bad luck that stalked him never slept.

A few days after landing, he received word that the government that had sent him had fallen and that his mission, which the new government considered useless, had been canceled, and that his salary had been cut out of the budget as an unnecessary expense. News of the catastrophe reached him among the sooty fogs of London. Furious though he was, he did not wish to return without visiting Paris, a city he longed to know, not only because of a natural interest but also in order to be able to praise or criticize it, as the occasion arose, with firsthand knowledge.

Stretching his first and only stipend as thin as a rubber band, he worked out a miraculous budget and spent three months in a modest boardinghouse on the Left Bank. But he had no more than settled there, and on the very afternoon that he was delightedly preparing to attend a solemn session of Congress presided over by Napoleon III, when he felt so ill that he had to forego the momentous occasion and take to his bed. Double pneumonia brought him within sight of the pearly gates. After weathering his illness without the aid of one word of French, Cousin Juancho spent his lonely convalescence in the Luxembourg Gardens, where the fallen leaves rustled softly beneath his footsteps and beneath the soliloquies he addressed to the gray autumn sky. His solitude, frequently besmirched by the mud of the streets and insults of cab drivers, increased his dislike for the wicked. When after three months he returned to Venezuela. he brought back a propensity toward heavy chest colds and a soul filled with nostalgia for snowy landscapes and high civic virtue. Uprooted for the rest of his days, he languished without hope.

III

Cousin Juancho's admiration for Europe, nourished on journals and catalogues, was to play an important role in our lives, although in a way diametrically opposed to the objective he desired and pursued for us with such keen interest. Evelyn, for example, had come to Piedra Azul at the repeated suggestion and advice of Cousin Juancho, so that from birth, he said, we should receive early notions of the sound mentality and the indispensable language of the English. Instead of teaching us English, Evelyn quickly picked up a Spanish patois devoid of articles, to which I have already referred, and her oppressive energy by contrast made us love all the more the pleasant indolence of everything around us and Mama's dulcet, affected, lilting Spanish.

Cousin Juancho had brought his relatives of Piedra Azul a big garden umbrella from London. His idea was that it should be fastened to the middle of an iron or wicker table, where beneath its circular English shade, after a fashion he had seen I don't know where, we should gather at five o'clock for tea and buttered toast. But Mama, Papa, and their guests, rocking rhythmically back and forth in rocking chairs on the porch of Piedra Azul, drank at four o'clock, or six o'clock, or whenever they felt like it, tall glasses of chilled soursop juice, or grenadine. And the forgotten, degraded umbrella made its rare appearance around ten in the morning, when, sheltering Mama, Evelyn, and all of us under its shade like a mother hen, swaying languidly from left to right, from right to left on the oxcart to which it had been affixed, it presided over our gay, noisy bath amid stones, soap, shrieks, and bath towels.

Our bath concluded, cool and our hair dripping pearls of water, we bunched together once more on the floor of the cart while Mama sat contentedly on a little bench closer to the oxen. While Evelyn and the driver, not without certain difficulties, got the heavy umbrella open and in place again, Mama sighed with pleasure in its shade and remarked calmly and complacently:

"Poor thing, it's old and ugly, but without it, my children, we could never come and bathe so pleasantly in this pool."

I owe Cousin Juancho a boundless debt of gratitude for having taught me from my earliest years to understand and love, in spite of all his insults and diatribes, the idealistic soul of my race. He imbued me with this knowledge and love by employing the pedagogical system that is, without any doubt, the most efficacious: that of example. In his violent harangues, he began by completely disqualifying Venezuela as a land forever lost to civilization, beyond hope of redemption. As his pessimism picked up speed, it came to embrace our whole southern continent until finally, with a leap across the waters, it fell upon Spain, fulminated her, and the sparks of the holocaust lighted on all the Latin nations. Above the catastrophe, only the British Isles, serene, happy, remained afloat.

How many lovable defects you shattered with your thunderbolts, Cousin Juancho, and how unwittingly, as you condemned them—reflecting each and every one in yourself—you invested them with grace and nobility. How much I was to learn from you!

Thanks exclusively to Cousin Juancho, before I had received any education or any notion of history, while older and more learned people found *Don Quixote* boring, I was lost in admiration at its kindness and wisdom. I followed with delight Sancho's simple chatter, I shoutingly called his attention to the fact that he was using the same proverb a second time, I played with his donkey, and the two of us winked at each other as Rocinante passed, so pompous and so bony. I finally came to love them all so that, like the Three Marys, I followed them tenderly on their road to Calvary and wept with tears and laughter at the amusing and touching martyrdom of their beatings and blanket-tossings.

Years later, when the snow of my heavy hair came to justify my name, as I traveled through certain old cities of Extremadura or Castile in Spain, where others found only poor roads, cooking that reeked of olive oil, and an absence of baths, as a result of Cousin Juancho's early indoctrination, I filled my eyes with ineffable horizons of deep, infinite beauty. It was always that familiar right arm moving eloquently and indignantly, still making signs and pointing among the joinings of the severe stones or the old vanes of the windmills of Don Quixote.

If I were to say that in the distant days of Piedra Azul my mind had been able to grasp such subtleties or even to know against

whom and what Cousin Juancho's praises and diatribes were directed, I should be trying to deceive you. I would be lying to put on
airs and would be guilty of bad taste. On the contrary, at the tender
age of five I was even a little backward. In that rustic setting, always
in a state of wonder, always with my lips a little open, like my other
sisters I had a pleasing, naive air of stupidity. We all loved Cousin
Juancho dearly, as one loves a big, gentle family dog that has never
bitten anybody. Our love ingenuously extended to include his shoes
and his clothes. In our ears there was no difference between his
magnificent oratory and the friendly barking of Marquesa. But little
by little those barks of his worked a subterranean effect in our
simple, unsophisticated little souls. As you can see, his image was to
become clearly impressed on us in its every detail like a bust carved
on one of those medallions hidden in the bottom of a trunk, and
which are brought out and gazed upon with loving eyes at long
intervals.

IV

Cousin Juancho wore his noble, well-brushed poverty with quiet
dignity. Along with his carefully concealed poverty, whose transparent devices at times were touching, there were two other things
about which he was sensitive: his real age and his four false teeth,
which had replaced those he lost as a young man in one of his
innumerable falls. Alas, expressions of both enthusiasm and censure,
as they came whistling through his lips, set his false teeth in motion.
And after emphatically stating: "One doesn't talk about age," without realizing it he revealed his own by the events he narrated. He
was born at the end of the eighteenth century, and at the time I am
telling about he was sixty-seven years old.

In addition to being always immaculately brushed, Cousin
Juancho was always dressed in somber black. Around his neck in
complicated folds he wore a wide cravat of dark silk, and he invariably
wore a solemn frock coat with long tails, and presiding over the tails,
two big buttons that buttoned nothing. He always looked as though
he were on his way to a funeral or to a session of Congress. His attire
never varied, and, believe it or not, this was the garb in which he

appeared bright and early in the morning in the halls of Piedra Azul. Dame Poverty at times indulges in these unexpected stubborn whims. It grieved Papa to see him like that, sweating and wearing out his frock coat. His kind heart tried to devise ways of counteracting this twofold evil, but without success.

It often happened that Cousin Juancho, in an endeavor to arouse Papa's complacent, indifferent soul to an awareness—even if only a momentary spark—of his sacred obligation to interest himself in his country's destinies, cornered him and laid before him, with the help of flailing arms and quivering coattails, dilemmas as horned as these:

"One of two things, Juan Manuel: either these liberals change their tactics and cease usurping the name of liberals, which they dishonor and betray, or I shall sever my connections with the party after telling them what I think of the whole lot of them. Don't you think that is my duty, Juan Manuel?"

After looking him over from head to foot, Papa would answer him with great concern:

"Cousin Juancho, I don't understand how you can go around all day with that black cloth coat stuck to you. The heat is enough to kill you. Put on one of my white drill coats, one of those I recently had made, as I've told you so many times. Put it on; I can't use them, and they'll fit you just fine. Even if it is only in the morning when the sun is high."

As for me, there was something else that aroused my curiosity so I could hardly bear it. When Cousin Juancho talked, while his beloved coattails fluttered at the height of my head, my upward gazing eyes never got tired of watching his lips. I would have interrupted him, but I never had the courage. On mine there hovered a question I had been wanting to ask for a long, long time:

"Cousin Juancho, when you talk how do you manage to move your teeth? How do you do it?"

Fortunately, my timidity was greater than my curiosity, and this most indiscreet of questions never was uttered. It would have been a knife driven in the heart of Mama's exquisite amiability, and it is possible that on hearing it she would have swooned at Cousin Juancho's feet.

Ever since, I have looked upon timidity as a great counselor and a trusted friend. Later, in my long peregrination through the world, how often it has walked beside me, a finger on its lips, like a guardian angel. Remembering what it had saved me from, I have cherished its memory, and from the gulf of silence have gratefully sent it my brightest smiles and purest kisses.

V

Of those anecdotes or narrations of Cousin Juancho's that did reach port, and which, without his suspecting it, revealed his pure Castilian spirit, there was one, perhaps the latest in his repertory, which was my favorite. Its actors were known to me, and not only were they present on the stage, but in the audience as well, which lent the story a flavor and animation all its own. Cousin Juancho took delight in it, and was still telling it with gusto years afterward, toward the end of his days. By force of repetition, it had become polished, its deadwood pruned away, its edges beveled, so that its form was one of rounded, smooth-drawn profiles. Mama was especially involved in it. Her figure occupied the foreground with the spotlight so strongly focused on her that he never began the story that she did not interrupt, her voice lilting in exasperation:

"Oh, Cousin Juancho, how many times are you going to tell that?"

But while it was hard to keep many of Cousin Juancho's stories from slipping off the rails, it was utterly impossible to halt one of his favorites once he'd pulled on his storyteller's seven-league boots and cleared his throat.

The anecdote in question could hardly have been simpler, but it was fascinating for all its triviality. How was it possible for two deadly enemies, triviality and interest, to run gaily hand in hand, you may ask. I cannot answer: there is the mystery, there is the spell, there is the unique quality of Cousin Juancho's art, which I shall never be able to convey to you.

The tale had to do with how, when, and under what circumstances Papa's and Mama's wedding had taken place.

"They got married in '46," Cousin Juancho would begin; "it was the month of March, on Easter Sunday. Carmen was fifteen, and Juan Manuel thirty-one. They wanted a splendid wedding, and it certainly was. They were married by the archbishop, and the bride was given away by her godfather, who was the president of the republic at the time. But as bride and godfather were leaving the house they had an accident that nobody could have foreseen, and that accident, as you will see, is the only thing funny about the story. . . ."

But it is useless to reproduce Cousin Juancho's words. Without his voice, his gestures, that indefinable warmth which is the soul or bouquet of the art of great narrators, they are meaningless. I can only assure you that when he began the simple story with the allusion to the "accident," everybody listened: if Evelyn was walking through the hall, for a moment her feverish activity abated and she listened; the servants listened; all we girls listened; even Aura Flor, the tiny despot, if she happened to be there in the arms of her nurse, with three fingers buried in her toothless mouth and a stern frown on her thoughtful forehead, impressed by the intensity of the atmosphere would have condescended to listen—and with pleasure, I guarantee it.

To tell the story in brief, drab words, the accident was that when the wedding party left the house, the leading carriage, in which the bride was riding, lost a wheel; and horses, coachman, bride, president, and all were turned over and dumped in the street. It was the official, solemn presidential carriage. In his old general's uniform from the wars of independence, covered with gold braid and decorations, the godfather crawled out of the overturned carriage like a snail out of its shell, helping the bride out as best he could; and although at the time he was going through a period of intense unpopularity and it was hardly prudent for him to rub elbows with the populace thus attired and bedecked, in view of the situation, in view of the fact that the church was not far off and that it was not easy to secure another carriage—a mark of great luxury and extravagance in those days—he swallowed his pride and discomfort and, facing up to both aggravations, announced with a gay, confident smile:

"All right, we'll continue on foot."

The guests who were following in carriages got out at once and, following the president's example, repeated his remark:

"We'll continue on foot."

So the godfather with his galoons, and the goddaughter with her orange blossoms, followed by the wedding party, proceeded up the street between a double row of onlookers and a double row of window gazers, who had thrown open the shutters, pouring a flood of light and comments on the dark street, for the wedding and the mishap took place in the early hours of the morning. The bride as she proceeded was hailed with compliments from all lips—but not so the general, who, as I have said, had many enemies. His term of office was coming to an end, and in spite of his great kindness and his past glories those were days of hostility and unpopularity for him. The moral: to run the gauntlet between two columns of onlookers and two columns of windows, it's better to be a bride than a general.

This was the story in its general outlines, moral and all. However, what Cousin Juancho called the "funny part of my story" was not confined to the mishap itself, as he thought, but resided in the gaiety that rejoiced the spirit, like a deep draught of cool water when one is thirsty, a gaiety and aroma which when it can be captured in words never is lost. It was only long years later that I learned this truth: overcome with surprise and nostalgia I discovered it one day in the yellowed pages from a book of old ballads, reading the account of another wedding party that had gone afoot with unpretentious simplicity. There they are: the nuptials of the Cid. If some of its fragrance can be made to perfume my dull version, you will capture the indescribable charm of Cousin Juancho's favorite story:

> *Behind them walked Jimena*
> *Her hand clasped in the king's;*
> *The queen, her godmother, followed,*
> *And the nobles of the realm.*
> *Through grilles and windows*
> *So much wheat was flung*
> *That the king's broad-brimmed cap*
> *Caught more than its share,*

And down gentle Jimena's neck
More than a thousand grains slipped
Which the gallant king removed.
Enviously spoke Suero,
So that the king might hear;
'Twere good to be the king
But better still his hand.

When they came to the gate
The crowd divided in two
And the king stayed to sup
With all who had been bid.

If you change the grains of wheat, which never grew in Caracas, for jibes at the president and cheers for the bride, you have the ballad of Mama's wedding party exactly as I heard it again and again when I was a child.

Ah, Cousin Juancho, the grace of your story! Now I understand why you lived in a state of constant indignation and why you attired yourself in your black funeral coat each morning. You knew that all were leagued in a plot to assassinate the simple, joyous grace of life, and as she was being buried bit by bit each day, each day you faithfully attended her piecemeal burial. But her death agony was long, and the breath of life persisted in her as long as you lived. And it was she who, like a faithful dog, sniffing at your coattails, trotted behind your modest funeral, and, motionless like the dogs carved on marble tombs, remained forever in the cemetery.

As I set down these words, two big tears roll down my cheeks, wrinkled as much by the rictus of sorrow as by the lines laughter has imprinted on them over the years. One of these tears is for the irreparable loss of the dear departed. The other, for the infinite sorrow it gives me to know that above the cherished ashes, always triumphant, always terrible, like an angel of vengeance with a flaming sword, barring the gate of all that is pleasant, we are left, not with grace and wit but, for our sins, with emphasis.

Vicente Cochocho

I

The weaknesses, the shortcomings, or imperfections of my soul, like those of most, are numerous, I admit. They have encircled me, gay and unabashed, all my life long, like a flock of sheep its shepherdess. Instead of my leading them, I have allowed them to lead me over the years, submissively and willingly. Thus they have grown attached to my person, and not one has strayed away; they are all here.

One that never—well, hardly ever—joined my flock is that highly contagious one designated in our times by that word of Anglo-Saxon origin: snobbishness. No, I am not and have never been a snob, except perhaps occasionally through indifference or boredom. As this weakness, when all is said and done, is a powerful force, my not being a snob has made me lose face in the estimation of people who seek out and exalt only those capable of crushing them under the weight of pretentious, sterile vanity. This shortcoming, together with my other weaknesses, has little by little given rise to my failures, which likewise follow me with a kind of fidelity, with a mildly ironic glee. I do not deny them. They had their origin in me. Like my children and my grandchildren, they are my life's work, my legacy. Let them go on following me, and God bless them all!

This exordium is to inform you that being an anti-snob whose life is dotted with modest failures, I am not ashamed to be seen in public with persons who are not presentable or who are shabbily dressed. I have just done this without your being aware of it when I entitled this chapter as I did: "Vicente Cochocho," named after an individual who, I must confess, walked the earth worse than shabbily dressed—hardly dressed at all. I ask your indulgence. Believe me when I say that the most unpresentable persons are generally the most interesting. It is my belief that the body all too often adorns itself at the expense of the spirit. It is a cruel conviction that it hurts me to admit, for it saddens me to think that the charming, the divine outer elegance of the body is a lovely, lowborn thief who, to bedeck herself, strips the soul of food and raiment, leaving it penniless.

So, worse than badly dressed, a hired hand of Piedra Azul—not even a sharecropper, without oxen, house, or fields—Vicente Cochocho was one of the tutelary friends of our childhood. For nearly sixty years now his bare black feet, stubby and fanwise, have ceased to leave the flower of their five toes on the dust of this world; but his obscure, beloved memory, so deserving of glory, has an honored place in my recollections. There he has his street, his statue, his sepulchre. He deserves them for his worth and his virtue, like the greatest of the earth. I know that all this will disappear one day—so have Nineveh and Tyre—but then and only then, buried amid my ruins, will his memory die with me.

Cochocho was not his name, but a nickname. Our venerated friend Vicente sported neither shoes nor surname. *Cochocho*—and I must ask your indulgence once more—means *louse*, but so contemptible a louse that it is not even listed in the dictionary. To find it one must go, I believe, to the savannahs of Venezuela and seek it out among the pelts or manes of the livestock. I don't know which—I never saw one—but to judge by its namesake Vicente, who wore the appellation with the same natural elegance as certain noblemen their title, a *cochocho* must be a horrible thing. Dear Vicente, in the peace of your eternal rest, do not take offense at this deduction. Remember that your art and your greatest glory was that of having made the ugly beautiful.

Vicente, who was a giant in kindness of soul, could hardly have been smaller in physical stature. He was barely four fingers taller than Aurora, though it must be said in fairness that she was well-grown for her seven years. Both dimensions, that of his soul and of his body, brought him close to us, who were small of size and in our innocence were drawn to goodness out of consonance or a love of harmony.

A powerful outer circumstance also contributed to our union

with Vicente, and this was our constant association. Vicente Cochocho's "official" capacity was cleaner of the irrigation ditch. This involved his spending four or five days every couple of weeks in the mud up to his knees, shoveling to both sides of the big ditch the sediment deposited by the water. As this activity was carried on at a distance from the house, Vicente was eclipsed from our view during this interval. But during the rest of the time his miscellaneous occupations were closely associated with the house and its outbuildings. Sometimes, but very rarely, he fed cane into the mill. It was a sight to behold him perched on a ladder to reach the three slow-moving cylinders like the other feeders. But he always managed, and the cylinders, without so much as a "thank you," majestically devoured the cane that Vicente fed them with so much effort. But, as I said, this did not happen often. Tasks more suited to his stature kept him hovering around the house most of the time.

It was Vicente who, as a rule, helped clean the stables and cure ailing horses and cows; it was Vicente whom Mama sent up trees to pick ripe fruit; it was Vicente who, mounted on a donkey, rode up the hills or down the trails after wood, banana leaves in which to wrap the *hallacas*, slippery elm for my hair, vegetables, alligator pears, brown sugar—or anything that might be unexpectedly needed in the kitchen. It was Vicente who mended doors and wired fences in the chicken yard, who hunted possums at night, who, armed with pick and shovel, dug the hole for some new plant Papa wanted to set out in the orchard or garden; it was Vicente who ruled the water like Neptune and, with feet firmly planted on either side of the sluice, raised the gate, releasing the tumultuous stream like a keeper letting a wild animal out of a cage, and it was Vicente who, squatting as close to the ground as his namesake to the cattle, patiently rooted out with a pointed knife he wore in his belt the spears of grass that stubbornly grew between the stones, flags, and bricks of the paths and patio of Piedra Azul.

To see Vicente Cochocho from a distance squatting down to weed the stones was like seeing a toad about to jump. In his flat, cordial head Indian and Negro had humbly come together, each in its place, meekly and without ever malevolently joining forces against the white man. The hair of his head, where the Negro predominated, was a thick, woolly mat, while that of his face, where the Indian held sway, was so sparse, so stiff, that we used to call him affectionately (it was Violeta who came up with it) "Vicente Cochocho, Cockroach Mustache."

Apparently, though like toads and lice he seemed to be of no special age, Vicente was old. His short, bowed legs, always on intimate terms with the earth and water, always bare to the knee, always bespattered with mud, never gave the impression of being dirty or neglected, nor did they arouse disgust. Are ferns that are kissed by the stream or dusted by the earth dirty? Do we feel disgust for roots reaching out of the ground through the friendly dirt and blessed rain?

But Evelyn, who saw things in a different light, had stated that Vicente was a filthy, loathsome creature who, being a louse himself, probably had a head full of them, and that, therefore, never for any reason were we ever to go near him. It goes without saying that our devotion to Vicente Cochocho, fanned by persecution and fed by being forbidden, grew by the hour. Love is not love unless it is opposed, nor is a friendship that does not involve sacrifice worth the name. As soon as we spied Vicente digging in the garden or squatting down to weed the patio, we ran and formed a loving circle around him. Then the least of his movements, the slightest word, which would have been fascinating under any circumstances, took on enhanced charm and value precisely because it was threatened by police intervention from Evelyn.

At bottom—I understand it now—the war to the death that Evelyn carried on daily against our beloved Cochocho had its origin in a complex, personal race hatred. For that reason it was relentless and without quarter. Evelyn's three-quarters of white blood cursed her quarter of Negro blood. As she was unable to bedevil the Negro in herself, she took it out on Vicente. She never passed up a chance to discredit him in the eyes of his admirers—that is to say, in our eyes—but without the least success. On the contrary.

She was implacable. If one of us had spilled soup or chocolate on our dress, Evelyn would stare for a moment at the miscreant in exasperation and reprove her:

"Because you don't watch what you're doing and are careless, you've got yourself all dirty. Just like Vicente Cochocho!"

Beneath the chocolate or the soup, our love for Vicente rose several degrees.

Or if one of us had been guilty of some lack of courtesy or breeding, Evelyn would inquire sarcastically, fixing the culprit with a withering glance:

"That beautiful, that elegant behavior—you learned it, I suppose, from your fine friend, Mr. Vicente Cochocho?"

The thermometer of our love rose higher.

If she came upon us unexpectedly huddled around Vicente in the middle of the patio, she swooped down on our circle of love, tearing it asunder and asking with devastating politeness that exuded venom:

"What have I told you more than thousand time? What is always, always forbidden here?"

Vicente knew only too well what was always, always forbidden here, and what we had been told more than "thousand time." Nevertheless, he never took offense. He went on patiently rooting out the stubborn grass with his knife. His soul did not know the meaning of hate. Belonging, as one might say, to the vegetable kingdom, he accepted without protest the iniquities of man and the injustices of nature. Submerged in the water, or clinging to the stones, insult him as they might, he went on impassively yielding his fruits and his flowers, good plant that he was.

II

Whether or not Vicente could be considered untidy or dirty was a moot point. It was a matter of opinion. But to accuse him of a lack of politeness was a manifest injustice. Nobody could have been more polite. But Evelyn, with her British and Protestant intolerance, was unable to appreciate the refinement of that rustic courtesy. We could. Nor could she or Mama or Papa or anyone appreciate the flavor of the noble, vintage Spanish that comprised Vicente's vocabulary. We could, and because we appreciated it we copied it.

Evelyn would correct us, assuring us that we were talking vulgarly; Mama would too, but they were both wrong. Right, or supreme good taste, was on the side of Vicente and us. Only many years later did I realize this. It was when I came to read López de Gómara, Cieza de León, Bernal Díaz del Castillo, and other authors of the period who came to America and generously bequeathed to us the Spanish that Vicente used, just as one uses a strong, solid, comfortable piece of old furniture inherited from one's ancestors.

Vicente would say, as they did in the magnificent seventeenth century, *ansina* instead of *así*, *truje* in place of *traje*, *aguaitar* instead of *mirar*, *mesmo* for *mismo*, and so on; his Spanish was, in a word, golden age Spanish.

Moreover, he employed a peculiar emphatic declination made up of various diminutive suffixes that he applied with equal facility to nouns, adjectives, adverbs, and gerunds, loading words with special nuances. If someone called him, he would answer, "Yes, sir, I'll be there in a jiffy, just a jiffy," which meant: "Happy to oblige, just give me a minute. A bit of patience, please."

If someone asked how he was feeling or how things were going, and he answered, "As you can see, here I am, worky, worky, work," this meant that he was happy to be working and that he did it willingly, but to little pecuniary advantage.

His courtesy was of a piece with his vocabulary. It too was noble and rich. Vicente never set foot anywhere, whether it was the kitchen or the coffee sorting shed, without asking leave in these words:

"God be praised!"

And glued to the doorway or the foot of the stairs, he would keep repeating the phrase, until an irate voice answered:

"For heaven's sake, come in and stop bothering!"

Vicente was incapable of keeping his palm-leaf hat on his head if he saw Mama go by, at whatever distance. As he chewed tobacco, he often spat through his teeth, it is true, but the skill and neatness with which he did it was a sight to behold. Nobody could have imitated him, and nobody could say where, when, or how he had done it. It was like a lightning flash—psst!—that flew through space and was lost in the distant bushes. Far from being a vulgar act, in Vicente it was a proof of respect and submission. He rarely did it when talking with his equals. As a rule it was a sign of perplexity. When he was being questioned by Papa, Mama, or Cousin Juancho, he would scratch his head, turning the matter over in his mind and then, like an arrow—psst!—hardly moving the muscles of his face, without ever leaving a trace where he should not, with unerring aim, he spat. Instantly the reply followed, a model of discretion and accuracy.

Our association with Vicente Cochocho gave us a better training in philosophy and the natural sciences than any textbook could have done. His spirit, at one with ours in its simplicity, strong with the wisdom of experience, held a fund of pleasant information that flowed from his mind to ours with the ease of a limpid, running brook. We besieged him with questions. Almost every one of them was punctuated with a "hmmm?" that represented the concentrated force of our curiosity and whose position varied, depending on the phrase.

"Why are there green guavas and yellow guavas, Vicente, hmmm?"

"Why do snakes bite, hmmm? Vicente, and eels don't?"

"Why is it roosters fight, Vicente, hmmm? and don't lay eggs like hens?"

"Why don't you, Vicente Cochocho, *topocho*, *rechocho*, Cockroach Mustache, have a tile-roofed house like the tenants, hmmm?"

To answer all these questions, Vicente imbued his replies with the noble philosophy of resignation. With regard to the eels, he said:

"Because they are good and protect themselves by their slipperiness without hurting anybody, and that's why people fish for them and eat them. Folks hate snakes, but nobody goes out to catch them. They're so evil they respect them."

As for the roosters:

"Because that is what they are supposed to do, fight, and they don't like to do anything where they can't be boss. Don't you see the badge of office in their crest?"

As for himself:

"Because I was born to be poor. Who ever saw a black hired hand living in a tile-roofed house?"

Papa had lived and ruled in Piedra Azul from earliest childhood.

He was, so to speak, the son of the whole plantation, and we were the grandchildren.

The old people called Papa "Young Juan Manuel," or "Young Juan Manuelito." The younger ones, "Don Juan Manuel." As for us, who were at one and the same time the grandchildren and princesses of Piedra Azul, we were addressed by the familiar *tú*, and as though we were princesses of Castile or Aragon, we were known by this long, sonorous title, which might have come from the verses of Jorge Manrique: the "Six Little Girls of the Big House."

Vicente, too, used *tú* when speaking to us, but as a sign of homage he never put "Miss" or "Missy" before our names, but "Lord," "Thou Lord," just as if he were addressing God.

For example, when he arrived on the donkey with a load of vegetables, fruits, and banana leaves, and we ran toward him deluging him with questions to find out if our orders had been filled, he would answer us one at a time:

"Yes, Lord, Aurora, I brought you your mangoes. Here they are."

"Yes, Lord, Blanca Nieves, I got you the white rabbit. They'll send it tomorrow, cage and all."

Or, "No, Lord, Violeta, don't hit the poor donkey, he never did anything to you."

It would be next to impossible to explain to you the delicate shades of meaning in Vicente's way of talking, for these nuances came not from the words themselves, but from the tone. What is a phrase without tone or rhythm? A corpse, a mummy. Oh, beautiful human voice, the soul of words, the mother of language, how rich, how infinite thou art!

As many times as I have attempted to explain how Vicente talked and how Mama talked, those two opposed poles; one the essence of rusticity and the other of refinement or preciosity; one in which rhythm predominated, in the other, melody; I have sadly realized the uselessness of my endeavor. The written word, I repeat, is a corpse. Why in this era of great inventions and startling innovations have writers not yet found a way of saying to this corpse, "Arise and walk"? Today, when everything is happy noise-making in the republic of letters, today when genius and novelty go hand in hand in blithe harmony, how have they not discovered the way of bringing this corpse to life? If I were a novelist of talent—two modest hypotheses—I would introduce the following innovation in the novel. Before I began to set down any conversation I would draw a musical staff on my page. At the left, in the usual fashion, I would indicate the clef, the key signature, and the time; then the measures with notes and accidentals, and then, below, the text, as though it were to be sung. A reader possessing the rudiments of do-re-mi would then have only to take the book in the left hand, mark the time with the right, humming the words. The characters of the novel would really talk.

I have just realized that what I have said is nonsense. Forgive me. The writer who did such a thing for the sake of greater verisimilitude or clarity would be held in utter contempt. The clarity that makes us pleasant keeps us from being admired. The incomprehensible, that which humiliates the spirit, is greeted by irritated and sincere applause whose real meaning is: "Bravo, bravissimo, we didn't understand a thing." A soaring imagination may take wing in darkness, which is infinite. God would not be worth adoring if he were comprehensible. Humble clarity is finite, frank, and poor. Clarity is as contemptible and comfortable as a pair of old shoes. I do not aspire to glory, or applause, or the admiration of the crowd; therefore, I can put on my comfortable old shoes occasionally.

Vicente Cochocho played the *maracas* at all the dances in Piedra Azul. To my ear, his conversation was always accompanied by the rattle or beat of a pair of invisible *maracas*. That's where it got its rhythm. If Mama, for instance, needed Vicente to bring her passion flowers or soursops in a hurry, she would lean over the railing, and call out:

"Vicente, are you there in the garden?"

From the distance came the reply:

"Yes, Lord!"

The "yes" could be represented by a whole note tied to an eighth note, with a hold, and one rattle of the *maracas*; the "Lord" by a quarter, a whole, and three rattles.

III

In addition to being a teacher of philosophy and natural sciences, player of the *maracas*, cleaner of ditches, cane feeder, and weeder, Vicente was the doctor, druggist, and undertaker of Piedra Azul. He was also, as will be seen, a soldier when the occasion arose, and a military genius. If his legs were spattered with mud, his bravery, spattered with deeds of valor and prowess, deserved to have fame throw open its doors to welcome him. But "Glory is only for those who seek her," a sage once remarked. Vicente, either because he was a philosopher, or because he did not feel himself sufficiently handsome and dashing to woo so great a lady, always turned his back on her, never drawing close enough to address one word to her.

In the field of military strategy, Vicente's genius exceeded his vocation; in that of medicine, his vocation exceeded his genius. As it is vocation that molds the true doctor, as medicine has its origins in mysticism, miracles, and the wisdom of the heart, Vicente, all activity, all self-sacrifice, all self-abnegation, Vicente, whom nobody ever called "Doctor Cochocho," was a doctor par excellence.

Papa did not think so. As medicine is a battleground of the most impassioned theories, the most ardent mysticism, and the most fanatical controversy, Papa combated Vicente's activities toward the sick on the plantation with wrath and intolerance. With the conviction of a zealot, he affirmed that Vicente's presence at Piedra Azul was a far more dangerous plague than typhus, dysentery, and yellow fever put together. Papa was prejudiced, no doubt about it. But as his power was absolute, Vicente's situation with respect to his sublime mission and with respect to Papa was that of the early Christians under the persecution of Diocletian or Nero. I don't mean by this that Papa was cruel, but that, threatened at every turn by his Omnipotence and filled with heroism, ever more strengthened in charity and faith, Vicente carried on his ministry in the shadows.

I believe that, as so often happens, Papa's righteous indignation concealed without his knowing it the keen, aggressive rivalry that always exists between two doctors dealing with the same clientele. Because I must tell you that, without study or degrees, Don Juan Manuel was a doctor too, after his own fashion. Mounted on his horse Caramelo, he too set out with his quinine pills, his thermometer, his mustard plasters, his physics, and prescribed remedies for the ailing. Vicente traveled on foot with his plantain leaves, ground plum root, lizard grease, blood of a rabbit killed in the waning moon, spells, prayers, and took Papa's patients away from him. Though the weaker of the two, Vicente had the advantage of his august vocation. In Piedra Azul all treatment and medication was free of charge. Therefore, completely disarmed inasmuch as he could not send his patients those staggering bills that do so much to uphold a doctor's reputation, Papa had to stand helplessly by, watching his practice dwindle away while that of his rival Vicente flourished.

Like every doctor, famous or obscure, unknown or celebrated, like every quack, sawbones, or great specialist, Vicente accomplished marvelous cures, and also at times lightning deaths that aroused great indignation and covered his name with opprobrium for a few days. Things soon returned to normal, and faith was restored. During the days when Vicente's reputation touched bottom, Papa's anger came thundering down on Vicente's defenseless head.

One day we witnessed the following solemn and painful scene.

It was in the afternoon. Papa had been shut up in his study with his overseer for a long time. Suddenly the door was flung open and, filled with arrogance and majesty, like an emperor on the balcony of his palace, Don Juan Manuel appeared at the railing beside his study, from which he dominated the broad esplanade or front entrance of the house. From there, in a stern voice that foretold the gathering storm, he called out to one of the servants:

"Go tell Vicente Cochocho to come here at once. I want to talk with him."

We shivered in our shoes in the face of the mystery that threatened harm to one of our fondest attachments, and we all ran, terrified, to witness the disaster.

In a few minutes, across the esplanade, smaller, squatter, more top-heavy than ever, there came our beloved Cochocho. As he never ventured to come up the front steps of the house, he approached the railing, and with his duck feet, his bowed legs, his woolly head, his palm-leaf hat in one hand, his machete in the other, he stopped, raising his head, like a frog confronting a lion:

"Lord?"

"Now, Vicente, you listen to me," thundered Papa, terrible and all-powerful. "I have just heard that the daughter of José del Rosario, over there in Quebrada Grande, had something wrong with her eye, and you went there and said the cure for it was the blood of a limpet, and you yourself caught the limpet, drew out the blood, took it to them, and they put it on, and the girl is now blind in one eye. You are a brute, and not only a brute, a criminal. Now, you listen to what I am saying, and don't forget it; for it's the last time I'm telling you: I swear, Vicente, that if you ever prescribe for another sick person here on Piedra Azul, I'm going to write to the judge of the district to send for you and to put you in jail for five or six years as a murderer. And so help me, I'll do it. Are you listening to me, Vicente? Do you understand?"

"Yes, Lord."

Vicente answered with bowed head, without omitting the hold and the three rattles of the *maraca*.

It goes without saying that he was at work more zealously than ever the next day, secretly hunting out limpets and herbs, grinding roots, going back and forth, north and south, losing many days' pay, fording flooded rivers, and spending sleepless nights at the bedside of his beloved patients.

The kindness and favors of Vicente Cochocho, like anything that grows bountiful and free, like wild fruits, like the golden mangoes of August, were held in no esteem at Piedra Azul. His self-abnegation often aroused irritation, and his greatest gifts were received like so many things which, though useful, are bothersome, a necessary but annoying shower, for example.

There existed at Piedra Azul a custom that had become law, a law worthy of the stern wisdom of a Lycurgus. When one of the field hands or any of his connections died, there was never any question. Papa took care of all the expenses involved in the funeral—except one, the coffin, which was Vicente's special charge. That is to say, the two doctors, each after his own fashion, assumed the expense occasioned by the death of their patients. As soon as Vicente learned of a demise, he went to the house—or, to be more exact, the cabin—of the deceased, arising before dawn if necessary, presented his condolences with his usual courtesy, and concluded:

"As for the 'urn,' you don't have to worry about it. I'll have it here this evening."

There were no wages for Vicente that day. He spent his morning going from place to place, to taverns, houses of the sharecroppers, cabins of the hired hands, asking everywhere if "by any chance" they happened to have a few boards or old boxes they could let him have. In truth it must be said that, in view of the circumstances, he was cordially received by all with an outpouring of generosity. Around noon, having assembled the necessary materials, he set himself up in a corner of the mill with saw, hammer, nails; and, with much pounding and banging, lopping off here, piecing out there, a rude coffin gradually emerged. When the basic carpentry was completed, he came to the house to ask Mama, with the timidity of all who ask a favor, and an expectoration of tobacco juice—psst!—as a token of respect, if "by chance" Miss Carmen María did not happen to have some black cloth she did not need. "Chance" never disappointed him. With an armful of black cloth, he returned to the mill where he cut the material skillfully and economically, coated it with paste, and fitted it on piece by piece until the patched box, stamped here and there with "Fragile," "Piedra Azul Plant . . . ," "La Guayr . . . ," gradually turned into a black coffin—a mass of pitiful humps and hollows, to be sure, but in the last analysis as lugubrious and ugly as the most expensive coffin. He never forgot to paste on the top two white strips in the form of a cross. His work completed, in the small hours of the night he hoisted the coffin on his shoulder and, trotting through the darkness, arrived at the mourning household, where he stopped at the door and:

"Praise be to God! Praise be to God!" he shouted to announce his presence.

From within, as was natural, came the irate reply: "What do you mean by making such a racket? Don't you know there's a dead person here, that the dead deserve more respect? Put the coffin down where it won't be in the way, and as long as you are here, sit down and have a cup of coffee and, if you want it, a glass of rum."

Having thus complied with the demands of the situation, all went on talking at the top of their lungs.

IV

Vicente Cochocho's bounty, like sunlight, spread itself on all alike, whatever the circumstance, rich or poor, mighty or humble, just or unjust. Vicente would risk his life to cross a flooded river to secure "yarbs" for a dying person, or to climb out on a fragile limb to reach a cluster of genips at the behest of one of us. He would stay up all night making a coffin or shaking the *maracas* without pause to make a dance a success. As you have observed, nobody ever thanked him for anything. Who ever remembers to thank the sun for shining or water for quenching one's thirst?

Although he loved dancing passionately, he never danced for the simple reason that nobody ever wanted to dance with him. As long ago as then and even in Piedra Azul, the pickers and sorters of coffee had their own brand of snobbishness. If the master of ceremonies went over to a group of guests and asked them to "dance just one little number with Vicente, to be nice, for the poor fellow had been playing the *maracas* all night, and it wouldn't lower any of you, or break a bone," they would snippily answer, "We'd have to be crazy; we're not going to make a spectacle of ourselves with that little shrimp who doesn't come to our waist; he's no kind of a partner for anybody." Poor Vicente, spurned, disdained, and resigned would go on playing his *maracas* until morning.

But if Vicente was passed over at the dances because of his complete lack of physical attractiveness, in compensation he had found a deep, undemanding love, a love that turned its back on sterile vanity, disdaining all material advantage, closing its eyes to the beauties of the body to fix them upon those of the soul. Vicente was loved for his moral attainments and with rare intensity, inasmuch as he was loved at the same time, without jealousy, quarrels, or rivalry, by Aquilina and Eleuteria. He loved them both without showing any partiality; they both knew this, and they accepted it with mutual, or, to be more exact, twofold generosity.

Aquilina and Eleuteria were neither very pretty nor very distinguished; on the contrary, they were on Vicente's own level and could give him a love that was all peace, without danger or storms, which is a more potent ingredient of happiness than elegance and beauty combined.

So that you will not be shocked or judge Vicente too harshly, I hasten to inform you that free love was accepted at Piedra Azul. It was as normal, as much the order of the day as, unfortunately, it is in our own times and as it was then in the rich, refined, aristocratic society of any of the great cities. Aside from slight variations of detail, basically the customs of Piedra Azul were worthy of a brilliant court. As my charming mother had never traveled and was ignorant of this remarkable coincidence, she used to complain to Papa, almost with tears in her eyes, that he could be sure of one very sorry thing, and that was that as far as customs were concerned, beyond the shadow of a doubt his plantation represented the lowest rung of the ladder. Filled with apostolic zeal, arising as much from a spirit of moral rectitude as of pride, just as she adorned the tables with antimacassars and vases of flowers, so she distributed advice, legitimacy, and nuptial blessings throughout the cabins of Piedra Azul. Papa took care of all funeral expenses; Mama, all wedding expenses. Her efforts on behalf of morality, like any endeavor that does not involve money, flourished. At times they flourished with satisfying results, but all too often the results were lamentable. As it inevitably and unfortunately happens everywhere, at Piedra Azul, too, most of the men, once the knot had been tied, gave themselves over to infidelity with remarkable dedication and plurality. In the shade of these strayings, jealousy, arguments, and scenes of violence thrived and multiplied, generally concluding in a brilliant symphony of blows. The victim nearly always turned up at the house, asked for Mama, told her her troubles, and without directly reproaching her, which would have been a breach of politeness, on the assumption that a word to the wise is enough, she concluded her tale of woe with such oblique remarks as:

"Oh, Miss Carmen María, you ought to see him; he's not the same man. I wonder if this could be a judgment of God upon me for my vanity. Whose idea was it for me ever to get married?"

Mama, torn with distress, sighing and raising her eyes heaven-ward, advised patience and resignation.

It goes without saying that as the irregularity of Vicente's menage put it in a class by itself, Mama rained warnings, complaints, appeals upon him daily without making a dent. Vicente was refractory to the marriage bond. Not because of that hardness of heart to which the Scriptures allude, but out of a deep-rooted, unshakable sense of fidel-ity. As neither the church nor the law sanctioned plural marriages, and as he could not put aside Eleuteria for Aquilina, nor Aquilina for Eleuteria, Vicente, firmly turning his back on marriage, divided his affections—by this time, undoubtedly platonic—between the two companions of different epochs of his youth whom a series of circum-stances had brought together one day in the autumn of his years under the sheltering roof of his rented cabin. By one of those miracles possible only to the truly good, like that of Saint Francis and the wolf, Vicente had brought it to pass that Aquilina and Eleuteria lived together in perfect harmony.

One day we girls, out for a walk with Evelyn, begged to see Vicente's house—which, as may be imagined, was a source of pas-sionate interest to us. Evelyn finally agreed.

The devout pilgrimage took place: walking, walking, we made our way to the shrine of our wonder. When we glimpsed it in the distance, topping a rise, half hidden among the trees, we ran as fast as we could to see who could get there first. Evelyn followed at a distance. The sight that met our eyes beneath the two trees was indeed of stupendous interest from the point of view of prehistoric simplicity. The thatched roof, smoke-blackened and tossed by the wind, hung desolately on all sides, touching the ground. Beside the door there was a bench made of a tree trunk resting on two forked sticks. On the ground three sooty stones conversed with the cold ashes of the hearth. A hen tied by one leg to one of the supports of the bench was cackling and flapping her wings in an attempt to get loose. In the middle of the yard stood a mortar, it too fashioned from a tree trunk, and on either side of it Aquilina and Eleuteria, each with pestle in hand, were pounding corn with evangelical zeal for Vicente's and their daily bread.

There are no words to describe the silent and mysterious indignation with which Evelyn, when she took in the implications of what she was witnessing, dragged us away from the cabin and its environs. The silence and mystery lasted until we got home, when she went into a low-voiced conference with Mama. In muted, outraged tones she stated that in addition to being the smallest, the ugliest, and the dirtiest of all the hands at Piedra Azul, to complete the picture and so nothing would be lacking, Vicente Cochocho was also the most "depraved," as she had just seen with her own eyes.

Inasmuch as the word "depraved" did not form a part of our vocabulary, we, too, went into a huddle to see if we could figure out what this new and terrible defect of our friend Vicente could be. As was to be expected, Violeta assumed the chairmanship of the meeting, and overwhelming us with her knowledge, stated ex cathedra that "depraved" meant all those whose thatch roofs were as dark and disheveled as that of Vicente's cabin, and that she had known this "oh, heavens, forever!" The next day Mama sent for Vicente and in the same plaintive voice that she employed when scolding us, she read him this sermon:

"In the name of God, Vicente, you can't go on living the way you do any longer. Evelyn went to your cabin with the girls yesterday, and she came back horrified. You have no idea of morality. Vicente, you are like the beasts who do not know that there is a God and have not heard of his commandments. At your age, Vicente, you ought to set an example, but, no, you are the worst of all, the ringleader. You can't go on like this. Either you marry one of the two, or else, Vicente, you live by yourself, like a normal human being, like a baptized Christian."

In adopting this laudable and positive attitude, my devout mother, obedient daughter of the church, had failed to note how many cruel, reprehensible acts are done with the best of intentions.

As was his habit when confronted with any dilemma, Vicente scratched his head, gave twist after twist to his palm-leaf hat, spat through his teeth with exquisite precision, and finally brought out between pauses and stammers: "As for getting married right away, God our Master knows only too well that I can't do it; to get married a man has to have a cabin of his own." Then he added conciliatingly:

"Now, aside from getting married, Miss Carmen María, any day now I'm going to satisfy you, I promise; but give me a little time. As soon as coffee-gathering time comes and they can get some work and get a few cents together, I'll send them away. I give you my word. But please be patient with me. It's just a question of a little while longer."

Mama, persevering and imbued with missionary spirit, continued plaintively wrestling with Vicente's conscience, while "the little while longer" went on indefinitely through all the coffee gatherings.

V

Nobody is a prophet in his own country. If Vicente's prestige was subzero in Piedra Azul, there were those for whom it ranked sky-high. "Cochocho from Piedra Azul," it will astonish you to know, was a name pronounced with respect and fear in many places. Two circumstances were needed to bring this about, it is true: first, for a revolution to break out; second, for some revolutionary general to request his services. If Vicente sent back the laconic answer: "I am at your command," Papa and the government could get ready—the former, for a boundless rage, the latter, for worries and defeats without end.

The day after sending in his message of acceptance—to Papa's utter indignation, for the situation always took him by surprise—Vicente would have mysteriously disappeared and along with him eight, ten, or fifteen hands, depending on the circumstances. To these absences caused by his military vocation, Papa added up on his fingers those occasioned by his medical vocation. As his two hands did not suffice for his indignation, he cut short the enumeration and summed up the disastrous tale:

"He is worse, far worse, than typhus, dysentery, and yellow fever put together. He is a plague, a veritable plague, a hailstorm, the seven-year locust. So help me, he's not setting foot on this place again."

The reports and comments soon began to come in:

"On that hill, or in this pass, Vicente is lying in ambush like a lion, wiping out the government troops. He doesn't let a fly get through."

Apparently, in questions of strategy, Vicente Cochocho was a pure and simple genius. Once he had received his orders from General X or Z, whom he was serving, Vicente collected twenty, thirty, or forty men, the number he judged necessary, and set off at their head. If, like Napoleon and Bolívar, his physical stature did not help him out, neither like them did he need any help. Other qualities made up for his lack of inches.

At the head of his men, his strategy all planned, went Vicente, making his way through mountain, plain, and wood with the assured sense of direction of a carrier pigeon. He would suddenly halt at some spot, peruse the ocean of woodlands and hills, stretch out his short arm quivering with genius, point with his finger to some determined point, and say:

"There's the place."

And there he lay in ambush with his thirty men, and God help anyone who tried to pass with warlike intentions. Traps, stratagems, attacks without number rained fatally down on the surprised enemy, however much better disciplined, armed, or numerous they might be.

Once the revolution was over, Vicente would descend from his Olympus to Piedra Azul, covered with laurels and with his forces intact.

Papa pretended he hadn't noticed anything.

The next day, Vicente was back in the mud up to his knees, cleaning out the drainage ditch, or squatting on the stones in the patio weeding with his same old knife.

Papa's forgiveness was one-third generosity and two-thirds hard sense. However much he might count and recount on his fingers calamities and deaths, Vicente was a source of far more advantages than disadvantages. With a foreknowledge of any brewing revolutionary movement that the most astute reporter might have envied, Vicente used all his influence to ward off any possible danger to Piedra Azul, and was a living guarantee.

If, say, a revolution broke out and Vicente was on the plantation because he had not yet been asked to assume the important role he was to play, he would suddenly come to the house, ask for Papa, approach him with a mysterious air, and winking one eye—a liberty he permitted himself only on such occasions—say in a low voice:

"I've come to let you know, Don Juan Manuel, that tomorrow at noon the revolution will be coming over the hill. They have given me their word that they will not come down and do any damage, but just to be on the safe side, it will be better for you to have the cattle out of sight."

Papa ordered the cattle hidden.

The next day, far in the distance, like a procession of ants, machetes gleaming and rifles blazing, over the mountain crest, beneath the magnificent midday sun, the revolution filed past.

One day, by one of those incomprehensible, almost miraculous turns of events, Papa was tipped off to the fact that Vicente was about to join the revolution. The uprising was scheduled for the next day. Just as on that other afternoon, when the hearing was held because of the medicinal failure of limpet blood, Papa, leaning over the railing, sent for Vicente. And just as we did that day, clustered about a pillar, we witnessed the event. The scene was repeated. Across the spreading esplanade, Cochocho, all ugliness, all politeness, the same as before, palm-leaf hat in hand, approached the railing. But this time, Papa, instead of throwing back his head awesome with majesty and radiating arrogance—on the contrary, with that solemn, moving tone we employ when we wish to dissuade a person from doing something which in reality is contrary to our own interests—began to harangue Vicente with a genial eloquence that overflowed with kindly, paternal advice. The speech, which lasted for some time, concluded with these words:

"You are risking your life, Vicente: you are ruining your health to serve the interests and ambitions of others. What do you get out of all this? What advantage, what profit, what good? None."

Vicente, his head bowed, and his hat spinning round and round between his fingers, answered never a word, but his silence spoke for itself: "I congratulate you on your eloquence, My Lord and Master, and I appreciate your interest, but for all your eloquence and your moving concern for me, I am joining the revolution tomorrow at dawn, for that matter has been decided."

As Papa took in perfectly the meaning of that silence, he changed his tactics. He solemnly offered Vicente, if he would give up the revolution, twice the salary he had been receiving and promised to build him a cabin on whatever site he selected, where he could also have a patch of land for his own.

Had Vicente's reply been somewhat briefer, it would have been worthy of a Spartan, of Guzman the Good—worthy, in a word, of going down in history.

"I have given my word to General——" (some well-known name I cannot now recall). "It was he who many years ago gave me the rank of captain. I have never had a pair of shoes on my feet, but I am not ungrateful, and I never turn my back on one who has been good to me. Not even if you were to give me all Piedra Azul, Don Juan Manuel, Vicente Aguilar's word has nothing to do with cabins or cornfields. It is not for sale nor can it be bought."

Under that magnificent answer Don Juan Manuel was crushed like an insect under a rock. In his defeat he had recourse to the weapon of the defeated: sarcasm. At this point he did toss his head back, and began to loudly exclaim with a forced, feigned smile:

"Oh-ho! But you are right. I had forgotten. I stand in the presence of the illustrious Captain Don Vicente Aguilar. Your humble servant! Go off, go off to the war, Sir Captain, and on your return you will undoubtedly be called upon to occupy the presidency of the republic."

Ah, the horrible opprobrium of those words, "Illustrious Captain Don Vicente Aguilar," far more harsh, far more cruel than the cruelest insults! That "Aguilar" was the worst of all. "Aguilar," on Papa's lips, was awful, more than you can ever know, more than he understood. The great have no way of entering the world of the small; they are blind, and unfeeling because of their blindness, and cruel because of their size. We, being small, grasped all the pain caused by that insult which was all the more insult because it was not an insult and simply Vicente's name, like anyone else's. Gathered about the column, on hearing that "Aguilar" pronounced with smiles and heard by us for the first time in our life, we were on the point of bursting into collective tears as on that day when Mama punished Violeta. And then the expression on the face of "illustrious Captain Don Vicente Aguilar"! Beaten with his own name, like a dog thrashed by its master, without raising his voice, lifting his orphaned eyes, whose beauty no one had ever noticed, which were like a bridge that led from the ugliness of his body to the beauty of his soul, he turned those eyes of a suffering dog toward us in search of sympathy. There he found it—and in what measure! With head hanging, without looking at papa or answering his sarcasm, he took his leave of him:

"Always at your orders, Don Juan Manuel."

And with a long, intense look at us:

"Goodbye, my little ladies. May God protect you, and the Virgin watch over you until we meet again.' And he left. That "until we meet again" never came true. We never saw him again. But that last glance of a faithful dog beaten for no reason was to accompany us for the rest of our lives. I have never forgotten it and it is still with me, still beside me, it still serves me as lesson and example.

Ah, far-off, forgotten Cochocho, sublime louse, doctor of the poor, humble god of mud, deity of coffins and the waters! The Divine Teacher must have foreseen many glances like that final regard of yours as he led his disciples up to the Mount and there spoke his last testament. In it he set down your obscure name, Vicente Cochocho, for you were meek, you were pure of heart, you were merciful, you suffered persecution for the sake of justice. Heir of glory, you rule today among the blessed, and yours, all yours, is the Kingdom of Heaven.

No More Mill

We were playing in the orchard one day. Violeta, whose love of adventure impelled her to the most daring feats, one of which was disobedience, with its promise of conflicts and punishment— Violeta, as I say, had gone to the dining room and got herself a knife. With it she cut off branches, whittled them to a point, and stuck them in the ground, saying:

"These are my cane fields: these are my coffee groves; these are my gardens; all this is my plantation, and nobody is to come near it."

One of the maids who was watching us came over and asked her to be good enough to set up her plantation without the use of a knife, for both Mama and Evelyn had absolutely forbidden us to play with fire, inkwells, or knives. Violeta told her to go away and stop bothering her with such nonsense. To wash her hands of all responsibility, the maid went off and told Evelyn. Evelyn arrived at the very moment that Violeta was sharpening a branch. The knife gleamed and flashed in the air. Seeing what was going on, Evelyn said firmly:

"Violeta, give me that knife."

No," answered Violeta.

Evelyn's authority translated itself from word to deed. Grabbing Violeta by the wrist, she took the knife from her with the other hand. Violeta, surprised and disarmed, gave her an insolent look, and in self-defense and in a clear voice said:

"____!"

Wham! Out came an epithet, unexpected, unqualified, and un-thinkable, fittingly applied as to gender and number, one single word.

Where had she picked it up? A complete mystery. That was one of Violeta's specialities, knowing things nobody else knew without knowing herself where she had learned it. In spite of the fact that the word was new, all the rest of us instantly grasped the fact that the word suited Evelyn like an ugly hat—that is to say, it fit her without flattering her. When the two maids who were present heard the term whose meaning admitted of no doubt, they began to shriek with laughter. With their mirth the appellation took on heightened proportions and enveloped Evelyn's person more closely. Outraged more by the laughter than by the unexpected word, Evelyn was speechless for a moment. Then she inquired:

"Where did you learn that word, Violeta, which has made mouth dirty, black as coal? Where did you learn?"

Violeta rubbed her hand over her mouth to see if it was really dirty, but she did not deign to answer. As Evelyn had to contrive some exemplary punishment, without waiting for the culprit's reply she suddenly arrived at this ominous conclusion:

"You learned it at mill! All right, no more mill, now or ever."

"No more mill," and all because of Violeta and the two maids! It was one of those infamous, arbitrary decisions that fall upon the innocent because of the violence of those in power or the crimes of a group. And without further explanation, the law went into effect as of that moment.

"No more mill!" What unprecedented punishment! What a tragedy!

To our rustic souls the mill was club, theater, city. There was no pleasure comparable to the hour we spent at the stream and in the mill. It seemed heaven to us, and we were right, it was. Everything about it pleased sight, smell, taste, ear. Just as the syrup boiled in the great kettles, so life in the vicinity of the mill bubbled frank and hearty. All the elements and all the colors met and came together there: water, fire, sun—all paraded unclothed and in harmony to the rhythm set by the great meek, majestic wheel of the mill. None of the ugly, inexplicable, gloomy boredom of factories moved by steam or electricity. No. There was nothing mysterious or hidden in the mill. Everything was in plain view. Everyone knew why things happened, and the door stood open to anyone who wanted to come in, the elements, people, animals.

First in importance, high captain and spirit mother of the mill, was the water. From on high it came piped in from the dam and flung itself upon the great wheel, singing its descent with a full chorus of plumes and spray. The slow-turning wheel trailed behind it with the rosary of its buckets, with intervals of empty space against a background of ferns and moss. To the turning of the wheel three masses moved; the cane oozing juice as it was crushed; the hands of the feeders moving among the canes; and the hands of the bagasse loaders who carried away the poor dead remains of the cane on leather stretchers to spread it in the sun. Dragged out into the sun by large rakes, the crushed corpses came back to life and blossomed into mountains: mashed mountains of bagasse, brides of fire.

In the vast, generous mill there were almost no walls or doors. Nothing was shut in. Everybody was welcome. The sun came in, the air, the rain, legions of golden, buzzing wasps in search of sweets. The slow ox teams came in with the broad carts piled high with tightly packed cane which the hands unloaded quickly and left piled on the ground behind the carts. And in search of sweets, like the wasps, came the children of the workers with a pan in their hands, asking: "Mama wants to know if you will be good enough to give me some scrapings or a piece of broken sugarloaf for *guarapo* tonight." Like the wasps, they were given their scrapings or piece of broken sugarloaf. Nobody was turned away.

In a swarm, with Evelyn and the maids following behind, buzzing and flying, like the wasps, like the workers' children, between the ox teams, the piles of cane, and the bagasse litters, came the girls in search of sweets, interfering with the work and getting in everyone's way.

The first thing we did was to rush to stick a foot into the hardened, grayish foam the cane sap formed as it went through a trough toward the boiling room. After imprinting on the foam the greatest possible number of feet, the next thing was to call out to Vicente Cochocho, if he happened to be present, and if not, to the group of loaders:

"When are you going to stop grinding? Hurry up, it's time now. Time for lunch. Time for lunch!"

To "stop the grinding" or to "lunch" was to halt the wheel and the cylinders and release the water through a cement conduit which emptied into a pool where, among vines, bamboo tufts, and a spreading *huisache* tree, we had our daily bath in the sunshine, to the roaring of the stream, amid the whirlpools it set up and the perfume the water released from the earth and the mossy stones as it touched them.

The big mill wheel and the noise of the water drowned out our voices. But by our gestures and moving lips the loaders knew what we wanted, and they limited themselves to answering by signs that it was not time to turn off the mill yet, and to round out their explanation they pointed out to us the pile of cane still to be ground.

While waiting for the water, we each ran our separate ways to one of the hands asking him to peel us a piece of cane. The peon had to stop what he was doing, select a cane, peel it with his machete, slice it into pieces, and each little girl went off with her sugarcane, sucking it and dribbling juice on herself. Up and down the mill they went, from one end to the other, and the more questions, the better.

I don't know about my sisters, but for myself I can assure you that here in the mill, waiting the moment for the water to be released, sucking stalks of cane with hands sticky and rivulets of juice running down my neck and arms, I spent the pleasantest hours of my life.

People did not gather at the mill to amuse themselves; that was what made it so pleasant and agreeable. To watch what was going on, one did not have to take a seat as in the theater and sit motionless without talking, for hours with a pair of opera glasses in hand, one's leg gone to sleep, watching gestures and listening to banalities against a background of painted cloth and boards. At the mill no one was expected, as at a dance, to whirl around solemnly on teetering heels in time to the music, nor was it necessary to mouth, with a sandwich in one hand and a glass of champagne in the other, all those commonplaces that most of our interlocutors, far more eloquent than we, affirm with such vehemence and assurance, so brilliantly, so emphatically.

What went on at the mill, so varied, so full of life and color, did not chain one's attention nor tyrannize one's movements. While watching the skimming cauldron, the twisting of the syrup, the molasses flowing through the pipes, the stirring of the thickening sugar, the filling of the molds, one could move freely from side to side like a dancer and at the same time suck cane, eat molasses candy, and think about anything one liked.

At the mill it was possible to fire a dozen questions at the sugar tester and walk off before he had a chance to answer, then ask the same questions of the skimmer of the first cauldron, without bothering to ask either of them first, "May I ask you something, sir?" At the mill solid body or winged spirit could go whither it listed, like the wasps, lighting here, there, when and where it pleased. Freedom of movement and freedom of thought—are not these two of the indispensable elements of happiness? Not to mention that delicious smell that kettles and pans gave off. Nor the beautiful golden hue of high-grade brown sugar of fine-quality cane. Or the drab color of the cheap variety from skimmings or poor cane. And the melodious cry of the tester calling out through a grating, like the angelus in the afternoon:

"F-i-i-ire!"

And the way everyone took his ease. Nobody in the boiling room, or the grinding room, or in the bagasse shed rushed about with brusque movements denoting activity, graceless and overbearing, as though shouting: "I am the big noise here; I am the one who makes the mare go, hurry up, look at me, look what I can do." None of that. Everything moved at a gentle pace in the friendly mill. Nobody was pretending to set the world on fire. The long process of sugar boiling, like the work of nature rather than industry, seemed to accomplish itself, in its own good time; little by little, bit by bit. The thirty or forty mill hands took part in the sugar making as though it were a birth: a little help, lots of patience, talk, and nothing more.

In a word, the mill was simple, good well-being. And Violeta had wiped it all out with a single word. Violeta was strong because she was enterprising and aggressive. Her words, as you have seen, like those of certain congressmen and senators, disrupted the calm course of life. Peaceful multitudes then had to suffer the consequences.

Now, with the severe sanction in force, before we could go to bathe we had to stay up the hill near the dam where the water poured into the pipe, at some distance from the mill wheel. To catch a glimpse of our beloved mill, we had to peep over the wall. With a great effort, standing tiptoe on a stone, we could manage to get eyes and nose over it, but rarely our mouths. There, as best we could, we proffered our daily prayer:

"When are you going to stop grinding? It's time for lunch. Go on, go on. It's time now."

A prayer that was swallowed up in the dark night of unnoticed things. Nobody paid any attention to us, inasmuch as, lost up there between the wall and the noise of the water, we could neither be seen nor heard.

In justice I must mention one thing. Although the prohibition was strictly enforced, as I have said, occasionally Evelyn gathered us together after our bath, and announced:

"Today, as you've all been good girls, you can come with me to the mill."

Our shrieks of delight were deafening, and our headlong flight wild. When all is said and done, I believe that if Violeta had never said that word with its disastrous results the memory of the mill would undoubtedly have vanished amid the myriad places, persons, scenes that lie buried under the dust of my memory as in a graveyard. Violeta provoked Evelyn's stern reprisal, and Evelyn's sternness saved the mill from oblivion. The mill gleams, the mill scintillates among my recollections.

Excellent Evelyn. Your good influence filled our childhood with joys and saved it from the bleak, the cruel boredom that afflicts the soul of those children who have everything, pitiful victims of satiety, frail buds blasted by disillusion. By forbidding us things and places, Evelyn imbued them with life. Breathing like God upon the dust, she gave it a soul, the soul that animates anything worth loving.

If my childhood was happy, if my childhood comes back to me, smiles upon me throughout the years, it is because it transpired in the arms of nature, and because, though channeled, it flowed as freely as a river between its banks. My sisters and I were never shut up within four walls, sated with candy, dolls, wagons, rocking horses, all those gloomy toys which, like the cares of adult life, bow down the shoulders of childhood. When one of us was given a doll, we fondled it as long as the novelty lasted. In two hours the sight of those staring eyes, those rigid legs and arms no longer interested us, and away with the dead thing! We never touched it again, and we were right.

We made our favorite toys ourselves out under the trees, made them of leaves, stones, water, green fruit, mud, old bottles, and empty tin cans. Like artists, we were possessed by the divine fire of creation, and like poets, we discovered secret affinities and mysterious relations between the most diverse objects. For example, we would take an old can and with a nail and a stone make a hole into which we fitted a stick as a tongue, attaching a pair of corncobs to serve as oxen, with two curved thorns stuck into each cob for horns, and with a reed for a goad. Our creation finished, we imitated the voice of the ox drivers, shouting at the stubborn corncobs:

"Gee-up, ox! Back, Swallow! Get over, Blaze!"

With the old can, the two cobs, and the four thorns we had made an oxcart with its team, and also a poem.

The rest of my life was to transpire under the same kindly and stern regime as my early childhood. Life imitated Evelyn; it gave me to taste of all its pleasant things, but sparingly, frugally, so that surfeit never dulled the edge of desire. The passing of the indifferent years did not carry off treasures of beauty, of love, or honors. I do not misprize my own bygone years, nor those that have not yet passed for others. Time, as it laid its lips upon my hair, has tenderly crowned me with the white snow of my own name, and has never left the teethmarks of bitterness in my soul. For all my seventy-five years, my heart still leaps up at the prospect of an automobile ride into the country for a picnic under the mountain sunshine, and my hands still tremble with excitement and impatience as they undo the knots of ribbon that adorn the surprise of a present.

Rain Cloud and Little Rain Cloud

I

Papa, as has been seen, fancied himself a doctor. His self-assumed vocation made him very health conscious: "The girls," he had decreed, "should always be out in the fresh air, it doesn't matter if they get tanned. For no reason should they ever go to Caracas, nor anywhere where there are a lot of people and they might catch measles, whooping cough, diphtheria, or scarlet fever. They should bathe in cold running water, not be too warmly dressed, get up early, and go the first thing and drink a glass of milk fresh from the cow."

These precepts were admirable, not for the hygienic advantages they may have afforded us, but for their moral therapy. Evelyn's strictures were designed to inculcate solid principles in us; those of Papa, solid health. By a happy coincidence, which neither of the two had thought out, they gave us in addition years of immediate happiness.

The order of the glass of milk fresh from the cow was, without doubt, the pleasantest of all. Not only because of the taste of the fresh milk, covered with foam in which we buried our noses as we raised the glass, holding our breath, and concluding with an "ah" of satisfaction and a pair of white mustaches, but also because of the atmosphere of the cow barn at six in the morning.

As attractive and almost as entertaining as the mill, the milking shed was backed up or guaranteed by the seal of hygienic approval. Evelyn would never have dared say: "You learned that in the barn. No more barn," as she had said: "No more mill." Because of this assurance, it was less valued but, as I said, almost as attractive.

The barn had in its favor the time of day. When at six in the morning each little girl, glass in hand, with Evelyn as group leader, walked the two blocks or so that separated the barn from the house, the sun gave off almost no warmth, the roosters, head and breast erect, gave us their good morning: "Cock-a-doodle-do"; the oxen, not yet spanned, were munching their fodder by the cabin doors; and as we touched the passing boughs or crossed the high grass, we were literally bathed in dew.

The ruler of the republic of the cows, by their choice and sovereign will—do not laugh, you will see that this is true—all wisdom, all good government, was Daniel the cowherd.

When we made our appearance in the city of the cows, Daniel, who had been up since four in the morning, had already, with the assistance of a stable boy, filled many buckets of milk. The order that prevailed was perfect: the order of the ideal future city. In the open air, under the sky and sun, each cow was happy and in her house—that is to say, tied to a tree or a post. Some had a tree— even a tree in bloom; others had only a short, bare post. Nobody complained and nobody was resentful; there was no class warfare. To each according to her needs, from each according to her ability. All was peace, all was light.

The four walls of the barn overflowed with milk and maternal love. Everything was noble, even things not generally considered so. Upon the bedding of straw, like the cows, like the buckets filled with milk, like Daniel and the stable boy, everything rested with complete naturalness. Nothing wounded sight or scent.

We were thoroughly conversant with the laws, the uses, and customs of the barn. We knew, for example, that the cow whose calf was tied to her leg had already been milked. That, on the contrary, those other calves still shut up behind the fence, restless, raising their muzzles over the bars, like the little girls above the wall of the mill, had not yet been weaned, nor their mothers milked. We knew this perfectly well, but this did not prevent our asking questions.

The minute we set foot in the barn, each with her glass, we ran to the group formed by Daniel, the calf, and the cow he was milking. The rain of questions began.

"Have you milked Rain Cloud yet, Daniel, hmmm? Why aren't you milking Rose Apple, hmmm, Daniel? Why don't you let little

Rose Apple loose? Look at it, Daniel, look at her, sticking out her head. Is it because she's hungry, Daniel, hmmm? Do you think so?"

Daniel had to armor himself with patience. We were a lot more trouble to him than all the cows and calves, who knowing the rules observed them, and best of all, observed them in silence, without asking things they knew perfectly well.

The cows, as you may already have noticed, had names similar to ours, without plagiarism on the one hand or the other, but pure coincidence. Daniel chose the cows' names with the same fine abandon as Mama ours. Being a plainsman, Daniel was a poet. Although his vein was by preference epigrammatic, he could be lyric when the occasion demanded. And the barnyard provided occasion. There Daniel showed the influence of the romantic school. So it was not strange that, traveling different routes, his tastes and Mama's should meet every morning between the four walls of the barnlot.

The cows baptized by Daniel were called as you have already heard, and there were also Elderberry Flower, Christmas Eve, Sad Widow, Pretty Girl, Sunshine (which Daniel and we contracted to Sushi), Bleeding Heart, Poppy, Never Leave Me, and so on to the number of twenty.

It hardly seems necessary to say that Sad Widow was utterly and without relief black, and that the coat of Christmas Eve, black too, was dappled here and there with all the stars of Bethlehem, and the shining orb that guided the Wise Men. Sunshine, on the contrary, was light, a golden brown that was in heartless, insulting contrast to poor Bleeding Heart, whose dingy, faded, indefinable hue neither rejoiced the heart nor pleased the eye.

Between the cows and their names there existed a kind of harmony or concordance that was lacking between us and ours. Aside from that, there was a resemblance that we perceived and that delighted us. They and we were daughters of Piedra Azul; the barn was close to the Big House, we were citizens and sisters of the same land. They were our wet nurses, and the calves, our foster brothers and sisters. So there was no call for us to put on airs or look down our noses at them.

To substantiate what I have said, I may add that there was one cow I haven't mentioned yet who, having been born with a white spot on her forehead, came into the world with her name ready made, so to speak. In spite of the confusion to which it gave rise, there was nothing that could be done about it. The cow was called Estrella. Do you think for a minute that the other Estrella—that is to say, my sister—felt lowered by this coincidence? Not at all. On the contrary, when she went to the barnlot, assuming that her name gave her certain prerogative over the rest of us, she would inquire with interest and pride:

"Have you milked my namesake yet, Daniel? I want you to milk her in my glass, for her milk is for me. Isn't that so, Daniel, hmmm? that her milk is for me?"

In reality, each cow and calf formed a single unit that bore the same name. In the group or family of Christmas Eve, for example, mother and son were equally Christmas Eve. This unification simplified discipline, making maneuvers and movements that needed to be carried out simultaneously coincide. For example, when the moment came to milk Christmas Eve, Daniel, wherever he happened to be, gave three long calls that filled and spread through the confines of the barnlot:

"Chri-i-i-istmas Eve! Christmas E-e-e-eve! Christmas E-e-e-ve!"

If Christmas Eve, mother, happened to be lying down drowsing, when she heard her name issue from Daniel's lips like a long wind sigh rippling through the grass of the savannah mile after mile until it is lost in the distant horizon—when Christmas Eve, as I say, heard the name, she got to her feet at once, and turned her head toward the calf pen. There Christmas Eve, son, was milling furiously around among his fellow prisoners, who in view of the circumstances let him through without resenting his butting and pushing. The stable boy had no more than lowered the first bar when over the gate came Christmas Eve, son, stiff-legged, dragging, tripping on and getting tangled up in his rope if he had one, stumbling, leaping, till he reached the side of Christmas Eve, mother, and began nuzzling her.

We could not understand how two persons, however close they were, could be called by the same name. This awkward, confused duality did not please us at all. If the truth be told, we separated the calf from the cow by employing a diminutive. The calves paid no attention to us whatsoever, but that was not important, inasmuch as they never obeyed anybody but Daniel, lord and high priest of the barnlot, whose clear voice of a muezzin announced the awaited hour of freedom and breakfast.

To us Poppy's calf was Little Poppy; Christmas Eve's, Little Christmas Eve; Rain Cloud's, Little Rain Cloud, and so on down the line.

II

As I have said, Daniel was a plainsman, born in the heart of the savannah. But he had spent most of his youth in the barnyards of the valleys of Aragua. There, for years, he had been looking after the cattle and making cheese, an admirable soft cheese that, wrapped in a banana leaf, like Candelaria's *hallacas*, came to be, under Mama's reign, the specialty and pride of Piedra Azul. With smiles and excuses for the rusticity of the gift, she presented it to all visitors.

Aside from the cheese, Daniel had brought to the valleys of Aragua his excellent system of cattle government, his muezzin calls, and the exquisite names of the cows, all of which were new to Piedra Azul and its environs. Like the plainsman he was, in addition to being an excellent cowman and an excellent epigrammatic poet, Daniel was crafty and covetous. Always conciliatory, always pleasant, his every act formed a part of a finespun web whose threads were invisible even to the sharpest eye. When Papa hired him to take charge of the cows, Daniel studied the situation for two or three days and then undoubtedly arrived at this conclusion: "You can keep this job, Daniel, without trouble or interference as long as you like, and you can make money at it." And so it was. The cows began to show just enough of a profit to forestall any danger of sale or breaking up the herd, not a penny less or a penny more. Daniel worked zealously all through the week, and on Saturday afternoon presented to Papa a perfectly balanced, carefully doctored statement of the sales of milk and cheese. In view of the exactitude of the accounts, Papa was unable to prove that they were inaccurate. And in the face of amiability with which they were presented, Papa found himself disarmed and powerless to question the figures.

Crucified by his own impotence, Papa would say:

"Daniel is an excellent dairyman, I never saw his like, but neither did I ever see the like of the way he robs me. Besides, the way he handles the cows is bad; he's got them spoiled, absolutely spoiled. I'd give anything in the world to get out from his clutches, but who could replace him?"

The order, the discipline, the muezzin calls, the names of the cows, and, above all, those songs he sang them while he was milking, melodious, monotonous, accompanying himself with the rhythm of the milk dropping into the bucket, everything, absolutely everything, as you will see, was policy, a Machiavellian statecraft that Papa summed up in a simple phrase:

"He's got the cows spoiled, absolutely spoiled."

Daniel's policy did not exclude wit, lyricism, pity, and gallantry. Not all was rapacity and selfishness, no. Along with these qualities went generous sentiments worthy of all praise. Daniel saw to it that the cows were well taken care of so they would give lots of milk, in the first place, and be so happy and contented under his rule (the paternalism of all dictators) that they could not get along without him. Papa, whose capacity was definitely a subordinate one in this arrangement, couldn't either. Taking all these factors into consideration, Daniel ruled wisely, as I told you at the beginning.

The milking procedure was as follows: After uttering his three musical calls or cries, a tuneful combination of assonance and dissonance impossible to imitate—"Chri-i-i-stmas Eve, Christmas E-e-e-eve, Christmas Eve!"—Daniel allowed cow and calf to come together in tenderness and milk for a short while. Then he stepped in. The calf was tied short to the cow's leg. Thus she was taken in, and the calf had to helplessly look on while the milk, which should have gone down his throat, went into the bucket. As Daniel never despoiled anyone without a flood of smiles, courtesy, and good manners, he would break into song as he began to milk, in verses filled with flattery and wise counsel.

The voice of Daniel swayed with every syllable like a palm tree in the breeze. The mother, lulled into drowsiness, spellbound by that siren's voice that showered praise upon her, while nostalgically recalling to her the echoes and laments of the fields where she had been born, let down all her milk. The calf, less sentimental, tugged at its rope from time to time until, convinced of the uselessness of its efforts, it finally resigned itself to the sight of that plunder, in illustration of the sacred law that might makes right. Perhaps taking into account the maxim that man does not live by bread alone, calf like mother gave in to the lyric pleasures of poetry and music.

Daniel, in heartfelt contentment, went on with his milking and his singing. While he spun out his verses, we girls, quivering with excitement, ran to watch the expression on the face of the flattered, milked-dry cow, observing the indubitable satisfaction she experienced at hearing her praises sung. For this reason we insisted that every word be clear and all the ideas within the grasp of our simple intelligences. Let us say that Daniel was singing this song which belonged in Rain Cloud's repertory—each cow had its own:

> *Rain Cloud,*
> *I've seen some right fine cows*
> *but none the likes of you.*
> *Your milk flows like the spring*
> *that keeps the blue lake blue.*

At the vision of that darkling, unknown lake, we all flung ourselves upon Daniel:

"Which lake, Daniel? Tell us, which lake?"

Daniel interrupted his song long enough to answer:

"Valencia Lake."

A chorus of protest:

"But, Daniel, she doesn't know that lake, she's never been to Valencia. How does she know what you're talking about? Why don't you tell her to give more milk than the river, or the millstream, or the dam? Hmmm, Daniel, why don't you tell her that?"

Daniel interrupted his song once more to answer laconically:

"Because neither *river*, nor *dam*, nor *millstream* fits the rhyme."

"You make it fit, Daniel, you know how to do it. What difference does it make to you? You make it fit."

Even though Daniel knew how to make any word or any idea

"fit," he had his fixed repertoire, and he did not like to introduce changes except in some special case of sickness, birth, or death. Therefore he silenced our objections with this conclusive answer:

"She understands, and the proof is that she lets down her milk. And if she doesn't, she'll just have to go on wondering. That won't hurt her. Nobody ever died from unsatisfied curiosity."

One Saturday afternoon Papa's indignation against Daniel finally came to a head, and the explosion was devastating. He was as collected as he was emphatic. He informed Daniel that he would listen to no excuses or explanations, and that he was to clear out of the barnyard and the confines of Piedra Azul as quickly as possible, that he was as sick of his tricks as he was of his amiability, and that, besides, he had a new dairyman, an honest, dependable fellow who could replace him most satisfactorily.

Daniel, always a model of courtesy, made no answer; there was no argument, no reference to the matter. With the greatest politeness, after telling Papa his address, he took his leave with the same ritual phrase Vicente Cochocho employed:

"Always at your orders, Don Juan Manuel."

When the news of his departure got around, one of the mill hands asked him whether, now that he was out of a job, he planned to go back to the valleys of Aragua. Daniel, with his unalterable good judgment, without sarcasm, resentment, or insolence, guided only by the canons of common sense, replied:

"No, I'll spend these two or three nights around here, in the neighborhood. I'll be coming back, you know."

Early the next morning the new dairyman, overflowing with honesty and industry, came to the house, asked for Papa, and announced to him:

"I have come to tell you something, Don Juan Manuel, those cows are out of hand. They won't let themselves be milked. They kick, and if I tie their legs, it's still worse: they won't let down their milk. As Daniel used to sing to them . . ."

Papa's answer was logical but tactless:

"Well, aren't you supposed to be the best singer in the neighborhood? Go ahead, sing to them! Show off your voice. This is your chance!"

Ah me, what an offense for the new dairyman! He was indeed famed as a singer, and this was a deadly wound to his artistic dignity. Drawing himself up proudly, he answered:

"For your information, Don Juan Manuel, I"—(at this point he laid his hand upon his breast)—"am ready to sing my *galerones* and *corridos* at a dance, and there are very few who are better than I either at the words or the music. But I"—(here he removed his hand from his breast)—"don't intend to sing to cows as though they were people. No, sir. Nobody is going to make me do that. The days of slavery are over. You find yourself another dairyman, Don Juan Manuel. Goodbye to you and the cows."

It is hardly necessary to add that, to our delight and that of the twenty cows, Daniel returned.

III

One tragic day, one fateful day, one sad day, a drama took place in the barnyard.

After a brief sickness, Little Rain Cloud was found in the calf pen, his legs outstretched and stiff as when in the cheerful dawn he went leaping toward the flowering tree in whose shade his mother, Rain Cloud, exuding peace and milk, awaited him. Horseflies were buzzing around his open mouth; his staring eyes were rolled up in his head, and his tail, his poor desolate, limp tail, lay stretched out on the ground as though disjoined from his body. That was something new, horrifying, irremediable. As though in a horizontal gallop, a frozen, motionless gallop over some invisible gate, Little Rain Cloud had gone to a better world.

Sick at soul, our heads peering over the fence, silent with grief, though bursting with questions, for a long time we gazed upon the innocent victim.

Finally we turned away from the funereal fence. Before our very eyes grief had invaded the barnyard. Rain Cloud's sorrow filled the air. All nature was hung with crepe, which was provided by the pitiful maternal lament. Tied to her flowering tree, alone and deserted, Rain Cloud lifted up her voice:

"Moo-ooo."

And raising her grief-stricken head, Rain Cloud supplicated every-thing around about her, her protecting tree, her namesake clouds, the sky, the sun:

"Moo-ooo."

There was no answer. The tree selfishly continued to display its flowers, the clouds drifted slowly by, the heartless sun shone on brightly, without a word of commiseration for the afflicted mother.

We, on the other hand, were expressing our sympathy in every possible and imaginable form, but Rain Cloud, so great was her grief, took no notice. We could barely sip our matutinal milk. Not one of us felt like burying her nose in the foam. Nobody breathed a deep "ah" when she finished, and naturally, nobody asked for more. No. With unfinished glasses in our hand, we went from the funereal fence to Rain Cloud's tree, and from Rain Cloud's tree to the fence, unable to think of anything else. At one of the stations of that *via crucis*, Rosalinda, one of my little sisters, unable to take her eyes off Rain Cloud, now become Sorrow Cloud, filled with pity and walk-ing backward, stumbled and sat down in a bucket of milk. With Evelyn clutching her hand, she had to leave the scene of the drama to change her panties and dress.

Meanwhile, all at once and without letup, the rest of us began to rain questions on Daniel which gradually turned from a steady drizzle to a cloudburst:

"You think he's really dead, Daniel? Daniel, do you think he can't be saved? Do you think, Daniel, that Rain Cloud knows it? Do you think that's why she's lowing, Daniel? Why don't you call him, Daniel, hmmm? Why don't you call him and see if he moves? Call him, Daniel, go on, say 'Little Rain Cloud.' Go ahead, call him, Daniel, please."

Daniel's laconic, negative answers left no room for hope and broke our hearts. Convinced at last that death was irremediable, we accepted the stern law. With our eyes fixed on Rain Cloud so steadily that we didn't even blink, when she raised her head once more calling upon the supreme powers: "Moo-oo-oo," we burst into a heartbreaking wail:

"Oh, Daniel, the poor thing."

If Daniel held out no hopes that Little Rain Cloud would ever rise again, on the other hand he was cheerfully optimistic with regard to Rain Cloud's suffering:

"Let her alone, let her alone. Let her have a good cry today till she gets it out of her system. I'll comfort her tomorrow, don't you fret. Just wait and see. The dead are forgotten."

Paternally solicitous, that very day, equipped with knife and the other necessary tools, Daniel skinned Little Rain Cloud to use the hide—you'll never guess—for a comforting disguise. The next morning he dipped the pathetic remains in brine and put that slashed, salty, abbreviated attire, so touchingly similar to that of the mother—the same reddish color, the same broad white belt around the middle, the same white forelegs—over the back of another calf. Making sure that the manifest imposture was within reach of the eyes and muzzle of the sorrowing mother, he tied the disguised calf to one of her front legs. Rain Cloud, all emotion after sniffing the beloved hide, which not only comforted her soul but delighted her tongue, happiness turning into milk, gave herself up to licking the brine with which the adored remains were impregnated. Like all idealists, she found pleasure in illusion, and in the salt the symbol of wisdom. Like so many unhappy lovers, she kissed the departed soul in a strange body. Meanwhile, the happy deceiver, sole heir of the departed, not only put on his attire, but guzzled his ration of milk.

The imposture lasted for several days. After that, the disguise and the salt were no longer needed. The calf, whom habit had legitimized, replaced the son. Daniel was right: the dead are forgotten. This does not mean that they are not deeply and sincerely mourned for some time. As Daniel knew this, too, while the crisis of grief lasted, comforting Rain Cloud and giving her advice, for several days he sang in a plaintive tone this song filled with philosophy and consolation:

> Rain Cloud, mourn no more
> Let thy heart's fond grief be stayed,
> All milk is turned to cheese
> And all sorrow is allayed.

Heeding the advice and lulled by the song, Rain Cloud was gently, gently consoled, while we, impatient, unable to grasp the role of the cheese, so alien to a mother's grief, fell like a swarm of flies upon the extraneous element in the middle of the verse:

"What cheese, Daniel, hmmm? What cheese?"

✿ Aurora

I

The charming, whimsical genie that carelessly whispered our names into Mama's ear happened to be right in one instance. His accuracy proved fatal. It's wrong to be right. To reap happiness it is not necessary to sow truth. Poor Mama, you knew it, you bore it tattooed on the tenderest fibers of your heart. This having been accidentally right once was to cost you floods of tears.

Aurora at seven was like the golden daybreak. Her skin pale, her eyes black, the last shreds of vanishing night; her fair hair like the first rays of the sun; her footfall light; her voice muted as if to guard the rest of the sleeping; her gestures; her sweetness; her pale beauty, all, all of her molded by the laws that govern the rising of the day. Aurora was the dawn. After having presided briefly over Mama's garden in bloom, gently, with a finger on her lips, she departed delicately and quietly just as it was dawning. Mama was right in naming her Aurora. Papa, too, was right when he barred the city for hygienic reasons. Aurora died shortly after we reached Caracas, when she was just eight, as the result of measles complicated by whooping cough.

I prefer to pass over this bereavement in silence. I will only say that Mama reached the end of her days with her grief unabated and unassuaged. Not for a minute did her behavior resemble that of Rain Cloud. The pain of that wound lasted as long as life itself. Ten, fifteen, twenty years later Mama was still weeping for Aurora. When she voiced her sadness, great though this was, it was imbued with that same exquisite rhetoric that characterized all her words and thoughts. The utterances of sorrow fell from her lips with a touch of dramatic art that was a little funny, which only made them more touching. Mama lamented Aurora often and in a low voice when she was alone; but, beyond this, Mama mourned Aurora just as often and in the same low voice when she was with people at the most unsuitable moments, in a form as inopportune as it was moving. It was like that her life long. When one least expected it: in a store, at the theater, when she was being handed her change, when she opened her umbrella in the midst of a rainstorm, when she gave the laundry to the washwoman or was trying on a pair of shoes, without rhyme or reason, Mama suddenly broke off what she was doing, and, raising her sweet eyes heavenward, would exclaim sighing, and in a tender, suffering voice:

"Oh, Aurora, my adored little daughter, why did you go from me, why did you leave me all alone?"

And as the word "alone" did not seem to her sufficiently strong or expressive, Mama often replaced it with the word "forlorn." This superlative of loneliness gave her much more relief:

"Why did you leave me all forlorn?"

Poor Mama asked the question to console herself, not because she hoped for any reply. It did not matter that her "forlorn" was drowned out by our shouts, laughter, or running. With her customary disregard for reality—she could hardly have been more accompanied and surrounded by people—Mama was obeying a deeper truth. For her words to reflect the state of her emotions, the word "forlorn" was indispensable. Out of generous homage to our departed sister, we never asked her why she thus compared us to a desert waste.

Aurora's death was the bitterest of all the misfortunes that followed our moving to Caracas, but it was not the only one. The path that led from the country to the city was uphill and rough.

Even though Papa ruled Piedra Azul with that absolute, careless authority of his, similar to God's both because of the pleasant hit-or-miss system that characterized his mercy and his justice as well as the way these were often flouted, in spite of his dazzling supreme authority, Papa was not the sole owner of Piedra Azul. It was the joint possession of himself and his two brothers. The day came when the property had to be divided. I think that Papa, with his rustic soul, naively believed, like his six little girls, in the golden happiness of the city. When he was confronted by the dilemma of dividing up the plantation or selling it, putting aside all sentimental ties, he decided to sell it so that, he said, he could go into business for himself in Caracas. And then he added:

"I'm tired of the country. Besides, we have to think about the girls' education."

Ah, me, "the girls' education." You were right, Papa; the time had come for us to enter through some gate the Valley of Tears.

After several weeks of interviews, letters, discussions, the arrival of unknown visitors who rode out with Papa through the coffee groves and cane fields and then returned, hot and talkative, to lunch, after several weeks of such incidents, one morning Mama gathered us around her and said:

"Daughters, Piedra Azul has been sold. That means, you understand, that the plantation is no longer ours. As we have to leave, we are all going to live in Caracas for good. There we will have a smaller house, you won't be able to bathe in the millstream, nor will you see the country—no, for the houses are built one beside the other there. You won't be able to run and shout the way you do here. But, on the other hand, you'll be able to see your two grandmothers often, your aunts, you will go to school, and you will have lots of friends. You are all going in the carriage with me next week. There, now you know."

The news filled our cups of happiness to overflowing. "We're going to Caracas, for good, next week!"

This was the shout of hosannah and ingratitude that preceded us wherever we rushed: in the kitchen, the barnyard, the mill, the surrounding cabins. In our need to share the news, we went shouting it to all we met, persons, animals, trees:

"We're going to Caracas for good in the carriage next week. Isn't that wonderful, wonderful!"

And we clapped our hands with glee.

That journey to Caracas, which was to bring us so many disagreeable things, provided us with one week of delirious happiness, our last week in Piedra Azul.

Finally the morning came. All crowded into a big chaise, the one that had so often driven Mama, amid packages, suitcases, dolls, baskets of fruit, candy, cheers, shouts, and peals of laughter—these last three so out of place in a final farewell—the straining horses finally moved, and we left Piedra Azul for good.

When our carriage, as crowded and humming as a beehive, bumping over the ruts of the lane, took the turn that finally blotted out the last glimpse of the Big House roof, like Lucifer after the Fall, like Adam and Eve after they had sinned, like Napoleon after the battle of Waterloo, all at once we had lost an empire. Humiliated, prisoners, in that moment we ceased to rule the world.

Poor noisy little girls in the crowded carriage! Like others older and wiser than us, we were ignorant of a truth that is never really learned—a truth I have not yet been able to keep in mind more than five minutes—which is that the most enticing change, the most alluring travels, in their monotonous variety reveal to us only one transcendent, cruel new thing: our utter human misery and our blithe ignorance of it, an ignorance forever lost in which living was so sweet.

II

The first thing we noticed when we reached Caracas was the absence of earth and water—by our standards, they were completely lacking. On all sides cement, boards, or bricks. A smattering of dry dirt in the patio and another handful in the backyard; two little fountains; two or three faucets in the kitchen and the bathroom, faucets that were unaware of how paltry they were inasmuch as they had never seen the millstream. The three or four drooping trees in the backyard did not afford shade for our games, and the walls that surrounded us on all sides were literally prison walls. Deprived of freedoms and horizons, shut up within the four backyard walls, our homesickness grew and so did our quarrels. The household expenditures that were effected in money—something unknown in Piedra Azul—were carefully curtailed. Instead of that cohort of servants that had been at our beck and call, we now had a single maid who looked after the five older girls. Only Aura Flor, as indifferent or imperturbable as a god, still had her own nurse. Evelyn had returned to Trinidad. Nobody scolded us any more. There was no longer anyone to salt or season the insipidness of life with prohibitions. Our whims that were born strong and numerous, without a watchful hand to prune them, smothered us in melancholy.

Mama, seated at a corner of the table, with a stubby pencil and a sheet of ruled paper, facing a new cook with splendid references and a deplorable "hand for seasoning," totted up the market accounts, delicately prolonging the final syllable of the various purchases:

"Plantains-s-s . . . meat . . . potatoes-s-s . . . coffee . . . spaghetti–i-i." A daily procedure that invariably wound up with: "You've spent too much today."

Gone were the days of abundance when Vicente Cochocho arrived with his donkey staggering under the weight of vegetables, alligator pears, plantains, brown sugar—all of which he dumped on the broad kitchen table under the angry vigilance of Candelaria. Who ever thought of itemizing the purchases with the monotonous prolongation of final syllables? Who ever said to him, in semi-dramatic tone: "Today you've spent too much?" Nobody.

A week in Caracas and we had become bitterly aware of the fact that we, the six daughters of the Big House, the ex-princesses of Piedra Azul, were nothing but ants, far worse off than most ants which, as they file along one after the other, are happily lost in their anonymity and uniformity. We, alas, were not cloaked in anonymity. When we were with other girls, friends or cousins, ants among ants, we stood out from the rest by reason of our ingenuousness, our rustic shyness, our rustic boldness, our foolish questions, our gaping mouths, our perpetual astonishment. It was impossible to be more ignorant, more sincerely, artlessly ignorant.

Our two first visits to the city abounded in mistaken conclusions and false discoveries.

The first thing we did from the day we arrived, the minute we set foot out of the house, was to start running, each going her own way. The new nursemaid, well on in years and somewhat asthmatic, unable to keep a firm grasp on the reins that Evelyn had guided with so steady, so careful a hand, this new and elderly nursemaid, confronted by this dispersion, stood bewildered in the middle of the street, addressing recriminations and wild threats to left and right that were totally ineffectual in their purpose of recalling us to her side. Scattered, given over to our observations, we didn't even see her. From our separate posts we called to each other at the top of our lungs: "Look, Blanca Nieves!" "Wait for me, Violeta!" just as though we were still running along the path to the barnyard. Everything was a source of wonder. When we came to a store we stopped before it, pointing with our fingers, and shouting: "A tavern!" The sidewalks for us were "trails": the lamp posts, "iron trees." When we saw a lady and gentleman walking gravely along arm in arm, we also stopped, and also pointing with our fingers exclaimed:

"A team of people!"

And that was not all. Our luxuriant ignorance welled up to include the whole city, like that of a troop of vandals who, instead of sowing destruction, sowed wonder.

The hats we had worn in Piedra Azul were simple, light palm-leaf affairs around which Mama had tied a bow after the pastoral fashion and which Evelyn jammed down on our heads with a single, practical idea: to protect us from the sun. These hats were so firmly affixed or attached to our persons that we never gave them another thought: they were like our ears or our hair. But those other hats, those city hats, which our devoted mother had hastened to get us the day after our arrival, those hats were another story. Almost always unnecessary, heavy with useless trimmings, held by an elastic under the chin, they were uncomfortable and always in a state of unstable equilibrium. There was no way to forget them. Nearly all of us, and nearly always, the minute we crossed the doorstep, feeling that wearing them was merely a sop to convention, jerked them off and carried them in our hands, proudly and painlessly, where we could keep an eye on them. Those which remained in their customary place, on an occasional head, city-fashion—or as in the case of Violeta so she could have her hands free—such a one, perched on a head, I repeat, immediately lost its center of gravity. Without the calculation or skill their use called for, unable as we were to gauge the space their volume required, we were always catching them on doorknobs, projecting window grilles, the elbows of passers-by. After which they remained tilted over our eyes, one ear, or riding on the back of our necks, in a direction opposite to where the accident or encounter had occurred.

On our second visit of exploration to the city, we happened to pass the cathedral. Its vast expanse, crowned by the tower, brought to mind our lost sugar mill, presided over by its chimney. One of us called out naturally pointing with her finger:

"A sugar mill!"

As always happened, it was Violeta who took the lead in the necessary investigation.

With the speed of an arrow she crossed the street, went up the church steps, pushed open the swinging door, went inside, and emerged pontificating with her usual practical sense, her hat over one ear:

"That's not a sugar mill. If it was, where is the cane? If it was a boiling room, where are the pans? And what are all those benches for?"

Meanwhile the nursemaid, at the end of the street, hurrying and puffing like a shipwrecked sailor against the horizon, was making frantic signs to us to wait for her, that one could not go into the church shouting, or hat in hand.

That same afternoon we had no more than got home when the nurse, who had not been able to catch up with us, without taking off her kerchief or anything, streaked across the patio to where Mama was sitting to announce, pale, and outraged, and unable to catch her breath:

"I'm not going out with those girls ever again. They don't pay me the least mind. They rush around the streets, each going her own way. They carry their hats in their hands. They bump into people. They point with their fingers. They go running into churches and come out shouting. They make me so ashamed. Besides, it's too much of a responsibility. Find another nursemaid to look after them. I'm leaving."

It is impossible to describe the deep suffering these words inflicted on Mama's exquisite sensibility.

"Good Heavens, daughters," she said with an anguished air and sibilant lilt, "when are you going to learn to act civilized? When are you going to realize, Mother of God, that we are not in Piedra Azul? Imagine going through the streets with your hats in your hands. And to go into a church shouting! And point your fingers at people! Oh, what will folks think of me? Don't mortify me like that, children. Behave civilized!"

III

In order to expedite our civilizing, the very next day poor Mama, with unwonted activity, entered us in a school. We were to begin to go regularly, morning and afternoon, to a house as clean as it was shabby and full of echoes about a block and a half from ours where two maiden ladies, as virtuous as they were poor, mournfully taught a dozen little girls their ABC's and the catechism.

There in a huge room, among Empire furniture and crocheted doilies, portraits of noble pose whose frames and canvas were the prey of moths and mice, where the holes in the matting revealed the underlying bricks and the mouldering ceiling yawned in leaks, there among the two distinguished gentlewomen and the twelve illiterate little girls, our civilization got under way. I must confess that it was at the cost of many humiliations, struggles, and defeats. Nations acquire civilization by fighting and suffering; so did we.

This, for example, is how I learned in a manner I never forgot, with the aid of pinches and slaps, the value of money.

Across from our school, or asylum of melancholy and learning, every afternoon a sweetmeat vendor installed herself, a white towel over her head and shoulders, a fly whisk, also white, in her right hand, and in her lap a big tray full of cakes, meringues, candied egg yolks, taffy, and coconut candies that glowed in the sun like precious stones. That vendor, with hieratic air, white coif, and enigmatic black face, was like a goddess or a fairy. Her sweetmeats, fanned by the perpetual motion of the immaculate, rustling strips of the fly whisk, were a kind of heavenly ambrosia that her hands dispensed in exchange for a penny. We were bereft of all hope of ever receiving them, inasmuch as Papa had stated:

"I don't see any call for rushing the girls into school; they'll have plenty of time to learn to read. But what I do think is important is to watch them carefully when they cross the street, and to see that they don't eat anything that may be contaminated by dust or flies."

Bound by this injunction, without ever having a penny of my own, I confess that, as far as I was concerned, not a day went by that I did not pay the vendor the tribute of the deepest, most reverent devotion. If possible, I stopped close beside her tray, with my hands crossed behind my back in token of awe, and gazed upon the cakes, the candied yolks, the taffy, the coconut candy, listened to the swish, swish of the fly whisk; and when I finally moved away it was with those heartfelt sighs produced by hopeless desires.

But the law must not be taken too seriously. It is the part of wisdom to boldly transgress it under the very nose of authority, always so ready to accept any collaboration or complicity that flouts it.

So one afternoon, just before setting out for school, I went to Mama and slyly and sweetly said to her:

"Mummy, dear, please give me a penny."

Either out of generosity or because she was thinking of something else, Mama gave me, not a penny but a silver five-cent piece, which because of its diminutive size aroused my suspicions. Nevertheless, I accepted it, and the better to guard it, decided to keep it clutched in the palm of my hand until I had a chance to use it. With my hot, sweaty five cents I got to school, and though during class I stumbled several times over the *p* and the *b*, I distinguished the *a* from the *w* with no trouble at all. The melancholy gentlewoman who was on duty that afternoon stated in a woebegone tone that I had known my lesson very well that day. Assurance engendered by a job well done, and with my five cents tightly clasped, I waited for the right moment, slipped out of the room without being seen, crossed the hall, sidewalk, street as fast as my legs would carry me until—eureka!—I reached the sweetmeat vendor. This time, without clasping my hands behind my back, I gave myself up to studying the contents of the tray, eager but tormented by the need of making a choice and by my distrust of the acquisitive powers of my tiny coin.

In a few minutes I was back in the hall of learning, and, spurred by that fatal, human longing to be admired, to dazzle the greatest possible number of fellow mortals with our good fortune, I went up to a group that was observing the customary practice of chattering behind the teacher's back:

"I went," I announced triumphantly with mouth still full—"I went across the street to the candy woman, I picked out a cake, and gave her a little penny and she gave me back four big pennies in addition to the cake that was so good, and I've already eaten it up."

The laughter, the scoffing, the hooting with which my brief speech was received by my audience was so loud, so humiliating, that Violeta, out of familial loyalty, coming to my defense with a generosity I had never before suspected in her, began to deal out slaps and pinches which the horrified glances and admonitions of the melancholy maiden lady or teacher were powerless to halt.

The fray, in which tablets and pages of clumsy, ink-stained writing began to fly, and in which I, naturally, had to intervene, was fierce and unequal. In it I lost the bow Mama had tied in my hair; as I squared off to deliver a tremendous right hook, I stumbled against one of the chairs, fell on the floor, and three of my pennies disappeared in the holes and rips of the matting. Meanwhile Violeta had brought the ruckus to an end in an unexpected, bloody manner. One of the peaceful bystanders, who had taken no part in the jeering or the fight except in the capacity of spectator, was losing her front baby teeth, and one of them was just about ready to come out. Violeta, as she laid about her, bumped into her or hit her without meaning to, and out came the tooth, all bloodied, which made a terrible impression. The noncombatant victim let out a stifled cry, and the fight was over. Violeta was covered with ignominy. Only then were we able to hear the words of the melancholy gentlewoman, who at the sight of the blood and the sacrificed tooth, repeated for the fourth or fifth time in her hoarse voice, addressing Violeta and me:

"It is plain that you come from the backwoods, where you've lived only with donkeys and calves."

The truth is bitter. I swallowed it in silence. Not Violeta. Violeta immediately answered the hoarse, melancholy gentlewoman that she was the calf, the donkey, and the ass. Naturally the reply elicited further reproaches, further humiliations, this time in the plural, and including the whole family.

IV

Thus, amid harsh lessons and startling revelations that enlivened the quiet passing of the days, culture started to blossom in our souls, or a knowledge of conventions, which is the basis of all civilization.

Two years went by.

The bygone days of Piedra Azul, haloed by an aureole of melancholy, gently tinged with the memory of Aurora who had gone from us, our golden age in paradise lost, became crystallized in the past. By the time I was seven or eight, thanks to this past, I felt myself an experienced person who, aside from certain trivial details, knew all there was to know about life and could smile indulgently at the memory of the gaucheries of my early days. Today, after seventy years, this confidence in my own experience, part of which is self-pride, is much less firmly rooted. Hard encounters with reality, the repeated discovery that our capacity for error is infinite, have finally convinced me of my lack of experience, and this has taught me humility and lends me a touch of that fresh, rosy wonder whose disappearance I deplored when I was seven.

In our conversations, whose leitmotiv was "do you remember?" the name of Piedra Azul cropped up at every other word. Convinced that we had abandoned a trove of happiness there, we sighed to possess it again, even if only for a few brief hours. And we hammered away at Mama—poor, sad Mama—begging her every chance we had:

"Mummy, when are we going back to Piedra Azul? Take us, Mummy, drive us there one day. Even if it's only for a little while. Why won't you?"

Mama did not want to revisit the old plantation. Not so much because it was a long, tiresome, dusty trip, but because her heart warned her that it is dangerous to go back to the sights and scenes that form the basis of our memories.

We pleaded so much that finally one day, after requesting permission from the new owner, again crowded into a carriage in the company of Mama and a big lunch basket, we returned to our lost paradise, thinking that our journey was taking us into the past, that Aurora, sitting on the forbidden railing, the railing across which judgments were handed down, would hold out her arms to us, while Evelyn, lifting us down one by one, would issue her usual warning:

"Careful with pretty dresses from Caracas. Not sit on ground."

But no, Aurora did not hold out her arms, nor did Evelyn lift us down from the carriage. Instead of the familiar shades, wherever we turned our eyes there had been painful changes. The new owner of Piedra Azul was a rich man, a great advocate of progress who was insatiable in thinking up and carrying out reforms. I may add that our beloved Piedra Azul, disguised now as something different, wept too with heartbreaking cries over its changes, over having lost us. The cries could be heard from far off.

The new overseer, radiating satisfaction, proudly pointed out to us the many sacrileges inflicted on our memories, and with an unfeeling, horribly impious smile asked Mama:

"You'd hardly know the place, would you? To be sure, it has taken a lot of money. . . . You know what all this has cost?"

And he named a fabulous sum.

Everything was changed. It was the triumph of wrong over right. What had been our parlor was now the dining room, and the dining room was the parlor. Where once there had been a door, there was now a wall, and where there had been a wall, a door now opened— flanked, if possible, by a window. Where our pleasant orchard had stood, the trees were all gone, and in its place lay a formal English garden; and the site of our fragrant flower garden was a smoothly mowed orchard where a multitude of exotic little trees raised their frail branches. What had become of Mama's roses and jasmines, which so often intertwined their foliage and their flowers? Where were the guava bushes, the big locust tree, the rose apples, the soursops, the myrtles? Where were the rustling bamboos with their velvet shoes, where miscreants could hide the evidence of their mischief? Like Aurora, like Evelyn, like us, they were gone.

The flagstones Vicente Cochocho had weeded no longer needed weeding, for the floor of corridors and patios was now of cement where nothing grows. In the rooms refurbished with hangings, new ceilings, and woodwork, the faint voice of Mama calling for Aurora was answered by an echo. In the barnyard, the peaceful barnyard that was the model of the future city, a stable had been built with stalls in which each cow vegetated all by herself as she inhaled the morbid selfishness of a closed house. The mill now had doors that bristled with signs reading: "Stay out!" "No smoking." The boiling room and the bagasse shed had been switched, too: only the wheel, the huge mill wheel, was in its place, presiding against its will over that horrible devastation, the poor faithful mill wheel, asking us timidly and lovingly, its arms opened wide, "What do you think of all this?"

Finally, when Mama went to the pool in search of the tutelar *husiache*, father of waters and shade of our baths, to ask there why Aurora had left her all forlorn, in its place she found a stone wall.

And that we should be spared nothing and to fill our cup of sadness to overflowing, one of our old hands with whom we talked gave us a bitter piece of news. Vicente Cochocho was no longer on the plantation because in all probablity he was no longer of this world. After having returned unscathed and triumphant from what was to be his final revolution, he set out one morning, as was his unalterable habit, to look for some herb or to carry a message to the rebels. Perhaps he fell into an ambush that had been set for him. Whatever it was that happened on that early, mysterious mission, Vicente never returned.

The field hand related this painful episode with horrible indifference, shrugging his shoulders, pursing his lips, and wound up with these conjectures:

"He was not a man to get lost. Either he took suddenly sick, or some enemy had him killed. Poor Vicente! He who buried so many, he who was so good at making coffins—you remember?—and there he lies somewhere in the woods without a coffin or anything. Maybe he fell into a ravine, or took sick and couldn't get back, or was badly wounded. Nobody knows. Anyway, the buzzards have eaten him."

Our lunch, which we ate on the grass beside the pool, orphaned of its protecting *huisache*, was silent and lugubrious. Few words were spoken; not a laugh was heard. The bread, the fried chicken, the hard-boiled eggs had the savor of sadness. Mama had been right. We should fold away our memories within ourselves without ever venturing to confront them with things and beings that life changes. Memories do not change, and change is the law of existence. If our dead, the closest, the most beloved, were to return to us after a long absence and instead of the old, familiar trees were to find in our souls English gardens and stone walls—that is to say, other loves, other tastes, other interests, they would gaze upon us sadly and tenderly for a moment, wiping away their tears, and then return to their tombs to rest.

When we had finished our lunch, we too, with one consent, wanted to return.

In a few minutes we were in the carriage, bumping over the ruts of the road, and as the trees and the slow-moving herds were left behind, our need to give vent to what we were feeling could no longer be contained:

"Oh, Mummy," one of us sadly wailed, "to see how they have cut down the *huisache* and taken away the barnyard, and then to have them tell us that Vicente Cochocho was eaten by the buzzards, it would have been better for us not to have come."

Between two hard bumps of the carriage and two deep sighs, Mama answered:

"That's what comes of being stubborn, my pets. Remember, I warned you."

Background and Criticism

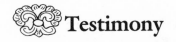 **Testimony**

JUAN LISCANO

Vicente Cochocho, I now understand, after rereading *Mama Blanca's Memoirs* fifty-four years after my first impassioned reading in 1933, functioned like the developing solution in photography: in his presence character traits are revealed not only of other protagonists in this delicious chronicle—among them the parents of Blanca Nieves; Evelyn, the black woman from Trinidad; the girls; Cousin Juancho—but of the country itself, nineteenth-century Venezuela with its agrarian economy, caudillo uprisings, large coffee, cocoa, and sugarcane haciendas, aristocratic, francophile minorities, malnourished, illiterate peasants, an exhausted treasury, and nonexistent industry.

In that unruly yet stagnant Venezuela, my parents were born. Ana Teresa Parra Sanojo and my mother were friends, though my mother was older. As a child I knew and above all watched that woman whose beauty and elegance disturbed my youthful libido. My mother was a flatterer when she chose to be and in my presence, after deliberately catching my attention, she would extol the beauty and intelligence of Ana Teresa.

The well-to-do of Caracas cooled off at the Macuto beach resort. For me those were unforgettable days: the grape sellers with their red fruit, the palm trees and the coconuts, the rocky shore where we would venture forth to watch the waves crash and the crabs scramble, the park with its dovecotes and doves, the houses with large patios, some in solemn Victorian style, the embankment, site of all meetings. My childhood still romps there as on that day when Ana Teresa Parra and my mother were talking and I, trying to shine before my friend, attempted to leap over a stone bench. My six or seven years were no match for the obstacle they wished to surmount. I landed against the hard cement edge and opened my knee amid cries of pain and sobbing. Ana Teresa and my mother fondled and pampered me no end.

Many years later, on the Basque coast of France, I wrote a long poem entitled "Meditación en Ciboure." This episode rose from the depths of my memory for whatever reason and I used it as an occasion for introspection, for going deeper into my own physical and metaphysical flesh wound. Ciboure is situated just opposite Saint-Jean-de-Luz. I now discover, upon rereading Teresa de la Parra, that in the epistolary inserted in the volume devoted to her by the *Biblioteca Ayacucho,* published in 1982, the Basque coast figures as the unforgettable location of her relationship with Gonzalo Zaldumbide. In 1927, she writes to him in a letter: "Dear Gonzalo, I have just left and I am thinking of you as usual: Guethary, then Bayonne: all our beloved towns of love and motoring." In another letter, from November 6, 1928, she writes: "Well, I've put on the ring and its weight, constantly tapping the ring next to it, produces a ting-a-ling that sounds like you. I think I'm still in Saint-Jean-de-Luz."

The coincidence of meditating between the fishing ports of Ciboure and Saint-Jean-de-Luz around 1962 or 1963 when I lived in Hendaye, twenty-one kilometers from Bayonne and near Guethary, and of recalling the very distant memory of the episode at Macuto without knowing that the region of the lower French Pyrenees had any meaning whatsoever for Ana Teresa Parra, seems more interesting to me than the very literary encounter imagined by Lautréamont, and adopted by the surrealists, to describe beauty: of a sewing machine and an umbrella on a dissecting table. The unconscious and the mechanisms of the psyche acting freely produce associations as inexplicable as the one I mentioned, for nothing in me was prompting the image of the author of *Mamá Blanca's Memoirs* in those surroundings, in that place, in that season, at that date.

Going back in time, I see myself at age seventeen, a boarding student at l'Ecole des Roches, near Evreux, in Normandy. This school followed the English model and had as its goal the creation of a plutocratic and aristocratic elite for France. There I experienced a most unjust experience of discrimination, one that culminated in my expulsion.

The school was not contained in one single building but was distributed among various central structures and many lodges where the students lived. The campus covered several hundred acres. From the start, they kept me in lodges with very few students. In Normandy it rains a lot, and I was often nostalgic for the tropics. One winter, that of 1933, I unexpectedly received *Mama Blanca's Memoirs*. The dedication read: "To my dear Juan Liscano: May he remember those times when he was the head devil of Macuto and I was not yet an 'author.' His old friend, Teresa." It was dated "Leysin, January 1933."

I devoured the book. It touched me deeply. In the Normandy winter and among the pages of the story, I saw and felt the tropical homeland of my nostalgia. And I lived with people of the countryside who reminded me of the ones I had known. I remembered the corrals, the patios, the ferns, Miguel Machado, the gardener at my house, his nighttime strolls with a candle in his hand, walking through the garden as if in a protective incantation, the peasants who came at dawn to the San Jacinto market to sell the produce they brought in from neighboring fields. Those evocations blended with the figure of the woman who signed the book Teresa de la Parra. Fragments of biographical anecdotes related to me by my mother set her in motion, dressed as she was ten years ago, wearing a wide-brimmed hat, her green eyes flashing in its shadow.

A country of haciendas reappeared. Those haciendas belonging to Mama Blanca and her sisters, that hacienda in the Caracus Valley where Teresa spent her earliest childhood and whose remote presence, from the end of the last century, she recreated in 1926 by writing the *Memoirs*. Teresa de la Parra is not only Iphigenia, the well-to-do young lady who gets bored and gets married, her soul lost, emptied of herself like the bride's dress on the chair, which seems to embrace it, abandoned to the rite of the marriage of greatest convenience; she is also that girl from the hacienda who discovers nature and the provincial modesty of Vicente the laborer, who discovers work in the sugar mill and the invasion of guests who, for a moment, divert her mother's attention. Teresa de la Parra's era is that of a Venezuela no longer in existence.

In 1931, she is diagnosed as having tuberculosis. So begins her long battle against it. She seeks refuge in friendship, "not love," as she states in her diary, published much later. In that final period, she and my mother begin seeing each other again. My mother has remarried, this time to Luis Gregorio Chacín Itriago. From 1929, the couple and their children from previous marriages travel to Europe. Chacín Itriago, who was the best of stepfathers, would hold a high diplomatic post from 1930 on in Switzerland at the League of Nations. In Geneva they meet Gonzalo Zaldumbide. He visits my mother frequently, constantly seeking news about Teresa. He arranges a marriage of convenience. (He did well for himself: diplomat, brilliant academic writer, he was a disenchanted, melancholy Don Juan. I remember him slumped in the confidential armchair looking at my mother.) He urges my mother to arrange a meeting with Teresa. He can't get her out of his mind. He wishes to see this beloved sick woman, his only love, who is undergoing a cure in the Leysin Sanatorium. Teresa and my mother speak over the phone. Teresa says no. She claims she has gotten very fat and wishes that Zaldumbide might retain the image he has of her from years ago. It was perhaps in these dealings with my mother in 1933 that the author remembered me and sent me *Mama Blanca's Memoirs*.

I wrote her an impetuous letter, expressing my admiration for the book and all that it stirred in me. Flipping through the pages of my copy of the book, I notice that I had underlined many lines, paragraphs, and even entire pages. I've tried to rekindle the reasons and emotions that prompted me to make those marks. One amuses and disturbs me. It appears among the first pages: "Adam and Eve sinned out of pride in their intelligence. In retaliation, God made it the source of most of our suffering and misery. Free of intelligence and its malevolent pleasures, humankind will be liberated from a Pandora's box of serpents." I also underlined, in the passage on Vicente Cochocho, the following: "I believe that the body tends to adorn itself to the detriment of the spirit. It is my belief that the body all too often adorns itself at the expense of the spirit. It is a cruel conviction that it hurts me to admit, for it saddens me to think that the charming, the divine outer elegance of the body is a lovely, lowborn thief who to bedeck herself strips the soul of food and raiment, leaving it penniless." And where a chapter on the poignant laborer ends, I marked these lines: "His soul did not know the meaning of hate. Belonging, as one might say, to the vegetable kingdom, he accepted without protest the iniquities of men and the injustices of nature. Submerged in the water, or clinging to the stones, insult him as they might, he went on impassively yielding his fruits and his flowers, good plant that he was."

I highlighted many other passages describing Vicente Cochocho in unforgettable terms with spirited parentheses. I also underlined the episode of Evelyn and the sugar mill.

Reading Teresa de la Parra's book was a milestone in my adolescence, like *Doña Bábara* by Rómulo Gallegos. In the melancholy of the rainy fields of school, I rediscovered the image of the hot countryside of Venezuela, decanted through the magic of literary writing. But while *Doña Bárbara* prompted nothing in me with regard to the author, Teresa's book returned me to her, to an indelible experience associated with the poem from Ciboure but also with a blurred childhood memory of a "tall woman in mourning," seen upon return from school on an afternoon invaded by the burning Caracas sunset, who "said my name through sad veils." I can no longer separate those verses from the photograph of Teresa, taken after the death of her patron, Emilia Ibarra de Barrios Parejo, in 1924.

I received Teresa's response to my letter, dated Leysin, February 14, 1933. I have preserved that missive with great care, not only because she was already a great author and I was a teenager with pretensions of being an intellectual, but because it confirmed for me those tendencies—let us call them idealist—which, with the passage of the years, led to a continuing interest in matters of the spirit.

After expressing her satisfaction in finding such a warm reception for her book, she praised the independence she discerned in my character as well as my enthusiasm for Venezuela, but she alerted me to a lack of *moral*—not intellectual—culture, "above all in men," characteristic of all of Latin America. Today I know the substance of that warning. It came from the very depths of her critical femininity, from her experience and knowledge. The story of María Eugenia Alonso is not hers alone, but that of thousands of Latin American women, some aware and others not, in a subordinate social position created by patriarchy and what is commonly called machismo.

The pathways of machismo are legion. One is fatuous seduction, Don Juan's deceit. María Eugenia Alonso accepted the sacrifice of marriage. Not Teresa de la Parra. But could she have escaped seduction, that narcissism in Don Juan, a man as sterile as he is seemingly in love with women? "Write me three little words whenever you can. You don't know how much they resemble your beautiful kisses. That kiss of the eyes and the written word is longer than the kiss of four lips and leaves a stickier trace on me than Guerlain red, which at least comes off with soap and water. Your red has not left me, Lillito, since last night . . . "Seduction by entanglement. Zaldumbide's wedding, his Don Juan behavior *d'annunziano,* his intelligent decadence, suggested or contained a self-destructive abandon. It would be mourned later. He would cry in front of my mother as he drove yet another beautiful Venezuelan lover to suicide. Machismo wore silk gloves. And lacked ethics; that spiritual ethic Teresa discovered when disease touched and purified her.

"You will see, the adolescent I once was would say, when you suddenly find yourself in that atmosphere, so pleasant and seductive in all other senses of the word. As I believe that true human superiority is not intellectual but ethical, I recommend you try to strengthen all the noble qualities of your soul; steep yourself well in all that is lofty in those old cultures so that they will always say of you not only that you are an intellectual but that you are a gentleman." She took leave with this: "Some day, perhaps, if God lets me live, we shall read the book together in Venezuela. . . ."

Mama Blanca's Memoirs was written between 1926 and 1928, a period of great activity for Teresa in her daily affairs and her literary social life. She is divided between her affective estate, composed of nostalgia for a country of haciendas and cities encircled and penetrated by vegetation, of that time in the nineteenth century governed by a mild bourgeoisie and patriarchal norms, and a relative modernity, felt more than thought and theorized, an existential, biographic consequence that moved her to write, to peek into another social world that was less conformist, that of the international "high society": diplomats, intellectuals, artists, journalists. The image of Teresa is that of a modern woman from the twenties. She is smoking with a cigarette holder, she is wearing pajamas; she is elegant. But deep within her persists her childhood attachment to the discovery of nature, of the country estates with their big houses and their servants almost like family, of a traditional way of life. Mama Blanca is opposed to the modernity of cubism, dadaism, surrealism, and other literary fashions. Teresa, through this personification of her inner self and her memory, puts a distance between herself and what she is experiencing, to strive for a sort of spiritual classicism, a direct writing, simple, authentic, that renders life— "the wings of life"—transparent. Her disease begins in 1931. She passed away five years later.

In a backwards Venezuela in which literature is divided between followers of Spanish romanticism and Latin American modernism, with its load of fin-de-siècle decadence and vague Americanist intuitions, the narrative of Teresa de la Parra, along with that of José Rafael Pocaterra (1888–1945) and Rómulo Gallegos (1884–1969) marked a reaction against the modernist aesthetic found in Manuel Díaz Rodríguez (1868–1927), its most outstanding cultivator.

Pocaterra was seduced by naturalism and realism, which in Gallegos attained epic and symbolic transformation. Teresa told the life of the affluent houses, penetrated the intimacy of women asphyxiated by a patriarchal world, of the childhood of rich girls on the haciendas, of universal femininity—thus inaugurating a literary wellspring which until then had been confined to the Southern Cone, to the burning, erotic poetry of notable women poets. Instead of lamentation in Teresa's writing there is confession; instead of rage, irony. Her writing rejects all emphasis, flows free of rhetorical embellishment, clasping the inner lives of its characters, practically a faithful transcription of daily speech into writing. María Eugenia Alonso is a well-to-do young lady who writes out of boredom, revealing with grace, irony, and even frugal dramatization, the way people act in her social milieu. At no point does she see herself as an author or pretend to be writing literature. Nor does she rebel from the depths of a demanding and tormented ego. She is an observer of herself, and for lack of the will to break away she submits to marriage, desiring a man who is not available.

Gallegos when he writes sings, wails, curses, hails, exalts, Poca-terra offers slices from a vivisection, denounces, uncovers tumors and decay of the soul. Teresa tells, in an intimate diary, in an intimate language, in white, transparent letters, the sentimental, psychic, emo-tional life of the women of Spanish blood at the beginning of the century, without any sociological, political, or psychological inten-tion. Her admirable stylistic mastery is based on simplicity, narrative efficiency, fidelity to speech and to feelings. An immense pruning of adjectives to reach the multiform yet natural noun. People's interior life determined by an environment, a history, and norms that consti-tute the glimpsed depths, precise in their imprecision, alive yet never specified by the author, delineated, accentuated, studied, described. A narration of interior events whose importance remains in subjectiv-ity. But that same distance grants the stories of Teresa de la Parra their universality and global transparency. The tree never blocks the view of the forest. And the forest is simply life, living, to be alive.

Mama Blanca's Memoirs and the Author Remembered

VELIA BOSCH

While 1926 has been given as the year *Mama Blanca's Memoirs* was written,[1] this date should be understood as heeding chronological simplification more than biographic precision.

Two clues tell of the existence of certain notes forming a possible draft or gestation of her second novel; they are a letter and a photograph—more specifically, the legend of that photograph. Let us first emphasize in one of her letters to Zaldumbide, the lines that speak of her contact with various smells and tastes, and the nostalgic passion revived by the sounds and music of the countryside as they call to others already lost:

We are still in Maracay . . . from the bed to the car and from the car to the river, the pasture, or the small lake. . . . The song that distracts my terrible impatience is also the song of your love which I see and watch and feel all around me, strolling at daybreak as at dusk, in the river's enchantement as in the Virgilian scenes of cowhands, and in the moon seen through rain trees, sponge trees, and cars when at top speed we race through the perfumed night.[2]

She writes this to Zaldumbide and poses for the camera a few hours later dressed in a severe and elegant black outfit, now frozen by the black and white of the photograph grown pallid with time. The group is sheltered from the harsh sun under the awning of the second deck of the steamboat *Tacarigua*. Teresa, Rafael Requena, and two other couples are leaning on the safety railings. The stern of the boat reveals the main deck below; the hull nestles against a thicket of mangroves.

The threads that will weave the story, or perhaps its hidden score, are there in the letter and the photograph, on the back of which Teresa had jotted down "Requena's Ballad."

> *When it comes to love*
> *I'm like a dog each day.*
> *Pat me and I'll leave,*
> *Kick me and I'll stay.*
>
> *I've seen some right fine cows,*
> *but none the likes of you.*
> *Your milk flows like the spring*
> *that keeps the blue lake blue.*
>
> *When I milk* Nube de Agua
> *she scares me half to death.*
> *The gushing milk resounding*
> *like several thunderheads.*

Here in these verses, hoarded in a family album, is the source of the milking song included in the chapter "Nube de Agua y Nube de Agüita" ("Rain Cloud and Little Rain Cloud"). Teresa copied and modified the second of Requena's verses; the first one she didn't use, and all she took from the third was the name of the cow, which would inspire the penultimate chapter of her work-in-progress.

Beginning with Christmas 1924, a silence envelops the creative process of the *Memoirs*. Months of European wanderings intervene: dances, neither writing nor reading, visits to museums, a talk here and there to hear Colette and who knows which "male celebrity." It is the time of "the gay vanity of the rags" and her standard of conduct: *"Tâche d'être belle, et tais-toi."*

Hardly had 1927 begun when she confessed to her friend, confidant, and depositary of the manuscripts of her novels, Rafael Carías: "I am wholly devoted to my "Mama Blanca's Memoirs" and have somewhat abandoned all else . . . . I believe this book, though not as difficult, will definitely be better than *Ifigenia*." And in October of the same year, concluding another letter to Carías, she writes: "The six little girls you are familiar with run around and stick their noses everywhere."

On the eve of another Christmas (1927?), she wrote to Enrique

Bernardo Núñez: "I have finally completed with honor my *Mama Blanca's Memoirs*. I have written it with great affection and find it entirely to my liking, which is why I am so fond of it."[3]

Without a doubt, the manuscript conceived in the notes of Maracay traveled on various occasions to Caracas. She once left notebooks, papers, and letters in the house of her sister Elia. Her crowded itinerary—Paris, Geneva, Italy; later, Paris, Havana, Caracas, Switzerland, Vevey, Corseaux—made her "feel by contrast the special flavor of all that is one's own."

The elaboration of the *Memoirs* continued in Maracay in December, in Vevey in Christmas, and finally in Paris. By then Carías had surely read the manuscript with her. In 1928, six months after her fleeting visit to Caracas, she recalled: "I have remembered you often, correcting my drafts with an eye to the unannotated Americanisms clouding the text. You were so right." In July 1928, the last installment of the *Memoirs* appeared in the supplement of the *Revue de L'Amérique Latine;* six months later, on January 29, she announced: "[The book] should be out any day now." Although she had not finished writing the forward, she wrote on June 28, "I have learned that my French *Memoirs* are floating around . . ." And in October: "In Vevey, I wrote the chapter in which Mamá Blanca is presented. I think you'll like it."

Her response to Garnier Brothers demonstrated her vigilance with regard to the final details:

As I infer from their letter, the Garnier publishing house proposes to publish my book at my expense with an immediate outlay of 16 or 17 thousand francs per copy. . . . Which is to say that I would lose a *minimum*, aside from my capital and work, of 17,000 francs! Garnier, on the other hand, would receive 26,700 francs! . . . [I] can't comprehend how a serious publisher could make an offer like that, or do they imagine that the honor they are doing by publishing my book comes so dear? In any case, it is no guarantee for an author, even when the publisher makes other offers, to entrust a work to a house that has the audacity to speak in such terms.[4]

We can conclude that the text was conceived in Venezuela, given the reference to Maracay (Requena) and the letter to Zaldumbide. The chapters and glossary were written between Caracas and her European travels; the manuscript was read. Between Vevey and

Paris, she gave the book its final touches for translation and its definitive publication in book form.

It is no mere coincidence that a Latin American work of such radical importance was produced, in certain fashion, in Paris. Pedro Henríquez Ureña discussed this in 1954: "France, since the beginning of the nineteenth century, has been our spiritual home and the spring from which we have gotten most of our information about European culture."⁵ It is fitting to present here one of the answers she granted the Colombian journalist Uribe Muñoz: "I take as my masters in the expression of the modern novel Anatole France, Alphonse Daudet, Maupassant, Catulle Mendés, and Valle Inclán. I consider them my masters because I believe they have influenced me the most."

We should view this questionnaire-reportage with a certain skepticism and take note of Teresa's closeness to Romain Rolland since her youth in Caracas (when she still signed her name as Ana Teresa): "Do you remember that you were the one who introduced me to *Juán Cristóbal* and that this book was very influential in my literary development?" (letter to Carías, July 1929). Perhaps she became fascinated by the pleasant simplicity and provincial lyricism of Daudet, but the instruction she acknowledges in her letter to the Nobel laureate of 1915 is more recent: "My dear *Teacher* and friend," she declares from Vevey in August 1929, "It seems that it was for you alone, and very near by you, that, unawares, in the full solitude of that golden autumn of 1927, I was writing that small book which you have chosen so sympathetically. Perhaps without realizing, you found the profound mark left on my soul when, still very young, in Caracas, a small, tropical city, I held your *Juán Cristóbal* in my hands." And referring to their proximity, she continues: "My *Mama Blanca's Memoirs* is simply a long letter, impregnated with my past, which I sent you from Vevey to Villeneuve. It took months to arrive and it was set in type. But you were the one I'd sent it to, I now see."⁶

In another letter to Carías, she writes: "As you can see, I am again in Vevey. Did you know that just recently I received a charming letter which was sent to me from Paris, having been originally posted from here? It was Romain Rolland . . . who told me that the six little girls of the *Memoirs* were his friends and played in his garden while he worked."

Accounts [by Teresa de la Parra] of the conception of *The Memoirs* show not only the characteristic stroke of reminiscence but certain stimuli awakened by her contact with Spain which made possible that particular assemblage of her maternal cultural heritage and her Latin American upbringing:

As you [Gonzalo Zaldumbide] did, despite her defects, brusqueness, and backwardness, I like Spain and my contact with her seems to seems to awaken in me spiritual energy and life, called forth by this evocation or journey through time. It is above all the people who cause me to feel this. Remember how we were always in agreement on this and how well we could see the conquistadors' voyage from Trujillo to America? And now I am sure that without my trip in 1927, I would not have felt the need to write *Mama Blanca's Memoirs,* that little book which, in spite of all, I continue to love with much fondness.

The second of Teresa de la Parra's books was published almost simultaneously in French and Spanish, four years after her first novel, *Ifigenia (Diario de una señorita que escribió porque se fastidiaba)* which had won the Grand Prix du Roman Américain au Concours in 1924. Her letters reflect a hopefulness regarding the receptivity of a certain reading public and the opinions of certain newspapers that had been hostile toward the subject of her first novel. Not so the French and Spanish critics, especially those who frequented the intellectual circles connected with the publisher Casa Editora Franco–Ibero Americana de Paris, the distinguished academics assembled in *La Revue de L'Amérique Latine,* and the publication *Les amies d'Edouard.*

During its author's life, however, *Mama Blanca's Memoirs* prompted fewer studies and editions, until the Venezuelan Academy of language promoted the repatriation of her remains from the port of Bilbao to the port of Guaira in 1947, and the Ministry of Education inaugurated its celebrated Colección Popular with an edition of the *Memoirs.*

It was the eminent essayist Mariano Picón Salas who, in a prologue to a selection of *Letters* by Teresa de la Parra published in 1951, referred for the first time to the political reasons for that silence toward the most representative works of Venezuelan and Caribbean literature about a society in crisis. Picón Salas said in this respect: "Many people, without reading the book and blinded by politics, superficially considered Teresa's work to be an elegant aristocratic account that did not speak to the passions of the moment."[7] Even more so than when greeted with silence, her life and work now fell into obscurity.

The years 1941–1947 was a time of revindication for the author and particularly for the *Memoirs*. The Caracas press of the period, *El Nacional, El Universal, Ultimas Noticias, El Heraldo,* and *La Esfera* print editorials, articles, poems and interviews devoted to honoring the memory of the writer who was returning to her homeland.[8] On January 28, 1947, the revolutionary government junta signs the decree authorizing the repatriation of her remains. The four-column headlines in *El Universal* on December 9, 1947, summarize the ceremony: "THE SOLEMN OBSEQUIES OF TERESA DE LA PARRA. AUTHOR LIES IN STATE IN THE ELLIPTICAL HALL. THOUSANDS OF PEOPLE PAID HER AN EMOTIONAL TRIBUTE. IN ATTENDANCE WERE THE GOVERNMENT JUNTA AND THE EXECUTIVE CABINET. STUDENTS FROM THE EXPERIMENTAL SCHOOL THAT BEARS THE NAME OF THE ILLUSTRIOUS WRITER GUARDED HER COFFIN. SPEECH BY THE POET JACINTO FOMBONA PACHANO."

One who is familiar with the historical-political events that took place in the Caribbean basin between 1927 and 1930 will be surprised by the evidence that attests to certain coincidental links between the author of the *Memoirs* and the rulers in power not only in Venezuela, but also in Cuba, Colombia, and Panama. The writer's itinerary through these countries during those years is due to various reasons: her attendance as a guest at the Congreso de la Prensa Latina, the talk she gave on Bolívar, and the talk she gave three times entitled: "Women's Influence on the Development of the American Soul." In 1927, when she traveled for the first time to Havana and Panama, Gerardo Machado, President of Cuba, was still respecting the constitutional norms, while in the isthmus region opposition was growing to the Arosemena regime, accused by the popular movement of serving the interests of the capitalists, and in Nicaragua, North American planes were bombing the region where Augusto César Sandino was operating.

In 1924, when she returned to Havana, her friend, President Machado, abolished the vice-presidency and extended the term of his government for another six years. From that moment on, Caribbean history would know him only by his surname and epithet, which have become a symbol of shame: "Dictator Machado."

On April 1, 1928, the *Diario de La Marina* in Havana published an article supporting Juan Vicente Gómez's regime in Venezuela; its headline stood out over a beautiful drawing by the Parisian portraitist, Messager: "Teresa de la Parra speaks to us with emotion of her Venezuela and with excitement about its progress." When she passed through Caracas, the city was swarming with popular and student demonstrations. As a result, Gómez's police shot the demonstrators down with machine guns, closed the universities, and sentenced the young people of the "Generation of '28" to hard labor on the roads and the rest to prison or exile. Teresa wrote to Gómez on April 12, 1928, enclosing the Havana interview and expressing her sympathy.

In Paris, *Mama Blanca's Memoirs* awaited her final corrections. Teresa would not return to Venezuela, although she would see Havana and Colombia again. The provincial newspapers in Colombia boosted the excitement surrounding her talks. *El Tiempo* headlines read: "Bogotá gave Teresa de la Parra a reception. There were people on top of the railway cars." It took twenty minutes to get through the crowds, from the train to automobile. In the photo, she appears surrounded by elegant women, distinguished by her physical and intellectual stature. Below it reads: "Teresa de la Parra in the Hotel Augusta, moments after her triumphant arrival."

The Colombian press of the day covered literary, social, and athletic homages arranged in her honor, printed poems dedicated to her serene, sweet beauty. One journalist insisted that she speak about politics; she refused, arguing: "[Imagine] that they made me out to have said that the president of Colombia, Abadía Méndez, received me in a ridiculous fashion. And beforehand, upon arrival in Caracas, the students lodged complaints because they considered me partial to the government. . . . No, no, no. We won't speak of government. I have said and still say that the dirtiest jobs are coal and politics. One almost always gets one's hands soiled."

Teresa's work was produced at the most difficult moment in Venezuela's history, with no democratic tradition, with associations, unions, and political parties being founded that, only much later, would allow intellectuals the possibility of ideological debate.

These fragments are from a long letter from Teresa de la Parra to Juan Vicente Gómez, dated June 18, 1923:

[With] the patience of a modest laborer and with all the enthusiasm of the artist who believes in his work, from dawn to dusk, two years in a row, polishing, correcting, perfecting, I have done nothing but write a book which at last, after such eagerness and such silent, steady work, I have just recently finished.

That book, which by its simple and pleasant form is an exponent of our culture and our current progress, a work from the years you have governed. . . . In order to publish it with a greater chance of success, I would like to have it published in Europe. . . . So then, can I count on your support in this enterprise? Whatever is possible, whatever is convenient, whatever you choose to offer me![9]

And finally, here is part of a letter written to General Gómez on a different occasion but under similar circumstances by the writer Rómulo Gallegos, future democratic president of Venezuela, a man forged in the crucible of family and civic virtue:

Please accept along with this letter two copies of the latest issue of *Actualidades,* which is devoted to a review of the formal ceremonies by which the National Government generously recognized the visit by the French sailors from the cruiser-school Jeanne d'Arc. As these ceremonies exhibited the principles of culture and cordiality with which you have customarily handled Venezuela's international relations, and at the same time made manifest the esteem in which our country and its Government is held among the civilized nations of the world—which is an act of great patriotism. . . .

If my contingent, which I have wished to offer to the patriotic endeavor perfectly realized by the National Government . . . is fortunate enough that you find it to your liking, please accept it as a token of our support and respect.[10]

Among the signatories to these declarations was Teresa de la Parra, the most ephemeral of them all. Three years before her death, the author of *Mama Blanca's Memoirs* and the creator of *Doña Bárbara* met in Barcelona. On the bastard title of his then famous novel, Gallegos wrote: "To the admirable author of *Ifigenia;* a tribute to Venezuelan letters, with my intellectual devotion and in testimony of my friendship." In the exchange of books, Teresa dedicated the *Memoirs* to him.

Translated by Mark Schafer

Notes

1. A date of 1926 was recorded by the historian and novelist, Ramón Díaz Sánchez in *Teresa de la Parra (Clave para una interpretación)* (Caracas: Ediciones Garrido, 1954), p. 62.

2. Letter to Gonzalo Zaldumbide, headed Maracay, December 1924, published for the first time in *Obra (narrativo, ensayos, cartas)* (Caracas: Biblioteca Ayacucho, 1982), p. 535. Unless otherwise indicated, all quotations from her letters are taken from this source.

3. Although its date is uncertain, this letter mentions events connected with defamatory articles about *Ifigenia* that appear in *el Universal* in Caracas in 1927 and refers to an article Teresa herself sent to that paper, published on March 31. The letter could be dated November 25, 1927 (Velia Bosch, *Lengua Viva de Teresa de la Parra* [Caracas: Editorial Pomaire, 1983], pp. 140–44).

4. From unpublished papers.

5. Pedro Henríquez Ureña, *Las Corrientes literarias en América Hispana,* 2d ed. (Mexico City: Fondo de Cultura Económica, 1954).

6. Armando Rojas, "Romain Rolland y Teresa de la Parra," *El Nacional* (Caracas), August 4, 1963.

7. Mariano Picón Salas, prologue to Teresa de la Parra, *Cartas . . .* (1951), p. 8.

8. Although born in Paris, Teresa gave Venezuela as her native country. Until now her account, *Datos Biográficos* written for García Prada, was the only one cited: "Born in Venezuela of a large family of six children." In documents examined for this edition, on an identity card, for place of birth, she wrote "Caracas," and on the next line, nationality, she wrote "venezuelienne." The card gives her date of birth as 6-10-1896. Her birth certificate, which we located, and a written account by her father put the exact date at October 5, 1889.

9. Letter to Juan Vicente Gómez, June 18, 1923, in Francisco Salazar Martínez, *Triunfo de compadre* (Caracas), pp. 103–95.

10. Rómulo Gallegos, letter to Juan Vicente Gómez, in Yolanda Segnini, *Las luces del gomecismo* (Caracas: Alfadil Ediciones, 1987), p. 135.

Piedra Azul,
or the Colonial Paradise of Women

ELIZABETH GARRELS

Though the setting for all but the first and final pages of *Mama Blanca's Memoirs* (1929) is the plantation Piedra Azul in mid-nineteenth-century Venezuela, Teresa de la Parra's second novel is an anachronistic colonial fantasy. To grasp this, it is crucial to understand certain terms to which de la Parra returns time and again in her letters, lectures, and novels. With Independence and the founding of the republic in the 1820s—so her reading of history goes—the colony lost its material strength but did not disappear. Political and economic power passed into new hands, becoming increasingly restructured around the liberal-positivist values of progress, capital, and competition. The colony, weakened but still alive, took refuge in "the very liberators who had been ruined by the war," that is, the *mantuanos* (the creole plantocracy, the *grandes cacaos*), whose prosperity had been linked to the expanded slaveholding regime of the eighteenth century.[1] After Independence, this creole elite was ironically rebaptized the *partido godo* (Gothic or pro-Spanish party), and, "stripped of power, . . . [it] was able to purify itself through adversity, and, divested of all material force, [it] continued to govern the *moral* life within the home. Its *influence* was healthy, and its intransigence was tempered by *tenderness* and *generosity*."[2] Thus it was, in de la Parra's words, that the "colonial spirit continued in effect throughout the nineteenth century, up to our own time."[3] And so it is, too, that inasmuch as spirit rules over matter in Piedra Azul, this plantation must be considered a colonial domain.

But let us be more specific about dates. The action that unfolds in Piedra Azul occurs in 1855. This date is buried in a text that ostensibly grants little importance to history. Two examples: the unnamed

136

president of the republic who gives Mama away at her wedding is in fact none other than Carlos Soublette, great-great-grandfather of Teresa de la Parra; the famous general who promotes Vicente Cochocho to the rank of captain becomes a trifling lapse in memory: "some well-known name I cannot now recall".[4] The elusive date of 1855 can be reconstructed, however, with relative ease. During the months in which the chapters devoted to Piedra Azul evolve, Mama, who was born around 1831, is twenty-four. Also, she was married in 1846 at the age of fifteen.

The date 1855 is of prime importance in the struggle between the spiritual and the material—between fantasy and reality—that is waged throughout the text. One year earlier, in 1854, the liberal president José Gregorio Monagas had decreed the abolition of slavery, an act that changed the legal status of some 20,000 people.[5] Although this historical fact also remains unspoken in the book, it is alluded to when the substitute dairyman angrily reacts to Papa's suggestion (Papa is owner of Piedra Azul) that he should induce the cows to give milk by singing them songs: "The days of slavery are over," he protests. Granted, it is impossible to know whether or not the institution of slavery had survived in Piedra Azul up to the time of Monagas's decree. It is even suggested that it may not have when Vicente Cochocho, a *zambo* laborer (a mixture of black and Indian), says that "many years ago" he was promoted to captain during his participation in numerous revolutions against the government. To engage in those guerrilla wars, Cochocho always abandoned Piedra Azul without his master's permission; upon his return he was scolded, but apparently not punished as a runaway slave would have been. (However, given the mixed status of labor on slave plantations, Cochocho could also have been a hired freedman working among legally held slaves.)

Even if slavery had indeed disappeared from Piedra Azul long before 1854, it can be asked whether or not the close coincidence between 1855 and the date of the abolition decree is purely accidental. The fact that it is in 1855 that Papa decides to sell the plantation "so that, as he said, he could go into business for himself in Caracas" suggests the existence of social and economic motivations in addition to strictly personal ones. Papa is not the exclusive owner of

Piedra Azul; he holds the title with his two brothers. "One day, it became imperative to divide up the value of the plantation," says the text, and "putting aside all sentimental ties, [Papa] decided to sell it". What could have prompted this division? Why would a traditional plantation owner decide to divest himself of his property in order to pursue a profession in the capital? It may well be that the country's economic and social climate was no longer so favorable to that class which, under the protection of Páez in the 1830s and 1840s, had attempted "to rebuild a plantation economy, by rapidly returning to slavery the blacks who had been emancipated during the Wars of Independence."[6] Although the novel sidesteps the problem by portraying Cochocho's revolutions as frivolous diversions, in reality as a guerrilla he was taking part in the growing wave of popular unrest and *caudillismo* that would explode scarcely four years later in the bloody Federal Revolution (1859–1863). This war would once again give vent to the old racial and class hatreds exploited by the Spaniard Boves at the time of Independence.[7]

There is something perverse about placing this idyll of Piedra Azul in a time of such historical intensity, but this gesture is symptomatic of the voluntary dematerialization of de la Parra's fictional world. Adopting a more sympathetic perspective, one might call it an elegiac testimony to the disappearance of a particular social formation sacrificed by the advance of history. Be that as it may, the Piedra Azul of Papa and his little girls exists, albeit tenuously, in blissful ignorance of history and material reality. Poised in the middle of the nineteenth century, it represents the colony because therein reigns—or so we are told—the morality of "the inner life of the home."

In fact, the plantation Piedra Azul is conceived as a great patriarchal family of the last third of the eighteenth century. When speaking of Simon Bolívar's plantation in the valley of Aragua, Teresa de la Parra calls it "the typical creole plantation, the almost biblical plantation where the slaves, who are a continuation of the family, bear the surname Bolívar or Palacios, which is the name of the master who is God and the father of all."[8] This concept of the eighteenth-century slave plantation recalls the famous letter written by Bolívar himself to the editor of the *Royal Jamaican Gazette* (1815) in which, motivated by pragmatic concerns of the moment, he stunningly falsified the true nature of race relations in his part of the Americas. An example:

The slave in Spanish America vegetates in a state of abandon on the plantations, enjoying, so to speak, his inactivity, the plantation of his master, and a large part of the fruits of liberty; and, as religion has persuaded him that servitude is a sacred duty, he is born and exists in this domestic dependency, considering his state to be natural to him, and believing himself a member of the family of his master whom he loves and respects.[9]

Teresa de la Parra's loyalty to this same idyllic vision of slavery is evident in her letter (November 29, 1930) to the Venezuelan historian Vicente Lecuna in which she consults him on her project—never completed—of writing a book on Bolívar: "In the portrait of the eighteenth century in which Bolívar was born, the slaves add a very charming touch."[10] Given this perspective, even if legal slavery did exist in Piedra Azul right up to the Monagas decree of 1854, it seems that this circumstance would have had little negative effect on the "charming" portrait of family relations linking Papa, the owner and "god" of his plantation, the black man Vicente Cochocho, a symbolic slave and practitioner of the "noble philosophy of resignation", and Mama and her six little girls.

The Feminine versus the Masculine

However charming the patriarchal relations in Piedra Azul may be, there is a certain tension or discord between Papa and Vicente, as there is between Papa and his numerous little daughters:

Father . . . suffered that flowery deluge [of girls] with such magnanimous resignation and such self-effacing generosity that from the first moment it wounded our pride and was irreparable. The misunderstanding was an established fact.

Yes, Don Juan Manuel, your silent forgiveness was a great offense, and it would have made for far better relations between you and your six little girls if from time to time you had shown us your disappointment in word and act. That resignation of yours was like a huge tree that you had felled across the pathway to our hearts.

Vicente and the six little girls, on the other hand, are drawn to each other in empathic identification, and there is a strong textual reason for this: they belong to the same semantic group—the feminine. As the author states in the second of three lectures she delivered on women in 1930, the colonial era is "naive and happy like children, or like those peoples who have no history. . . . Devoid of politics, of the press, of war, of industry and of business, it is a long vacation for men and the reign, without chronicles or chroniclers, of women."[11] Children, the common people (slaves and laborers), and women form a holy alliance in this, the reign of women and the "long vacation for men."

Here it is appropriate to elaborate on those qualities that the novel defines as feminine: irrationality, an identification with nature (the ahistorical), spirituality and its corollary, an indifference to the material, an apparent resignation to the injustices proceeding from the masculine domain, an impulse toward reconciliation, and a marked preference for orality in verbal artistic expression. The masculine, for its part, is characterized by a materialist or, more accurately, positivist mentality, an identification with history and politics, rebellion and violence (war), intolerance, the imposition of restrictions, and a marked preference for the written and printed word (literature and the press) in verbal artistic expression. The book's feminine characters are Blanca Nieves (and Mama Blanca), Mama, Cousin Juancho, Vicente Cochocho, and Daniel. Papa, Evelyn, Violeta, and the new owner of Piedra Azul are masculine. The editor—that is, the first-person narrator of the Foreword—does not belong to the world of Piedra Azul, but rather to the modern world where other standards prevail. As a contemporary professional woman, she is a rather uneasy mix of the two categories.

Granted, in the residents of Piedra Azul one can also perceive degrees. At times the feminine characters exhibit masculine traits; the converse is also true. The dairyman Daniel is adept at "Machiavellian statecraft", and in this sense he belongs to the masculine sphere; nonetheless, his identity as a traditional (oral) poet and his class rivalry with Papa (laborer versus master) mark him as feminine. Mama, like Papa, cannot appreciate the flavor of "golden age Spanish that Vicente used," and in this respect she stands outside the purely feminine alliance that binds the children to the "common" people. (The little girls, however, do appreciate Cochocho's speech, "because children and the common folk, either out of ignorance or because of their dislike for abstractions, know how to harmonize things with words—to bring words to life—and have the unique gift of transforming language"). At any rate, though Mama fails to recognize the merits of Vicente's speech, the two of them are indisputable masters of the spoken word: he represents "the essence of rusticity," and she "the essence of refinement or preciocity"; in his speech "rhythm predominated, in the other, melody." That is, even though Mama is "well read," she is clearly associated with orality. In fact, we need look no further than to her "poet's temperament, [which] scorned reality" and which therefore earned her full rights of citizenship in the feminine sphere.

It appears, then, that in Piedra Azul one's gender may be subject to partial redefinition according to the characteristic under scrutiny (attitude toward politics, language, etcetera), and also according to the semantic position one occupies relative to another person at a given time. Vicente Cochocho, for example, represents the colonial slave by virtue of both his proximity to the little girls and nature and his distance (differentiation) from Evelyn. Even his participation in the guerrilla wars—a masculine activity—takes on, as in the case of Daniel's "Machiavellian" politics, a feminine connotation to the extent that one focuses on the popular, antioligarchic character of this behavior. But this free play of movable signifiers in Piedra Azul is subtle, and in the end does not notably disrupt the fundamental sexual identity of each person.

Mama Blanca and Cousin Juancho, however, are immune to such shifts, for both are invariably feminine. Incapable of managing her money and blessed with the "temperament of a magnificent artist and a subtle, exquisite intelligence nourished not so much on books as on nature and on life's daily banquet," Mama Blanca is one of those beings "miraculously unsuited to the present" who, against all odds, continues to live in the colonial past. (De la Parra's second lecture from 1930: "Who among us has not lived a bit in colonial times, thanks to some friend, some relative, or some old serving-woman miraculously unsuited to the present?")[12] Indeed, Mama

Blanca has studied the art of anachronism with an excellent teacher, her cousin Juancho. She admits to his having taught her how to conceal poverty with poise and style, but in fact her debt to him is much greater.

Cousin Juancho is an avatar of the ridiculous Quixotes of the nineteenthth-century Spanish realist Benito Pérez Galdós; we might cite, for example, Don José Relimpio y Sastre and Frasquito Ponte, of *La desheredada* (*The Disinherited*, 1881) and *Misericordia* (*Mercy*, 1897), respectively. But according to the value system of the *Memoirs*, Cousin Juancho is not ridiculous; on the contrary, his absurdity is judged sublime. In short, Cousin Juancho is a Frasquito Ponte seen through the eyes of the Spanish "Generation of '98." The scorn of the "Ninety-Eighters" for Galdos's bourgeois realism is well known, as is their active defense of the "reason of unreason," programmatically associated with Don Quixote. In many ways, de la Parra's novel partakes of the most conservative tendencies of the "Generation of '98": their idealization of the past and of intrahistory, their love of pipe dreams (*el ensueño*), and their defensive irrationalism. Moreover, the book is conscious of its debt to this generation. The inspiration of a passage like the following is unmistakable:

Thanks exclusively to Cousin Juancho, . . . while older and more learned people found *Don Quixote* boring, I was lost in admiration at its kindness and wisdom. . . . [And later] as I traveled through certain old cities of Extremadura or Castile in Spain, where others found only poor roads, cooking that reeked of olive oil, and an absence of baths, as a result of Cousin Juancho's early indoctrination, I filled my eyes with ineffable horizons of deep, infinite beauty.

Besides elaborating on the feminine, this open enthusiasm for the Spanish heritage filtered through the "Generation of '98" serves yet another purpose. In the Latin American intertextual debate over civilization versus barbarism (liberalism versus tradition) in which the novel engages, especially with its last chapter, "Aurora," this pro-Spanish sentiment represents a clear profession of antiliberalism.

Although Papa is a focal point in the text for the masculine, he does not display its most negative qualities. These are demonstrated by Evelyn, the mulatto housekeeper from Trinidad who is aggres-

sively "positivistic," "authoritative," "oppressive," and "intolerant."
Exercising constant "police intervention" with a "general staff" of
three nannies, her "regime" is, as the novel states, a "military dictatorship." Moreover, Evelyn declares a "war to the death" against
Vicente Cochocho, motivated by "a complex, personal race hatred."
Her conduct unequivocally places her at the opposite pole from
feminine generosity. Blanca Nieves's sister Violeta, "whose down-
to-earth soul [*alma positivista*] completely coincided with Evelyn's,"
is another strong male character: she is "enterprising and aggressive" ("Violeta's aggressiveness was insatiable"), she displays "rebelliousness" and "despotism," and she is always "ready to stand up for
her rights." The text explicitly identifies her as a male disguised in
female form: because of her "spirit," she is the son (Juan Manuel)
whom Papa always wanted to have. Finally, completing the group
of unadulterated "males" is "the new owner of Piedra Azul," who
"was a rich man, a great advocate of progress who was insatiable in
thinking up and carrying out reforms." In fact, the triad formed by
Evelyn, Violeta, and the new owner of Piedra Azul embodies what
Teresa de la Parra conceives of as the unleashed masculinity of the
republican era.

By comparison, Papa is considerably more benevolent and inept;
for instance, he is not a good enough businessman to hold onto
Piedra Azul. Though decidedly masculine, Papa has a colonial mentality: he lives in that "long vacation" during which men are supposed to have let women rule, and so the power of the feminine
controls and softens his masculinity. In Papa, the author shows us a
man who is somewhat marginal to the feminine universe of Piedra
Azul: the girls do not notice his absences, and his laborers calmly
and habitually disobey his orders. He never ceases to be God, however, although the God of Piedra Azul is not "the terrible God of
the Inquisition," but rather the creole God, pampered and agreeable, who, according to the author, prevailed in Spanish America
after the explusion of the Jesuits in 1767.[13] Papa is said to have
exercised "absolute, careless authority, similar to God's both because of the pleasant hit-or-miss system that characterized his mercy
and his justice as well as the way these were often flouted." Simply
by her reference to the "pleasant" disorder of his governance, de la

Parra identifies both this particular God and Papa as feminized beings, for disorder (as distinct from anarchy) is a concept she always associates with women. (The reader is directed to the author's first Bogotá lecture of 1930, in which she praises women, whom she considers disorderly by nature, for subversively shuffling the labels imposed on things by men.)[14]

Equally noteworthy is the paradox contained in the words "absolute and careless." Being omnipotent, the amiable and absent-minded Papa is still threatening. The novel's first chapter, "Blanca Nieves and Company," assiduously develops the metaphor of Piedra Azul as paradise, Papa as God, and the little girls as Adam and Eve. Here, the female narrator plays with convention when she says that the girls enjoyed several advantages over their prototypes, including that of disobedience: "We could sneak off and with complete impunity gorge ourselves on all the guavas we wanted without God casting us out of paradise." Yet toward the end of the book the convention reasserts its rights, and the guavas assume all the bitter taste of an ironic prophecy. For it is, after all, Papa who expels his daughters from Eden.

Childhood as Paradise; or The Impossible Alliance of Women, Children, and the Popular Masses

Although Teresa de la Parra could say in 1930 that the colonial era was "the reign of women, without chronicles or chroniclers," the fact is, in this novel the metaphorical colony is inseparable from childhood. The loss of innocence (or the knowledge of death, as in the cases of Nube de Agüita and Aurora), the departure from Piedra Azul, and the beginning of education—that is, training for womanhood—are all one and the same. The young Blanca Nieves experiences each of Mama's periodic absences as a "heartbreaking occurrence," a "mournful interregnum," "an unpleasant thing indeed, an interval as dark and gloomy as the tomb." But Mama Blanca as narrator has sufficient experience to know—though she does not and probably would never say so, even to herself—that the periodic expulsions from Piedra Azul that Mama must suffer are part of the price she pays for being a woman: Mama goes to Caracas every fifteen or sixteen months in order to give birth. Papa, in his double role as paterfamilias and God, is responsible for all the expulsions from Piedra Azul (he makes Mama pregnant, and he sells the plantation). In the final analysis, Papa controls the material destiny of both his big and little women.

Here we see one of the basic inconsistencies of Teresa de la Parra's colonial paradise. A fully realized alliance among women, children, and the popular masses is impossible because—among other things—women are adults, not children. Between girlhood and womanhood there is puberty, and once this threshold is crossed, one enters, never to return, the problematic and hazardous world of adult sexuality. The text of *Mama Blanca's Memoirs*, narrated by an old woman who endeavors to reconstruct her impressions as a girl of five or six, seems to take little interest in such matters, with the exception of Vicente Cochocho's ménage à trois, a situation that is dismissed as being "by this time undoubtedly platonic." However, beyond this single direct remark, the book refers to adult sexuality through "muteness" and "mystery." On occasion these rise to a "low-voiced conference," like that used by Evelyn to speak to Mama about Cochocho's sexual behavior. Similar to the girls, who overhear but who lack the necessary verbal competence to understand the word "depraved," it may be that many readers have failed to capture this mute discussion of female sexuality due to their inability to recognize the signs.

One of the signs the novel uses to discuss female sexuality is the novel *Paul et Virginie* (1787), by the French writer Bernard de Saint-Pierre. In this instance, the treatment of the theme remains mute because it rests on intertextuality. In *Paul et Virginie*, woman's sexuality gives rise to misfortune; for example, the two characters who are mothers lead a life of penitence for having had sexual relations with a man. Even more significant, Virginie's puberty serves as catalyst for the story's tragic dénouement. If the moral of this little eighteenth-century "pastoral" is that "our happiness consists of living in harmony with nature and virtue," it is clear that nature unredeemed by virtue can be a destructive force, which, in the mature human being, takes the form of passion and sexuality.[15] A recasting of the myth of paradise (like *Mama Blanca's Memoirs*),

Paul et Virginie establishes rigid equivalences among innocence, happiness, childhood, and the colonial island countryside, on the one hand, and, on the other, among sin, suffering, maturity, and Europe (the immoral "city" of the topos *beatus ille*). In *Mama Blanca's Memoirs*, Mama continually reinvents *Paul et Virginie*— "the story of the two little children"—because it is the "favorite" of her daughter Blanca Nieves. This little girl will grow up to be Mama Blanca, who will graft her old association between the island and Piedra Azul onto the entire structure of the story of her early childhood. (Or is it the editor, exquisitely trained in literary conventions, who exploits these parallels in order to lend the book that very symmetry that she disparagingly associates with literature in print?)

The significance acquired by the family chaise offers a prime example of how the harsh sexual lesson of *Paul et Virginie* becomes interwoven with the substance of Mama Blanca's recollections. Mama makes her inevitable trips to Caracas "in a two-horse chaise." This same chaise appears in the reelaborations of *Paul et Virginie*, dreamed up by Mama and Blanca Nieves:

Instead of taking a ship for France—pretentious word whose meaning was vague—Virginie, as natural as could be, set out for Caracas in a chaise just like Mama's. On her return, she was caught in a river flood.

The girls' exodus from Piedra Azul and perhaps even the calamitous wreck of the impossible return, described in chapter 8, also take place in the chaise. The chaise, then, serves to expel females from their particular idyll: it is the vehicle that carries girls and women to their confrontation with reality. It is semantically linked to the delayed punishment that awaits every girl for the sin of not having been born male, the very sin that gives rise to the "misunderstanding" between Papa and his six little girls:

The truth of the matter is that we never disobeyed him but once in our life. . . . This great act of disobedience took place at the hour of our birth.

The case of Mama, with her periodic disappearances, reinforces the interpretation that woman's true punishment is motherhood— that is, pregnancy. Motherhood, marriage, and economic dependence are three names for the same predicament. For the "decent" woman (the virtuous upper- and middle-class woman), mother-hood does not happen outside of marriage; at least, this seems to be de la Parra's premise in her fiction and her lectures. The combination of motherhood, marriage, and financial vulnerability constitutes the extreme of women's dependence on men. The cases of both Mama in the *Memoirs* and María Eugenia Alonso in de la Parra's first novel *Ifigenia* (1924) support this thesis.

If the author's writings bear out this interpretation, then it is no coincidence that we meet the protagonist of the *Memoirs* only at either end of her long life.[16] Both Blanca Nieves and Mama Blanca are free of the physical realities of motherhood. The first has not yet begun to serve her sexual sentence, while the other has already completed it. Both, therefore, inhabit worlds in which the oppressive weight of masculinity is diminished: one dwells in her childhood paradise, the other in "her ivory tower" where "she lived as solitary as a hermit." The two are thus able to consider themselves relatively happy.

Mama, on the other hand, embodies one of the options available to women during their reproductive years. Others are represented by the "two maiden ladies, as virtuous as they were poor, [who] mournfully taught a dozen little girls their ABC's and the catechism," by Mama Blanca's daughters-in-law, by the editor of the Foreword, and by the ghost of María Eugenia Alonso, *Ifigenia*'s protagonist, who should at all times inform our reading of the *Memoirs*, for she is the editor's negative alter ego, and perhaps even an unmarried version of the daughters-in-law. The options that exist for the years between menarche and menopause are notably inferior to the agreeable lives of Blanca Nieves and Mama Blanca. Mama, who is evoked from the childhood of Mama Blanca, seems a happy woman, though we learn that she reads books because she is idle and isolated, and that this isolation, a condition of her marriage to Papa, deprives her of opportunities to express her natural "social charm." No such lack of opportunities will follow her move to Caracas, another material circumstance dictated by her husband. But with this move, her family becomes subject to the rule of money and discovers the strain of a household budget. An analogous process of economic decline condemns the two "distinguished maiden

ladies" to running a "school or asylum of melancholy and learning."
Here we see one of the few means of earning a living that was open
to "decent" women in Latin American cities during the last century:
running a small school for girls became the fate of many an unmarried woman who had no male relative to support her and who
would not "lower herself" to the labors of the common people.

On the other hand, Mama Blanca's daughters-in-law are
twentieth-century women: elegant *señoras* who live in constant
competition with each other, they are portrayed in *Ifigenia* in the
person of Mercedes Galindo. Both Mama Blanca and her friend
the editor have contempt for them. The editor is a woman of
letters, a professional writer. We are not told if she supports herself by writing, but she is a woman whose self-definition comes
from her work, not from her marital status. Finally, María Eugenia
Alonso, a young woman with a certain intellectual promise, is
impelled by financial necessity as well as by her education to com-
mit spiritual suicide when she marries a little despot whose veneer
of refinement fails to hide his true nature—primitive, barbaric, and
uncouth.

Of all these women, only Mama is able to live under colonial
conditions, and this only metaphorically and only until 1855. The
others inhabit republican Caracas of the nineteenth and twentieth
centuries. Especially in twentieth-century Caracas, which is the Caracas of de la Parra, as well as of the editor, the daughters-in-law, and
María Eugenia, a young woman cannot possibly follow in the footsteps of her great-grandmothers. Because of the profound disloca-
tion of the colonial hierarchy, the material conditions have ceased to
exist that supposedly made the lives of the married and unmarried
ladies of long ago tolerable and even enviable.[17]

Thus two principal factors limit de la Parra's colonial matriarchy.
One is woman's material condition—her body and her economic
dependence—which even in Piedra Azul undermines feminine
power and allows men to have the final say. While on the literal
plane the novel seems to belittle the importance of this material
factor, other levels of the text serve to confirm it. The second limit is
imposed by the eruption of history into the characters' lives. The
abolition of slavery in Venezuela symbolically marks the end of the

señorial era and the beginning of the modern period, the latter being characterized by the many forms of social instability so troubling to the author. If the colony was ahistorical ("as naive and happy as children and as those peoples who have no history"), the republic is history itself: constant change, violence, and the predominanance of men. With the sale of Piedra Azul in 1855, the aggressive masculinity of Evelyn and Violeta prevails over Papa's milder variation. And with the demise of that universe, which seemed beyond the reach of history, even Evelyn and Violeta lose their freedom to adopt masculine identities: Evelyn suddenly abandons both the family and the novel to return to Trinidad, and Violeta moves with her sisters to Caracas, where she will undergo a successful transformation into a proper young lady.

Translated by Elizabeth Garrels and Amanda Powell

Notes

1. *Mantuano*: name given to the creole plantation aristocracy of Caracas in the eighteenth century. *Gran cacao*: another name for this group, which refers to the source of their wealth in cacao production. "Segunda conferencia," in *Obras completas de Teresa de la Parra* (Caracas: Editorial Arte, 1965), p. 713. (This lecture belongs to a series of three public talks that de la Parra delivered in Bogotá, Colombia, in 1930, under the general title "The Influence of Women in the Formation of the American Soul.") Unless otherwise indicated, all translations in this essay are the joint work of Amanda Powell and myself.

2. Ibid., pp. 713–14, emphasis added. One can begin to appreciate how Teresa de la Parra continually establishes the same valences: Colony + morality + influence + tenderness + generosity + female.

3. Ibid., p. 713.

4. The unnamed president has to be the conservative Soublette because of the date of Mama's wedding (1846). On the relationship of the author to Soublette, see ibid., pp. 735–36.

5. Nicolás Sánchez Albornoz, *The Population of Latin America: A History*, trans. W.A.R. Richardson (Berkeley and Los Angeles: University of California Press, 1974), p. 145. Lieuwen claims that the law of 1854 freed 40,000 slaves (*Venezuela* [London: Oxford University Press, 1961]).

6. Tulio Halperín-Donghi, *Historia contemporánea de América Latina* (Madrid: Alianza, 1972), p. 192.

7. *Caudillismo*: the phenomenon of leaders whose rule was personal rather than constitutional and who frequently established their own armies.

8. "Tercera conferencia," *Obras completas*, p. 750.

9. Simon Bolívar, *Escritos políticos* (Madrid: Alianza, 1969), p. 87.

10. Teresa de la Parra, *Cartas* (Caracas: Cruz del Sur, 1951), p. 17.

11. "Segunda conferencia," *Obras completas*, pp. 711–12.

12. Ibid., p. 713.

13. "Tercera conferencia," *Obras completas*, pp. 745–46.

14. "Primera conferencia," *Obras completas*, pp. 689–90.

15. Bernadin de Saint-Pierre, *Pablo y Virginia*, trans. Luis Cernuda (Madrid: Espasa-Calpe, 1967), p. 7.

16. In fact, Teresa de la Parra uses similar terms to define the protagonists of *Ifigenia* and the *Memoirs*, María Eugenia and Mama Blanca, respectively: "Situated at the extreme opposites of life, they remained with me for some time; one told me of her desire to live, the other of her sadness at having left life behind" ("Primera conferencia," *Obras completas*, p. 684).

17. Ibid., pp. 684–87.

 **Sequential Narrations**

JOSÉ BALZA

It could be startling to enter this frieze (or sequence or "well-stitched embroidery") in which so many exquisite and subtle doors open, through the rough, savage, and—why not say it?—bestial precinct of the corral. Here we find the cows, Daniel the dairyman, the bull calves, and the seven little girls of Piedra Azul. Such simple elements, however, may have functions in the story that are less direct and simple than milking the cows, drinking the glass of fresh milk, and assisting the little princesses in waking up with the hacienda.

The "republic of the cows" unfolds, as it should, in a rural setting. The father has instituted the custom—it is one of his only commands—that every day the girls must drink a glass of milk fresh from the cow. Scarcely have they awakened from dreams when another stimulating apparition assails them: the opening of the body, of the senses, to the new day; they walk from their home up to the corral through the dew, through the forceful stand of bushes. Somehow or other the fence of injunctions, represented by their governess Evelyn, is annulled in the course of this walk. So attentive to nuances, Teresa de la Parra grounds herself above all in this scene in the girls' speech. They are the ones who pester the milker as he works with occasional phrases, questions, and exclamations. That assured speech confirms that we are in a new territory.

Now the little maids receive their first nourishment of the day, they play, talk, but above all, find themselves in the calves. The bond stems from their names; just like Carmen María, Daniel has handed out names: this calf is Flor de Saúco [Elderberry Flower], that one Nochebuena [Christmas Eve], that other one Rayo de Sol [Sunshine]. The possible link between the calves and the girls is synthetically determined by the animal named Estrella [Star], like one of the girls. Her feelings of pride and fraternity turn the animal into her "namesake." Destined to study, to see themselves in their delicate mother, to be beautiful, at this moment the girls shatter all of these assumptions. As they drink the milk and watch the cows being milked, not only do they lose the identification their mother has so rigorously established, but they adjust to other customs, to other latitudes.

We are well aware of how mistaken Carmen María's method was for choosing her daughters' names; well do we know how problematic nut-colored skin is in a girl named Blanca Nieves [Snow White] or rebelliousness in someone supposed to be a meek Violeta [Violet]. In the corral, things don't happen that way. Each cow has exactly the right name, not only because the image each name evokes coincides with the animal's appearance—Viuda Triste [Sad Widow], Nube de Agua [Rain Cloud],—but because each animal recognizes itself in that sonority and responds to it quickly.

Such a miraculous fit of ideal image and reality is due in the corral to its chief priest. It is Daniel the cowherd. A man of the plains, from the savannas of Aragua; the way he offers the glass of milk to the girls is the same way he makes the extraordinary handmade cheese that gives Piedra Azul its renown. Daniel's powers range from handling cows and achieving a magnificent production to his talent for giving them names and above all, his ability to be a poet with a preference for epigrams. Daniel's poetry disturbs the girls, who look to the cows to understand it; it simplifies the animals and constitutes the free circulation of lyricism within the hacienda. We could discover many mysteries and tonalities of language in this novel, but this is the only spring from which gushes the song to sudden inspiration and to immovable laws: the song to the unity of the moment with tradition. Delivering his couplets, Daniel obeys his pure talent; no one has taught him and no one is going to correct him. To take away his words, strip bare his intimate rhythm, would place his voice in danger of becoming live sound, like the lowing of a cow, like the girls' exclamations.

Everything cannot be perfect. "Daniel was astute and predatory." The peaks of his song (and its power) are his alone. They are foreign to moral conventions. Daniel brazenly swindles—although in such a way as to be unprovable—the owner of the hacienda. The latter, in one of his few emphatic gestures, throws the farmhand out, but the cows as well as the feeding schedule oblige him to call Daniel back again. (Let us not forget that in the corral the man who really gives the orders is Daniel and that in Piedra Azul, the father is perhaps only "a figure . . . of the third order.")

For the girls, Daniel's nature as a supreme artist is revealed with the death of the calf. To trick the cow named Nube de Agua [Rain Cloud], he takes the hide off the dead calf, puts it over another animal, and both his tunes and the disguise keep the cow giving her best milk. If we had any doubts about the involuntarily divine character that envelops Daniel—this mask of life for death, this playing with animality and dread—the narrator will unsuccessfully associate them with the mother's pain when she loses Aurora.

So when something (grief? destiny?) forces us to accept that life may be covered by death (or vice versa), when we recognize that the irrational experience gives just the right names to the right beings, when in a landscape of vigorous bushes, of dew and dawn, conventions are muddled or forgotten, it is because we are in a unique environment: that of intuition, of instinct, of vague and steady forces. And this is what happens to the girls as they leave the big house and enter the corral. One part of them ceases to be and is joined with the other: the animal energy, the poetry behind its amorphous splendor. The corral, Daniel, the cows, and the girls, upon being brought together, form a mandala of mysterious vectors: of the unconscious dream, of the conscious dream. Animality and digestion; sound and meanings.

Through this unintentional door, we have tried to enter the world of Piedra Azul. Should we follow the logical, transparent and enchanting order that Teresa de la Parra offers us on Mama Blanca's doorstep, we would be unable to look at the back side of the tapestry. Perhaps the world of Piedra Azul is not really what we read in the *Memoirs*. It is not frivolous when one of the girls, faced with the union of cow and calf under one name, says to herself in amazement: "We could not understand how two persons, no matter how close they were, could be called by the same name. This awkward, confused duality did not please us at all."

"You read it if you want to, but don't show it to anybody," is the request with which Mama Blanca, at the end of her life, hands to her exegete the original text of her memoirs. Of course, the text will not be presented, for while we peruse the memories written down by the old woman, we are only reading through the recipient of the bundle. "Some five hundred sheets of linen paper." (If Blanca Nieves's, [Snow White's] mother was born in 1831 and is twenty-four years old when the narrator is born, her childhood years—through age seven?—must take place between 1855 and 1862.)

We already know that out of curiosity and chance, a girl befriends the old woman. With no familial bonds, they establish a tie between them based on those "mysterious spiritual affinities that in the commerce of souls weave the brief or enduring web of sympathy, friendship, or love, which are separate stages in that supreme joy of mutual understanding."

The supreme joy of mutual understanding: the carrot and the stick that lead the inheritor of the bundle to the act of publishing (or reading) it. This is important, for she is the one who gives us access to the world of Mama Blanca, that original voice that immediately produces two effects: that of disappearing and that of projecting itself. First of all, she alone hands us the "seven golden keys" to enter that kingdom of memory, but her instantaneous appearance in the foreword or prologue scarcely allows us a glimpse of her. We know something of a childhood and the hypnotic force which attracts her to Mama Blanca; we also will know that years later she corrects the originals. Then she disappears forever.

A strange phenomenon, however, seems to keep her suspended throughout the work. There is such intensity in the memoirs (its paradoxical quality of *immediacy* is so vivid) that the recipient of the bundle seems to be looking over our shoulder, always accompanying us. Perhaps this specter comes from the sensation provoked in us by the phrase "Don't show it to anybody." We find things out as the heiress reads on.

This is the sense in which we have tried to use the term "frieze"[1] to designate the narrative composition of *Mama Blanca's Memoirs*. With a glance one can highlight one scene or character and then others. But they are all within arm's reach, immediately apparent, with the same degree of relief and light. The inheritor of the writings disappears (or appears,) Blanca Nieves might be the central character, but Evelyn and Vicente Cochocho, Daniel and Cousin Juancho are of equal rank. Many molds produce a single relief (that charge of immediacy on which the action rides?).

Of course the mother is Piedra Azul itself, but like fairies, who only err on minor details (as in choosing the girls' names), she sustains two amiable errors within the boundaries of the hacienda: Violeta and Evelyn. The former, her personality diametrically opposed to her name, is the leader of the flock, picks her destiny and that of the other girls, rebels, ignores the sirens' song. A fatally practical temperament makes her suspect everything or exhibit an unquenchable curiosity. She even dares to tread on the terrain of linguistics and dreams (realms of Blanca Nieves [Snow White]) when she states very pompously how *depraved* "all those people are whose thatched roofs are damp and unkempt as Vicente [Cochocho]'s hut."

, Violeta, as a character, dominates us right away: she overflows with life, a taste for action, spontaneity. That is why on occasion her father celebrates the girl's behavior for the son he never had. "I believe that in Violeta's body lodged the spirit of Juan Manuel the Desired, and this was the main reason why he had never been born: for six years he had walked the earth disguised as a violet." Perhaps the particular way in which Violeta dominates the progress of the narrative derives from her gestures: she has no past, no history to round out. Her destiny is built on deeds, she is a character who is always in action, and such gestures distinguish her by her liveliness from all the lives presented (Cousin Juancho, Cochocho) but inexorably evoked. Administered by the elderly Mama Blanca and racked with pains and laughter by the little Blanca Nieves, an important psychic current in the book is concealed in Violeta's adventures and decisions: humor. She lets loose comic situations, faces them or resolves them. And if to that we add that such situations are not recollected but occur before our eyes, we are a little closer to the unforgettable effect Violeta has on the reader. (By inevitable contrast, Violeta is the salvation of María Eugenia Alonso; the humor and independence in each lead to different perspectives.)

It is precisely in *Ifigenia* that María Eugenia as well as Mercedes Galindo obsessively worship civilization and foreign culture. They don't utter a sentence without inserting a phrase in French. The fashion and customs of Caracas are meager in comparison with absolutely anything Parisian. In *Mama Blanca's Memoirs,* it is different. Evelyn not only turns out to be a stranger in the territory of Piedra Azul (as do other participants) but is not from Venezuela either. Meticulous, tidy, very proper, Evelyn comes from Trinidad exclusively for the purpose of teaching the girls English. They, blossoming and savage, turn her into just another plaything. An instrument of power for the mother, the black woman is made fun of at every turn. She carries out basic duties and even promulgates a *wicked law*—"No more sugar mill!"—but she never manages to teach English and her poor Spanish is mutilated in the end.

● With Evelyn, the worship of all things foreign is, in Teresa de la Parra's eyes, tempered. Neither admiration nor reserve: a warm confidence in the pedagogical power of the foreigner (although this is not borne out), a hygienic means of integration, even while it may be the butt of jokes and laughter, but nothing more.

The father, Daniel, the laborers, Vicente Cochocho, and Cousin Juancho are the dark voices set against the chorus of the mother, Evelyn, and the little girls (who really form a single unit). The protagonists of *Ifigenia* are established in order to sketch out the plot and to support the shifting psychological construct of María Eugenia. They also modulate the great themes of the novel: money, feminine dependency, doubt. *Mamá Blanca's Memoirs,* on the other hand, is a book solely of characters; they are so rounded out (literally, in the case of the men) that at times we see them looking right into the chasm of deep symbolism. But having touched those abysses, Teresa de la Parra's fluidity and irony maintains the vitality of her characters, strangers to meaningful *entelechies*.

Among them, curiously conspicuous as much for his symbolic caliber as for his own internal force, is Cousin Juancho, who takes his place with ease in the *Memoirs* but who at the same time stands up perfectly well in our world, in the actual history of Venezuela. Although he is very old for the little girls of Piedra Azul, he never ceases being the "cousin" his customary visits have turned him into. Intelligent, nonconformist, lucid, and at the same time scattered, absolutely incapable of solving his own problems, he lives nevertheless proposing grand solutions for all the country's woes. The Venezuelan left has known so many Cousin Juanchos in the twentieth century.

⊘ Juancho complains about the condition of the roads, accuses the government of corruption, brings the English teacher to the hacienda; he exists through his baritone voice, made to deliver speeches in the academies and to tell amusing anecdotes. But it gives the author cause to dedicate these brush strokes to him, terrible and playful: "He was like a dictionary: the same partial unity within the same overall disjointedness"—which does not keep her from viewing literature rather severely: "The dictionary is the only pleasant and peaceful book whose amiable incoherence, so resembling that of Mother Nature, gives us a rest from logic, oratory, and literature."

How well Cousin Juancho, in his ambivalence, epitomizes an entire political reality! His honest, spotless character resembles the "idealistic soul of the race." He is utterly incapable of hypocrisy, of climbing up the ladder, of obsessively seeking power; at the same time, he is more equipped than anyone (by his knowledge of history, his capacity to reflect, his immense wealth of information) to be a brilliant figure in Congress or in government circles. But his rhetoric and his penetrating analytical ability are fragile and frail, as incoherent as the black woollen frock coat he wears in hot weather. Mama Blanca perceives in the Cousin Juancho's vast political visions the advent of a United States of Hispanoamerica, of fabulous significance to the destiny of the continent . . . provided our character doesn't concern himself with equal intensity with a grease stain he might notice on someone's clothes. And she corroborates how, in the mouth of Cousin Juancho, the speeches, anecdotes, and advice are interrupted, repositioned interchangably, how they "rambled up a thousand bypaths." The lucid personality of the visionary turns out to be as dull as that of a more ignorant person. Fragmentation, constant disparity, waves that will not solidify, make him totally immature despite his long life. Contemplating that "sort of well-stitched embroidery" that turns out ro be Cousin Juancho's character, it is not difficult to divine indications, outlines of so many of our politicians. However, it is no less disturbing that despite his clarity, Cousin Juancho's moral caliber leads him to join the liberal party when he is, in essence, a conservative. All in the spirit of contradiction?

And so we come to Vicente Cochocho, one of the most studied and compared figures in Teresa de la Parra's work. The author's imaginative method is already defined for this moment: the characters appear like beads on a necklace. And even though each of them exerts an effective *tension* over the others, nothing announces them in chapters prior to their depiction. They are trotted out abruptly, definitive and unanticipated.

Vicente Cochocho is marked by an American multiplicity. The other characters take part too in that significant scattering, but the humble peasant of Piedra Azul has in his psychology a magnificent, worldly craftsmanship. "Badly dressed, a hired hand," his name is that of a lowly creature, and he performs the most rudimentary and dirty tasks of the hacienda. One rung up, he takes care of and cures the animals. He lives in close affinity with the plant world, whose secrets he wields for good as well as for evil. His ugly form expresses itself in a golden tongue: classical Spanish, which, according to the author, is spoken as if preceded by strict musical clefs. Perhaps all these characteristics define an archaic range for Vicente's dimensions. For even his frugal obedience to his boss disappears when echoes of the revolution reverberate through the province. Cochocho then takes on the rank of a strategist, a leader.

The childhood years of Mama Blanca take place, in fact, amid the uprisings and the capricious appetite for power that linked one war to another. A Venezuela filled with violence surrounds the enchanted world of the six little princesses.

• Magician, military man, doctor, our character is also a master of the affairs of death: in solidarity he builds coffins, attends to the sick. And he lives with two women! In Mama Blanca's fond recollection,

Vicente is already an old man when this occurs, and his loves ought only to be platonic, but in this way she indicates to us that up to the end of his life, Cochoco follows a very personal erotic tradition.

If in the center of Piedra Azul is the family house, the sugar mill, the corral, and the peasants' huts, if so many lively characters—the girls, the animals, the adults—all live together in this space, if the hacienda as a whole corresponds by name to a little blue halo of tenderness and storytelling, it is because Vicente Cochocho protects that fable. The boundaries of Piedra Azul are those of Vicente Cochocho's heart: angel, protector, his energy makes possible the blue halo, the dreaming, and the happiness. Thanks to him, no one invades or destroys that luminous space; his power elevates this territory to the highest status in a violent country: that of commanding respect. Only one person exercises power over Vicente Cochocho: Carmen María, the mother, that delicious and romantic woman who makes all the decisions.

Initially, because of the narrator's link with Carmen María (her mother), and later, through the delicate and funny portrait the girl draws of the woman, we find ourselves drawn by a whirlwind of sympathy toward such a seductive character.

The mother attends to the house through her servants; she prepares her girls for daily life, for elegance, and for the future; she consecrates the marriages of her employees (at times with the same misfortune as when she names her daughters). She is seen harmoniously tied to her husband, but the focus of that union does not let us see that, in fact, Don Juan Manuel barely figures in the life of Piedra Azul: he is only shown having quarrels with Daniel and Cochocho, without even managing to have his way. He is, according to Blanca Nieves, a "minor" figure. Stylized, romantic almost to the point of sentimentality, the beautiful mother of Blanca Nieves opposes natural corresondences (in the girls' hair, in the peasant couples). She conducts the social life of the hacienda, administering visits and other trifles; she has a peculiar way of speaking with pauses that might be exquisite laments; she initiates her daughter into the world of fantasy, telling her comfortable, well-known stories, enthralling her so that she might submit to having her hair done.

All this pampering and feminine transcendence makes us smile at the mother's caprices. But it also prevents us from seeing how if anyone orders, controls, and decides all that goes on in Piedra Azul, it is Carmen María. Behind the wasp-waist bodice and the charming smile is an exacting will, an imposing cadence, an absolute mastery of the place and its inhabitants. The enchanted world of the hacienda maintains its equilibrium with the rest of the country by Vicente Cochocho's intervention, but he along with the other inhabitants of the place obey an exquisite, dictatorial leader: the mother.

The sober and transparent writing of the *Memoirs* tells us precisely what it has to say. The fluidity of style, the hint of humor, and the design of its characters enchant and convince. Such refinement, however, might eclipse other tensions that are less delicate and fair than they seem. That is the impression we get of the society of Piedra Azul as seen from the corral.

Considering Daniel's earthy lyricism and basing ourselves on the intuitive vectors which the animality of the place seems to liberate, we have observed how Cochocho—complex and versatile—brings together such varied qualities as heroism or amorality, while Cousin Juancho, despite his vision of salvation for the nation, is ruled only by doubt.

Perhaps we would have found such a reading impossible had we not taken Daniel as our starting point. His behavior makes him immediately prone to suspicion (instead of limiting himself to milking, he sings and robs.) But to suspect him is to suspect everyone.

Thus we come to that pleasant shadow, Carmen María, the mother. Woven with tenderness and exquisite tones, every move she makes is wrapped in a magical aura. Looking from the corral, we find, nevertheless, that as she carries out her motherly functions with elegance, she enforces the language of tyranny in the guise of femininity.

We can thus doubly appreciate the image of the "embroidery": its empty spaces, its clefts not only mark the reliefs, the whole form of the stitching, but also let through deceptive light, disguising the weave. The frieze of the *Memoirs* exists with its clear depressions and projections, but if we aren't careful (in our first reading,) we will miss the "mysterious duality": despite its obvious harmony, in many instances the embroidery has been reversed.

Translated by Mark Schafer

Note

1. The frieze: a successive totality in movement before the spectator's eyes. Teresa de la Parra retained the idea of writing a "series" with the anecdotes and characters from this novel, as indicated in a letter she sent to Enrique Bernardo Núñez).

Mirror, Mirror, in Mother's Room
Watch Us While We Tell and Groom

DORIS SOMMER

Probably because Mama Blanca taught me to meander along conciliatory and syncretic narrative paths, I sometimes imagine her meeting up with Doña Bárbara, the unnaturally aggressive cattle boss of Rómulo Gallegos's 1929 novel. And if I needed a justification for imagining the meeting, I could quote Blanca's own (un)reason, not so much a lack of reason as an awareness that there was no need to be reasonable: the only excuse she gives for letting herself combine, distort, and reframe the stories her mother told her is, "Nobody told me I couldn't" (51; 33)]. Even without her lead, though, getting Bárbara and Blanca together is hardly arbitrary for the reader who notices their coincidence of time and place, as well as the thematic similarity between two books about women who occupy the center of their rural Venezuelan worlds until they are deposed by men who dispute property and propriety.[1] Through these disputes, and the changes they announce, both novels comment on the process of social modernization. By every other comparison, though, the books could hardly be more different. Their narrative trajectories and linguistic strategies, even their ideological implications, probably have some relevance for what may broadly be called literary criticism. But I am moved to leave that ground for a moment as I imagine the two books in terms of a possible confrontation between the "personifications" of barbarous dissemination in one and of playful permutations in the other. My own feminist longings and readerly desire for poetic justice make me unable to resist a temptation to shift the discursive ground from interpretation to active listening.

Instead of analytical categories, the two female protagonists begin to loom independent from their texts, like participants in a very intimate, unscheduled but unavoidable, consciousness-raising session. Deposed and displaced, Bárbara would surely have found an empathetic interlocutor in Mama Blanca, the exile from paradise where she had learned how to listen to everyone. Their hypothetical conversation, as I choose to imagine it, would manage to get beyond the inevitable racial and class differences, although Bárbara's resentment toward the aristocratic breeding of the white woman—white to her very name—would surely make her wary of sharing indiscreet confidences. But Blanca's unaffected tone, the nostalgia for Violeta that this exorbitant guest would evoke, and especially the discreet but knowing questions with which Blanca would make room for Bárbara, would soon generate a friendly dialogue. They would tell each other about their respective stories, stories already written and, perhaps, those they might still write. Bárbara's resistance to this sort of intimacy would necessarily falter as she considered the self-legitimating possibilities of the narrative strategies developed by the author of her own memoirs. Incredulous, she would ask how Blanca managed to organize her chapters so unsystematically, or how she could side with hired hands over her father, the legitimate authority of the place. "What, you? A five-year-old authority? Don't make me laugh. . . . You're right; why not laugh?"

Giddy from the twists the girl imposed on her mother's stories, I can hardly be expected to keep the novels about Blanca and Bárbara straight. And even if that were possible, I am convinced that Blanca would have experimented with a dialogic (con)fusion between the two, had she heard the tale of a nostalgic old lady and the one about a despoiled woman rancher. The same five-year-old girl would surely have imagined them as I do: sitting together in the garden, sipping hot chocolate, chatting and remembering a Venezuela "*tan relejos*," "so very long ago." The girl's own habit of blending and twisting her mother's stories is so contagious that it becomes useless for me to refrain from the narrative mixes that she herself prepares. How else can we listen to these compatriot and contemporary books after Blanca's mother confuses error with charm, and especially after the girl herself charms us with irresponsible listening?

Now the scene of her deceptively passive activity hardly seems promising. She is sitting in front of the big mirror in her mother's bedroom, this and every day, watching her mother comb out curls set in the morning. Like a penitent for the sin of having straight hair, or like a convict for esthetic crimes with an insistent parole officer, Blanca Nieves suffers the daily humiliation of being only temporarily improved. But the Hegelian intuition of the ward tips her off about the power she exercises over the warden. If curls were the mandate, since curls are beautiful and "a woman's first duty is to look her best," Blanca's black head of hair would have to remain cooperatively still in front of that disciplinary mirror. So her captive captor was forced to concede to a coterminous demand: to captivate the girl with stories as long as the curling process lasted. And just as the result of the curling would produce a pleasing excess, so the telling would be excessive, because Blanca Nieves sometimes insisted that the stories be repeated with unprecedented borrowings from other stories, with tragic endings required by some caprice and comic endings by another. The girl dictated, unpredictably, and the mother dutifully narrated. While her mother curled her straight hair, adjusting stepmother Nature to higher esthetic standards, the daughter was also stamping her creative will on the stories that she demanded for entertainment. Like her hair, those stories were mere raw material, the pretexts for supplements that never achieved stable or definitive shapes. In front of the great mirror that conspired in the daily ritual, mother and daughter supplemented all they wanted. This is certainly not the mirror that some female autobiographers complain can only frame them in the male gaze. More like Luce Irigaray's penetrating speculum, it is an instrument that promises to reflect on feminine interiority.[2] This mirror is a screen for aimless projections, a compensatory diversion, a forced freedom to recount without being held accountable to models, or to nature.

We may also want to read this scene of manipulation as a figure for the primal scene of Hispano-American creativity, akin to the self-arrogation of authority by Domingo Sarmiento (one of Argentina's founding fathers) every time he saw a hint of himself in an imperfect model. ("I felt I was Franklin"—he says, for example, immediately to ask himself a bit aggressively, "and why not? I was very poor, just like he was, a diligent student like he was." That is, a veritable "Franklincito" before discovering his own person in someone else's book.)³ Contemplating themselves in the mirror of European and North American art, Latin Americans create specular distortions that return very different images or "identities" from that of putative models. The difference is not always parody but quite often represents a "correction" or an improvement of the adoptive parent culture, as one can argue from Latin American rewritings of Rousseau, Chateaubriand, Scott, Stendhal, Cooper, Balzac.⁴

Along with the acknowledgment of foreign authority comes the greater measure of local authority that can respect models and supersede them at the same time. Blanca's straight hair is evidently acknowledged in the curling process, but the rectilinear matter is returned with pleasing twists every time Blanca's mother wins her battle against nature. And the European stories come back from the mirror equally transformed, domesticated, and perfected in various and contradictory ways. Far from being content with the foreign stuff, or from repeating it in servile imitations, the childish narrator was learning from her mother how to tangle, tie, and adjust the malleable matter in ways that kept giving it new life. There was no reason why established plots always had to coincide with their traditional developments, as little reason as there was to make names identify with their subjects or to make genders coincide with sexes.

Frustrated, bored, or offended by the ending of Bernardin de Saint-Pierre's *Paul et Virginie*, for example, where the chaste girl prefers to die in the storm at sea rather than expose her limbs by swimming safely to her lover, Blanca Nieves sometimes demands a happy reunion. At other times, though, she makes all the characters die together in a final cataclysm. On hearing "Beauty and the Beast," to mention another example, she decides that the metamorphosis at the end is an extraneous concession to those who cannot truly love. So she has it omitted, charging that it is an offense to the noble Beast, and to her dog, Marquesa, whom she identifies with the hero. "How wonderful!" Bárbara would interrupt, slapping her thigh and throwing her head back to laugh outloud. "You cast the bitch as hero!" "Of course," Blanca would giggle, "it was the only thing I never changed in that story."

"You remember, Mama, the Beast is to remain Beast, with his tail, his black hair, his ears and everything, and he is to marry the Beauty like that. He is never to become a prince. You won't forget?"

Mama took due notice.

Naturally, *Paul and Virginia* at times had a happy ending. Virginia, miraculously saved from the flood waters, married Paul and they lived happily ever after. But if it so happened that my soul felt a vague, voluptuous desire to immerse itself in grief, then I let things take their course.

"Mama, let it rain terribly hard, and the river rise, and the little girl drown, and then everybody die."

Mama unleashed the elements, and the scene was covered with crepe and corpses.

Little Snow White is infectiously willful, with her requirements for stories to fit her childish moods, with the liberating lack of discrimination that lets her daydream about her mother's wedding on hearing *El Cantar de Mío Cid*.

Reading her extravagant or extraneous demands, and watching them take pleasing shapes in the makeup mirror, goads me to reflect back on possible narrative twists and to wonder what Bárbara and Mama Blanca might have said to each other with their first introductions. "Good afternoon, I am Bárbara. I mean, I am called Bárbara and that's been a problem." "Oh, names are so absurd," Blanca would say with soothing levity, "it took me all these years and all these white hairs to fade into mine." Doña Bárbara, trained to recognize the indelible mark of barbarity in (or as) her calling, would be surprised to learn that in Piedra Azul names didn't announce characters with some supposed allegorical immediacy; instead, they alluded indirectly, almost against the grain, in the same way that the stories Blanca Nieves demanded were hardly self-identical but rather capricious misrepresentations.

As for the visual language of faces and physical features (so expressive of hero Santos's superiority, his beloved Marisela's unwashed nobility, and Bárbara's unnatural appeal), it was no more reliable a code than other words in Piedra Azul. Marquesa was one incongruous example, another was the gentle peon nicknamed for a stinging bug: "Vicente Cochocho, who was a giant in kindness of soul, could hardly have been smaller in physical stature." These representational disencounters, multiplied throughout the memoirs, are instances of a general (and merciful) crisis of authority here. So perhaps it will suffice to mention only one more emblematic failure to find transparent correspondences between expression and experience: the evident authority that the father wields is hardly a controlling force, since Vicente Cochocho and cowherd Daniel can both lord it over the master's "absolute" power. Like Blanca Nieves under her mother's beautifying authority, the master's underlings understand his dependence on them. Daniel leaves graciously when Don Juan Manuel fires him for evident but undocumented cheating, because the employee knows long before the soon-desperate employer that he will be called back to resume serenading the now spoiled cows. And the patriarchal outrage caused by Vicente's multiple marriages or by his occasional leadership of regional revolutions do little more than humiliate him and the master who is caught between principled pronouncements and his inability to let Cochocho go.

By contrast, Gallegos forces the hierarchy, and the supporting verbal correspondences, into a tidy construction. That Santos Luzardo is meant to rule, that his ranch "Altamira" is meant to command an encompassing vision, Bárbara to be banished, and "El Miedo" ranch along with her, are all announced by their names. Hardly insensitive to verbal and narrative waywardness, *Doña Bárbara* is determined to erect a tight allegorical defense against surprises. Reaching its goal so directly, her name fixes her as an immobile sign; and she suffers the same fatality that dooms Aurora. "Poor Aurora," Bárbara would agree, "and poor Mama," because by now she will have caught on that, thanks to the fissured nature of language, and to the desire that language cannot (and perhaps refuses to) satisfy, words usually fail to name adequately. Luckily, the effort to name can become a continual game of hide and seek, frustrating for a "positivistic soul" such as the governess Evelyn, but hilarious in the disordered and aimless affections of Mama and Mama Blanca. If, by a paradoxical disfunction, the symbolic order occasionally functions the way it pretends to, it can produce a glimpse of what Lacan called imaginary harmony—a postulated, prelinguistic immediacy between child and mother before spoken interventions by the father teach a rhythm of cleavages. That preconceptual, even prehuman, harmony is the rapport that some fathers imagine the mothers to foster; but mothers may choose to evade this dubious and debilitating honor, preferring to play in the gaps that the "order of the father" (of Gallegos, for example) dreams of closing up.[5]

Whereas Violeta, that absurdly improper proper noun, gives the blunder of Blanca's name a friendly context of family resemblance, it is Bárbara's stark significance that allows us to savor Mother's irreverent linguistic freedom. *Doña Bárbara* is not just a contemporaneous fiction; it is the founding novel for Venezuela's first populist party, Acción Democrática. On that ticket, Gallegos himself would become, in 1948, the first freely elected president of the country. Focusing for the moment on Violeta, both novels are about women who are also men. Bárbara is the "personification"[6] of the seductive land and of lawless usurpations, an oxymoronic obstacle to the hero's demand for legally binding terms.

Published after his disciples had already gone to jail or to exile for opposing Juan Vicente Gómez, *Doña Bárbara* is Gallegos's fantasy of return and repair. He stages the reconquest as a tale of triumphant civilization, in the person of aptly named Santos Luzardo, who has come home to the llano after graduating from law school in Caracas. His first intention was merely to sell the family ranch and to spend the earnings in Europe. But the llano makes claims on its rightful master, and Santos stays to put his ranch in order. In the process he must subdue the barbarous woman who has been rustling his cattle and seizing his land. Her very identity as a domineering woman is a signal for censure, a rhetorical trespassing of populism's gendered code. Meanwhile, his newly fenced-in property adds newly diversified dairy products to the original meat and hides, and production develops with factory efficiency. Borders, fences, frontiers are civilization's first requirements, the kind of writing that refuses to risk barbarous misreadings.[7] Indecisiveness was precisely the semiotic transgression that gave seductive charm to the llano—with its hallucinatory circle of receding mirages—and to Bárbara's exorbitant sexuality, her "imposing appearance of Amazon [*marimacho*] put . . . the stamp of originality on her beauty: there was something about her at once wild, beautiful, and terrible."[8] For Gallegos, her jumbled identity is literally a mess, a monstrous transgression of neat social constructions of nature, a threat and obstacle to the oppositional logic that positive progress depends on.[9] He measured Bárbara's hatred for men and the fear she engendered by a criterion of inviolable Nature in which those feelings amount to depravity, even though he must have been aware of the arbitrarily—almost legalistically—drawn distinctions between legitimate and illegitimate sentiments.[10]

But in the *Memoirs*, by conspicuous contrast, virile Violeta is loved by everyone: her admiring sisters, her amused mother, and not least of all by her gender-lonely father. And if Mama Blanca could have met Doña Bárbara, it is possible that she would have loved her too. At the very least, she would have perceived Bárbara's uncontrollable energy and a certain pride in womanly independence as evocations of her beloved Violeta. As for Mother Nature, she loses all authority to real mothers in this book, because her work is sometimes unfeeling and almost always unfinished. A fatherly text, like Gallegos's, may take nature to be a sacred ground; but mothers seem to take her as a challenge to their own creative authority. Blanca Nieves here is more amused than disappointed about her mother's nominal mistake, an innocent joke that brought laughter but never malice from other people. But she is furious with that false mother, Nature, for giving her straight hair, a cruel joke that had to be corrected each day at her own and her mother's expense. Nature was merely a "cruel, heartless stepmother. But as Mama was a mother, she defied her in a struggle without quarter, and the stepmother was defeated and thwarted."

Gallegos's novel continually forces itself into a straight line—with possibly compromising flashbacks about Bárbara clearly marked off as prehistory—aimed at positive, economically rational change. Proper language and legitimate propriety are two sides of the same civilizing coin whose purchase is never at issue. If the relationship between language and legitimacy is admittedly allegorical here, it is not attributed to metaphoric leaps from one system of representation to another, the kind of moves that predictably fall short of a close fit. Instead, the allegory presumes a metonymical (perhaps tautological) structure, from the legal implications of authoritative language and from the authority conferred by a linguistic construction called law.

By contrast, so much of Teresa de la Parra's novel seems to take place in one single moment, a single and sonorous moment that exchanges time for space and gives room to the most diverse and equally legitimate codes in a world doomed by positive and rational change. The mother's aristocratic disdain for referential language, the father's incontestable but also inconsequential pronouncements, the English-speaking governess's absurdly ungrammatical insistence on being proper, Vicente Cochocho's popular archaisms, Cousin Juancho's pleasing and pointless monologues, cowherd Daniel's precisely modulated calls to each of his bovine wards. Finally, there are the little girls whose indiscriminate imitations produce a democratizing effect among these codes and whose permutations construct flights beyond linguistic pluralism. It is something like a playfully postmodern instability, inspired perhaps by the mother's genteel disregard for "reality," far more inclusive than hers and as irreverent about the signifier as about the signified.

Hardly discursive obstacles, the linguistic failures and maladjustments between desire and experience describe a playing field where Blanca Nieves and her mother enjoy re-creation. It was also the space enjoyed for a while by María Eugenia, the young lady who wrote a diary out of boredom in Teresa de la Parra's first novel.[11] Certainly in this second one, the disencounters constitute no communication crisis between mother and daughter, presumably exiled into a linguistic diaspora from which there is no going home. They no doubt understand each other very well, precisely because of their shared disappointments with a symbolic order in which, for example, hair should mean curls although it cannot always mean that. The current and future mothers make themselves accomplices in covering over the difference between reality and desired ends.

But the process of curling, shaping, and deceiving becomes more than a compensatory process; it becomes a series of willful, creative impositions that inevitably reinscribe the gap. If, in Lacan's terms, that order belongs to "Poor Papa, . . . [who] took on in our eyes the thankless role of God," it may be because he demands that it work. He yearns to reconquer the supposed originary harmony by insisting that desire be satisfied, that signifiers *mean* what they signify, without stopping to take creative advantage of the disappointments. He yearns, for instance, to reproduce himself perfectly in a male child who could carry on the legitimating name of the father. Each year, his renewed insistence would send his wife off, heavy with child, to Caracas where she would deliver another daughter. The mother, evidently, was taking her own sort of control of the paternal order, enjoying the annual and irremediable slips between intention and issue, an excessive production that nevertheless could not satisfy the father's unmovable desire. "The truth of the matter is that we never disobeyed him but once in our life. But that single time sufficed to disunite us without scenes of violence for many years. This great act of disobedience took place at the hour of our birth." Being born female was the original sin that had them expelled, not from maternal harmony but from the divine order of paternal paradise. Yet thanks to the exile, these little women were also let loose in a fully humanized world where the constitutive distance between desire and realization, language and experience, gave them room to play. If they had been born male and fully legitimate for the father, perhaps their unauthorized games would have taken longer to develop.

A study in contrast is Primo Juancho, the girls' aging uncle who demonstrates better than anyone the mechanisms of verbal misfirings. But he seems stubbornly to delay any acknowledgment of a systemic difficulty. The impoverished old gentleman shows all the intellectual disorder these memoirs associate with great spirits, but he resists calling it that, because he worships positive programs even if they don't work. When one scientific scheme fails him, another quickly takes its place; the value of scientific thinking itself is never at issue. Juancho's verbal aim was as far off the mark as Mother's, but not by a choice that would make the best of an impossible system. He wanted to *make* a difference, not just to play with it. He would dream, for example, of being appointed to powerful government positions, but he "could not govern or direct anything, not for lack of ability, but because of too much thinking. His learning was his ruin." This is one unmistakable hint that at the end of the novel, after the plantation is sold to appease the father's family, the successful modernization of the new owner (let's call him Santos) is accomplished thanks, precisely, to the modernizer's limited knowledge. To organize anything rationally one has to make choices, to exclude, to resolve debates in favor of one speaker, in favor of one code of conduct, just as "Santos" would do in Piedra Azul and in Altamira. It was a narrowness that could not contain Juancho.

(Dis)ordered arbitrarily, like an unbound dictionary that includes everything in scattered juxtapositions and metonymical relationships that need no hierarchy, and composed also like this almost static novel that recognizes Juancho's particular brand of purposeless heroism, and like Mama Blanca herself, with her noisy failures in every practical venture, Cousin Juancho's exorbitant humanity gets in the way of his own projects.[12] In equal measure, his un–self-conscious flair for traitorous language manages to articulate, not the desired projects, but rather his loyalty to "the idealistic soul of my race." English-speaking Evelyn, for example, was brought into the household by his insistence so that the girls would learn her "sane mentality and indispensable language." What happened instead was that Evelyn learned Creolized Castilian, and spoke it badly, without definite articles. So the paradoxical result of Juancho's efforts to "Europeanize" the plantation was to instill there a love for indolent tolerance and for "Mama's dulcet, affected, lilting Spanish."

Juancho would even trip himself up quite literally when his ideal code (alternately and conflictively positivist and chivalric) might fail at the moment of the communication he yearned for. This happened, for instance, when he slipped on a fruit peel and fell on top of the very lady to whom he was preparing to bow on the street. The indignant woman made an inappropriately insulting remark, because she could never have understood this "master of etiquette." If we understand Juancho, and love him, perhaps it is because by now Blanca Nieves has taught us how admirable linguistic (verbal and gestural) misfires can be, especially when they attempt to respect a disinterested code of behavior out of date and dear to the same degree. Juancho lives from one disaster to the next without admitting that a quixotic pattern trails behind, a weave of idealized notions repeatedly surprised in their encounter with reality. And reality here is, by contrast, nothing more than a discourse that refuses to be surprised, exiling whatever is unpredictable as, by definition, unrealistic. It is a fatal discourse for Cousin Juancho whose ingenuousness amounts to an ethical posture. As if to ensure our empathy, or at least to dramatize his almost helpless sense of wonder, these memoirs continually confront us as readers with the impossibility to predict anything, or to hold onto the stereotypes that might make our reading less hazardous, and perhaps less rigorously ethical.

It should not come as a surprise, therefore, that the young woman and friend who "edits" Mama Blanca's posthumous memoirs criticizes herself for organizing, clarifying, and polishing what the old lady called, aware of how writing distances what it brings into focus, the "portrait of [her] memory." The young professional writer might have defended herself, nevertheless, by noting how Blanca Nieves loved to put her mother's stories in order, giving "unity to the whole." But the editor surely recognized a difference in the two procedures. Blanca Nieves would weave her stories together and take them apart, without worrying about achieving a final form or how they would be received by an anonymous public. Her future friend deviated by submitting Blanca's loose pages to the kind of logical *Nachträglichkeit* that the vogue for biography imposes on diffuse material. The difference comes into relief against the background of continuity between these characters, since the old writer's pains to cultivate the young one suggest a transfer of mantle. Their contiguous relationship (literally at the piano or at table) accounts, in fact, for much of the charm of their friendship. But the editor could not have forgotten that her indiscriminate transfer of text to a faceless public violates the old woman's confidence.

Now you know, this is for you. It is dedicated to my children and grandchildren, but I know that if it came into their hands they would smile tenderly and say: 'One of Mama Blanca's whims,' and they wouldn't even bother to open it. It was written for them, but I am leaving it to you. You read it if you want to, but don't show it to anybody. . . . This is the portrait of my memory. I leave it in your hands. Keep it a few years more in my memory." And thus it was kept for some years.

Since the publication of memoirs and biographies has become one of the more fashionable indiscretions, cutting here, padding there, according to the taste of biographers and publishers, I have been unable to resist the trend of the times, and so I have undertaken the easy and destructive task of arranging the first hundred pages . . . to bring them to the public. While I have been arranging them I have felt the eye of the reader fixed upon me like that of the Lord on Cain.

We readers, titillated by the illusion of conspiracy, read on; but this rather conventional ploy of arousing voyeuristic interest is more than that here. It is also a staging of the forced displacement narrated in the following pages, a proleptic loss of privacy with the sale of the plantation and the move to Caracas, which also amounts to the loss of a pointless freedom to make and unmake texts.

By extending the continuity from Mama Blanca, through the editor, to a general readership that can identify with the story, the introduction frames the impersonal process of modernization that will end Blanca Nieves's private haven and her narrative. And after her irresistible decision to bring the memoirs out, the modernizing agent reinscribes her fatal, Cainlike guilt every time she transcribes (or invents) Mama Blanca's objections to fixing words in writing. "As many times as I have attempted to explain to you how Vicente talked and how Mama talked, those two opposed poles, one the essence of rusticity and the other of refinement or preciosity, one in which the rhythm predominated, the other, the melody, I have sadly realized the uselessness of my endeavor. The written word, I repeat, is a corpse." For the price of that guilt, however, the editor gains the purchase of a conflicted—modern—freedom. It allows her to resist a traditional and maternal authority by submitting to the contemporary sway of market and fame. It is as if she had learned from Mama Blanca herself how to perform inside the contradiction between codes. Writing is a death that, paradoxically, assures the memory of what it has killed, not the death of "meaning" that might concern a more rigorously deconstructive reading so much as of musicality and gesture, always an impoverished but also repeatable representation.

Far less tortured or coyly self-deprecating, the narrator of *Doña Bárbara* sees things differently. For this modernizer, the flatness and public visibility of writing are great advantages, not lamentable losses. They are the preconditions for distinguishing written and generally binding law from oral tradition, which amounts to distinguishing civilization from barbarism. This mandate to draw neatly demarcated terms of opposition would have been dangerously impatient with the plurivalent heteroglossia that survived in Piedra Azul. Blanca Nieves would find out that, after a while, Bárbara was left with no space between signifier and signified in which the feminine subject could enjoy re-creation. On the contrary, that space for enchantments, interpretations, seductions was the measure of Bárbara's abnormality. The same kind of verbal and gestural freedom that made the naughty little girls of Piedra Azul charming made Bárbara the target of a linguistic cleanup campaign. Her independence and power were interpreted as the wages of hatred, perversions of her female nature. By wedging a space between the word woman and her aggressive, virile persona, Bárbara had dared to untie the bond between virility and virtue, father and fatherland, and had sent the entire rationally demarcated system into motion. Obviously she had to be eliminated.

In Piedra Azul, by contrast, nothing is eliminated; all the rational and irrational discourses cohabit in common-law polygamy, if not altogether legally, like Vicente and his two wives. Ancient and noble traditions, together with popular practices, eccentric superstition, races, generations—all occupy the same inclusive and static space. Everything coexists and each element enriches Piedra Azul, although the adults don't see it that way.

But Evelyn, with her British and Protestant intolerance, was unable to appreciate the refinement of that rustic courtesy. We could. Nor could she or Mama or Papa or anyone appreciate the flavor of the noble, vintage Spanish that comprised Vicente's vocabulary. We could, and because we appreciated it we copied it. Evelyn would correct us, assuring us that we were talking vulgarly; Mama would too, but they were both wrong. Right, or supreme good taste, was on the side of Vicente and us. Only many years later did I realize this. It was when I came to read López de Gómara, Cieza de León, Bernal Díaz del Castillo, and other authors of the period who came to America and generously bequeathed to us the Spanish that Vicente used, just as one uses a strong, solid, comfortable piece of old furniture inherited from one's ancestors.

Vicente would say, as they did in the magnificent seventeenth century, *ansina* instead of *así, truje* in place of *traje, aguaitar* instead of *mirar, mesmo* for *mismo,* and so on; his Spanish was, in a word, golden age Spanish.

The very archaisms, preserved by Teresa de la Parra as a precious inheritance of the original "American" language, were being presented at the same time in *Doña Bárbara*. And just consider the difference in presentation. Coming from Bárbara's daughter Marisela, they really do seem to be the vulgarities that Evelyn and the girls' parents thought they heard in Piedra Azul. For Santos Luzardo, a man obsessed by the ideal of a centralizing and efficient language, variations are disturbances, or they are reduced to the opposition between correct and incorrect usage, and always, ultimately, between civilization and barbarism. By contrast to Sarmiento's pampa and to Gallegos's llano, Piedra Azul knows no barbarism. The narrator doesn't perceive it because her memoirs don't represent a fight to the death between two cultural–linguistic systems where the Other is almost by etymological definition barbarous, or foreign. Bárbara is, of course, the Other, the one who competes with the Father.

It is possible that while she listens to Doña Bárbara's story, Mama Blanca may come to the same conclusion about Other being unfairly coded as evil, because there is abundant reason for thinking that the apparently ethical difference between civilization and barbarism is, as I have said, also a proprietary difference between *mine* and *yours*. In my imagined epilogue for their books, the two women would certainly develop a profound friendship based on their common and rending experience that made them ex-centric. They are already absent from their ideal contexts, an absence that both allows for and obliges them to write. In one case, it is in order to supplement the emptiness that nostalgia leaves; in the other, writing is the caricature of another writer that banishes Bárbara and makes her absent.

Long before she sat down to write her memoirs, Mama Blanca evidently knew the value of distances, between names and people, between experience and the "portrait" of a life that she was writing. Her editor is no less sensitive to the calculus of loss and gain when she describes the papers "fastened together at the back by a narrow silk cord whose color time and the touch of [her] fingers and those of the departed had blurred." By extension, she is also describing how our hands caress the same pages and occupy an analogous position to hers in the chain of absences that paradoxically make our association possible. But Bárbara would only begin to conceive of absence as an opportunity now that she was far from the llano and planning to write her own story. Her version might take advantage of Mama Blanca's appreciation for what was missing, her flair for narrative mismatches and contempt for absolutely binding signification, because in the other version, his version, Bárbara's history seems so terribly present. It pretends to be as coherent as if a person could signify anything so categorical as evil.

Gallegos declares the immediacy of his writing in the very first words, "Who goes with us?" where present tense and first-person plural question the reader as participant. He writes as if interpretation and slips of meaning were entirely conquerable. And when he appeals to literary subtexts, as in the case of "Sleeping Beauty," it is not to remark on a literary continuity that may be affecting his own production. It is rather to enlist an apparently transparent allegory for didactic purposes, where Beauty is a figure for Marisela or Venezuela. But now that Gallegos has put us on the track of the allegorical possibilities of using fairy tales, Bárbara, or Blanca, or we, may continue to experiment where he stopped.

Minds that lack the necessary discipline may wander beyond Gallegos's demarcations. We may think, for one obvious example in this epilogue, about the fairy tale of Snow White while we reread his "Sleeping Beauty." And perhaps by this path of associative reading, as well as through the writerly leads given by Parra's heroine, we can imagine a feminist rereading of *Doña Bárbara* through Snow White. In the fairytale version, the heroine is a good little girl, good fundamentally because she *is* a little girl. That is, she is innocent because, at her prepubescent age, she lacks the maternal power to reproduce herself in daughters. The mother (stepmother here, in order to underscore their discontinuity) is necessarily evil, basically because she exercises power that challenges the father. Sandra Gilbert and Susan Gubar offer these provocative observations and add that the supposed real mother in the story had died shortly after giving birth, as if that very demonstration of maternal power somehow annulled her validity as mother.[13] This apparent absurdity, and the radical separation of mother and daughter (Bárbara and Marisela) in this story so basic to our Western narrative habits, represents a kind of Oedipal struggle between parent and child in which father is the prize. It is a construct of familial relationships that has by now been shaken by tools in feminist psychoanalysis that describe female development as a process of continuity and extension with the mother and by a feminist literature that disarticulates inherited models.[14] There is probably no better example of the literary assaults on the oedipal model than *Las memorias de Mamá Blanca*, where the spatial figures of extension and metonymy become the very principles of narrative organization. Here the bedroom mirror is no magic mirror on the wall to judge competing women's worth, no determining voice of the absent and desired father as in the fairy tale, but the projection screen for a mother's hands entwined in her daughter's hair while they become accomplices in creative daydreaming.

If Bárbara had the chance to write her own story, inspired as much by the "evil" (enterprising) queen as by that other Snow White, the naughty, oxymoronically dark one, perhaps she could have extended her entrepreneurial plotting to include literary plot making in the demonic reflections of her own witch's conjuring table. There she would surely have enjoyed the twists she could give to some of the neat lines of the patriotic "epic" named for her. The heroic genre, always told with the suffocating self-respect of the victor, was no place for a woman's willful tangles. Perhaps, in the untidy novelized result that her literary conjuring might produce, there would have been more room for mothers to be accompanied by their daughters.[15] In Gallegos's version, mother and daughter get together too, but as antagonists, when Marisela barges into Bárbara's bedroom to confront the "witch" who is casting a spell on Santos. The women fight (over him) and Santos overturns Bárbara's advantage by breaking in to save the girl.[16]

It is entirely possible that my rereading against the grain of *Doña Bárbara* may seem a bit perverse, and short of perverse it may be at least anachronistic or irresponsible. No one should forget the importance of Rómulo Gallegos as figurehead for the "Generation of '28" that opposed dictator Juan Vicente Gómez. And of course it is true that his 1929 novel did much to build bases for the victorious populism of Acción Democrática. The educator, author, and president was, without a doubt, "progressive," advocating as he did a binding legal system as well as economic development that would promote general prosperity and welfare. To a great degree, modernization did, in fact, equal social improvement. And there is no question that it was preferable to Gómez's outmoded authoritarianism that organized the state as if it were his personal estate.

Perhaps the one halting worry that I would like to voice in the dialogic pause that Bárbara would give to Gallegos's epic flow is an observation about a certain rhetorical and emotive continuity between populism and personalism.[17] Both kinds of political culture tend to be centralizing under the leadership of a practically cultlike figure. And although the centralizing project in a populist novel like *Doña Bárbara* grounds itself in a legal and apparently impersonal system, the victorious result seems suspiciously like the problem it has conquered. With even more clarity than the novel, the movie script that Gallegos prepared in 1939 dramatizes the coincidence. The problem that Santos has come to resolve is the absolute power that Bárbara wields on the llano. And the solution celebrated at the end of the movie is the equally absolute power that Santos has wrested from her. By then his cousin and possible rival for real estate has conveniently died, Marisela has learned to speak correct Spanish, and Bárbara has taken the lady's way out, disappearing into the background. First she and then he are in control. Between them is what might be called a metaphoric relationship, a semantic substitution that, however radical, does not destabilize the verbal organization. The invariable is the protagonist's position as leader. This simple observation suggests the possibility that some authoritarian habits might survive in a populist project that, say, could not satisfy the popular demands it helped to formulate.

It seems hardly promising, by contrast, that Teresa de la Parra was never really concerned about progressive or popular demands. Some of the affectionate pages she dedicates to Vicente Cochocho, whose Afro-Indigenous body bore dirt as carelessly as any extension of nature, are painfully patronizing. Even her feminism was, in her own words, quite moderate and never went so far as women's suffrage.[18] For many readers she is conservative, even reactionary in the strictest sense of the term, given her pride in illustrious forebears, the charm and refinement that distinguished her in elegant society, and her alleged nostalgia for colonial life.[19] Parra's short life of shuttling back and forth between Spain and France—with short stays in Venezuela and visits to Cuba and Colombia—was given to the re-creation of a lost world. Poignantly absent from Venezuela (and from her truncated childhood), Teresa de la Parra knew how to turn distance to literary advantage. One might call her compensatory writing project reactionary, in terms of literary as well as political history, because it reverts to the episodic, loosely articulated, "*costumbrista*" literature that produced static "portraits" of rural life, the same word Mama Blanca used for her memoirs. This characterization, though, is excessively simple; it comes from the kind of political imagination that reduces everything to left and right, to good and bad, to a binarism as proper and constraining as Santos Luzardo's language. Instead of forcing her toward one pole or another, one might place her more commodiously on an anarchic tangent. If her persona Mama Blanca is conservative, it is because she wants to conserve everything, from Vicente's seasoned archaisms to the most unpredictable variations on the modern, like the special brand of Spanish without articles that Evelyn perfected. Blanca refuses to thoughtlessly equate new with improved and thus leaves room for those whom history, and even her adored mother as well as her "all-powerful" father, would marginalize and finally erase. What is more, she orchestrates a rhythmic and melodious polyphony from the equal linguistic marginality of each inhabitant of Piedra Azul, a concerted simultaneity of sound supported by the contiguous and metonymic mapping of the place, where it would be impossible to substitute anyone (metaphorically) without sacrificing the general effect.

With an analogous and imitative gesture, I might find a tangent from which to preserve the politically promising aspects of this novel: its tolerance, flexibility, and the merciful "incoherence" of its multiple voices.[20] If one cared to extract a moral from all this, it could be suggested, perhaps, that marches of progress might take note where and on whom they step; otherwise, progress may turn into something else, as it did for some critics of Acción Democrática when it "progressively" silenced internal voices that challenged party leadership. To step (or sidestep) gingerly might be preferable, especially when the horizontal move promises a capacious utopia.

Notes

1. Their authors' literary "collaboration" dates at least from 1920, when Parra published "Diario de una caraqueña por el Lejano Oriente" in *Actualidades*, a magazine edited by Gallegos. See Velia Bosch, "Selección, Estudio Crítico y Cronología," in Teresa de la Parra, *Obras completas (Narrativa, ensayos, cartas)* (Caracas: Biblioteca Ayacucho, 1982), p. 696.

2. For the contrast, see Bella Brodzki and Celeste Schenck, introduction to *Life/Lines: Theorizing Women's Autobiography* (Ithaca, N.Y.: Cornell University Press, 1988), p. 7.

3. Domingo Faustino Sarmiento, *Recuerdos de provincia* (Barcelona: Ramón Sopena Editor, 1931), p. 161.

4. See Doris Sommer, *Foundational Fictions: The National Romances of Latin America* (Berkeley and Los Angeles: University of California Press, 1991).

5. See Luce Irigaray's discussion of the imaginary as a male "blind spot," that space separating the boy from his mother while positing a primal unity, in "The Blind Spot of an Old Dream of Symmetry," in *Speculum of the Other Woman*, trans. Gillian C. Gill (Ithaca, N.Y.: Cornell University Press, 1985), pp. 87–89. See also Irigaray, "Questions," in *This Sex Which Is Not One* (Ithaca, N.Y.: Cornell University Press, 1985), p. 164: "I am trying . . . to go back through the masculine imaginary, to interpret the way it has reduced us to silence to muteness, to mimicry." See also Patricia Yaegar, *Honey-Mad Women* (New York: Columbia University Press, 1987), on playful strategies as against a French feminist idea that language is always alienated.

6. Rómulo Gallegos, *Doña Bárbara*, trans. Robert Malloy (1931; rpt. New York: Peter Smith, 1948), p. 29.

7. Ibid., p. 137.

8. Ibid., pp. 45–46.

9. For an excellent study of *Las memorias*, which includes a suggestive comparison with *Doña Bárbara*, see Elizabeth Garrels, *Las grietas de la ternura: Nueva lectura de Teresa de la Parra* (Caracas: Monte Avila Editores, 1986). Another perceptive comparison, more generally between feminism and "*mundonovismo*," appears in Francine Masiello, "Texto, ley, transgresión: Especulación sobre la novela (feminista) de vanguardia," *Revista Iberoamericana*, nos. 132–33 (July–December 1985): 807–22.

10. If a case had to be made for the prevalence of stereotypes like Gallegos's, many writers could be mentioned, among them the very popular José Rafael Pocaterra. The heroine of his aptly and allegorically titled novel *Tierra del Sol amada* is described like this: "she encarnates the great spiritual *patria*, which gives herself over, offers herself entirely, whose body flourishes and then disintegrates, self-denying, like the dark roots of a race." Quoted in Pedro Díaz Seija, *La antigua y la moderna literatura venezolana* (Caracas: Ediciones Armitano, 1966), p. 494. Of Teresa de la Parra's work, Díaz Seija calls it less objective, more inductive and feminine.

11. For a fine reading, see Julieta Fombona, "Teresa de la Parra: Las voces de la palabra," in de la Parra, *Obras completas*, pp. ix–xxvi; but I evidently quibble with the contrast she suggests (p. xxii) between this first novel (where words are obstacles to meaning) and *Memorias* (where words fit meanings perfectly).

12. Arturo Uslar-Pietri appreciated Parra's writing for similar reasons. "El testimonio de Teresa de la Parra" begins, "There was a time, marvelously imprecise and static . . ." However, to judge from his quick overview, he misses much of the slow-motion detail: "In *Mamá Blanca* Teresa painted the portrait of our grandmothers. A world devoted to security, resigned to pain." See *Letras y hombres de Venezuela* (Mexico: Fondo de Cultura Económica, 1948), pp. 148–53.

13. Sandra Gilbert and Susan Gubar, *The Madwoman in the Attic: The Woman Writer and the Nineteenth-Century Literary Imagination* (New Haven, Conn.: Yale University Press, 1979), p. 37. "The real story begins when the Queen, having become a mother, metamorphoses also into a witch—that is, into a wicked 'step' mother: ' . . . when the child was born, the Queen died,' and 'After a year had passed the King took to himself another wife.' "

14. Nancy Chodorow, *The Reproduction of Mothering: Psychoanalysis and the Sociology of Gender* (Berkeley and Los Angeles: University of California Press, 1978). The relationship is not always a happy one, of course, because the daughter's only recourse for limiting her mother's consuming power is to submit to paternal authority.

15. I refer to the distinction made in M. M. Bakhtin, "Epic and Novel," *The Dialogic Imagination*, trans. Caryl Emerson and Michael Holquist (Austin: University of Texas Press, 1981), pp. 3–40.

16. Gallegos, *Doña Bárbara*, pp. 178–79.

17. Patriarchal political rhetoric, which in our century has often described a struggle between a legitimate father (people) and the usurper (dictator or imperialist) or the body and love of the wife/mother (land), is the basis of what I have called a populist culture. For a more developed discussion, see Doris Sommer, *One Master for Another*.

18. Teresa de la Parra, "Influencia de las mujeres en la formación del alma americana," *Obras completas*, p. 474. She defends women's rights to careers, "fitting for women with fair pay. . . . I don't want, as a consequence of my tone and argument, to be considered a suffragist. I neither defend or object to suffragism for the simple reason that I don't understand it. The fact of knowing that it raises its voice to win for women the same attributions and political responsibilities that men have frightens and disturbs me so that I could never manage to hear out what suffragism has to say. And this is because I generally believe, in contrast to suffragists, that we women should thank men for resigning themselves to take on all the political work. It seems to me that, next to that of coal miners, it is the most difficult and least cleanly work that exists. Why demand it?

"My feminism is moderate."

19. In the second of three talks she gave on the "Influencia de las mujeres en la formación del alma americana," Parra corrected, or responded defensively to, a common (mis)perception: "My affection for the Colony would never bring me to say, as some do in lyrical moments, that I would have preferred being born then.

No, I am quite happy in my epoch and I admire it" (ibid., p. 490). See Mariano Picón Salas's description of Parra, the creole Circe: "so beautiful a woman, who could be seen at all the parties with her splendid eyes and her bearing of a young Spanish marquise who dressed in Paris and could tell us about episodes and anecdotes that dated back a century, because she had heard them from grandmothers and from old servant women" (*Estudios de literatura venezolana* [Madrid: Ediciones Edime, 1961], pp. 266–67).

20. Of course, one may choose to draw connections between Teresa de la Parra's ideological position and the bald manipulations justified by the socialist rhetoric that she admires in the cowherd Daniel:

The ruler of the republic of the cows, by their choice and sovereign will—do not laugh, you will see that this is true—all wisdom, all good government, was Daniel the cowherd.

When we made our appearance in the city of the cows, Daniel, who had been up since four in the morning, had already, with the assistance of a stable boy, filled many buckets of milk. The order that prevailed was perfect: the order of the ideal future city. In the open air, under the sky and sun, each cow was happy and in its house, that is to say, tied to a tree or a post. . . . Nobody complained and nobody was resentful; there was no class warfare. To each according to her needs, from each according to her ability. All was peace, all was light.

But this praise occurs in a novel where other systems of organization or disorganization receive equal applause. And if one thinks of the liberties the girls take with everyone, or of Juancho's flagrant failures and the other's anachronistically poetic posturing, among other practices, it may be seen that Daniel's government represents one point of this portrait, if not a delicate scoffing at the "future city."

TERESA DE LA PARRA

Mama Blanca's Memoirs

Translated by Harriet de Onís
Translation revised by Frederick H. Fornoff
Doris Sommer, Coordinator

THE PITTSBURGH EDITIONS OF LATIN AMERICAN LITERATURE

"Parra reconstructs not only the forms of her own life, but the life of her country and, more than that, elucidates, as Virginia Woolf did, the inner life of women in an overtly patriarchal world."
                                        —Louis Antoine Lemaître

Raised on a sugarcane plantation in Venezuela, Teresa de la Parra (1889–1936) spent most of her adult life in Paris and died in Spain of tuberculosis. She is remembered for two novels, *Iphigenia, Diary of a Bored Young Lady* (1924) and *Mama Blanca's Memoirs* (1929), crafted with the subtlety and stylistic delicacy of Virginia Woolf and Katherine Anne Porter.

Mama Blanca's Memoirs re-creates the lost world of later nineteenth-century plantation society. The "memoirs" tell the story of six little girls growing up on a sugar plantation outside Caracas under the ostensible patriarchy of their father and the madcap maternity of their beautiful young mother. In language at times comic, often lyrically hypnotic, de la Parra creates a series of vignettes and portraits, embellishments on her own memories, for a haunting portrayal of a particular culture and a distant time.

Despite its popularity in Latin America (though often read as a book for children), *Mama Blanca's Memoirs* has yet to receive the full recognition it deserves in North America. This translation by Harriet de Onís, revised by Frederick Fornoff, captures the flavor of de la Parra's feminist flair. Critical essays offer historical and literary perspectives on the text.

The Pittsburgh Editions of Latin American Literature are based on the Colección Archivos, a landmark series of critical editions of twentieth-century Latin American fiction, poetry, and essays. This important collection was created through agreements with the governments of France, Italy, Spain, Portugal, Argentina, Brazil, Colombia, and Mexico, with funding provided by ALLCA and UNESCO. The translations in the Pittsburgh Editions will make this valuable and influential body of literature accessible to North American readers.

UNIVERSITY OF PITTSBURGH PRESS

Cover ... s Book Design; cover art: "Figura bajo la trinitaria" by Antonio Edmundo Monsanto. Courtesy Fundación Galería de Arte Nacional and CINAP, Venezuela.

ISBN 0-8229-591